SIDELINED LOVE

THE CRESTWOOD UNIVERSITY SERIES
BOOK 1

EMERY PAIGE

EMERY PAIGE PUBLISHING

Cover Illustrator and Designer: Andra Murarasu

Editor: Chrisandra's Corrections

Proofreaders: Sisters Get Lit.erary Author Services, EAL Editing Services

❀ Created with Vellum

For my Mom,
Without your unwavering support and optimism, this book
would be nothing more than a dream.
Thank you.

AUTHOR'S NOTE

Thank you so much for taking the time to pick up Sidelined Love. I did want to take the time to also give you a list of content warnings.

This book isn't dark, but your mental health is important and I want you to make the best choice for you.

PLAYLIST

Here - Alessia Cara

Miss Americana & The Heartbreak Prince - Taylor Swift

Falling - Harry Styles

What Was I Made For? - Billie Eilish

Crash & Burn - Jesse McCartney

invisible string - Taylor Swift

Houdini - Dua Lipa

Photograph - Ed Sheeran

Someone To You - BANNERS

Love Again - Dua Lipa

Teenage Dream - Katy Perry

Castles Crumbling - Taylor Swift, Hayley Williams

favorite kind of high - Kelly Clarkson

You can check out the playlist on Spotify

1

HAILEY

If I could, I would pay someone to drag me out back and put me out of my misery by any means necessary.

But luck isn't on my side.

Instead, I'm forced to do what I consider to be a soul-sucking job. Well, it's not the job, it's my boss.

"Large Americano!" I call out, but nothing changes.

My fingers tighten around the steaming paper cup as the heat from it begins to seep into my skin. I'm staring for a moment at the woman who ordered the drink, but, of course, she's not paying attention. It's taking everything in me not to snap. I have to maintain a positive customer experience for the patrons of Brewed Beginnings.

In order to calm the urge to scream, I take a moment to center myself and then I say it once more. "Large Americano!"

The woman's eyes meet mine. I gesture to the drink before sliding the cup across the counter without looking back at it, knowing it won't fall off the counter from having done this a million times before.

How hard is it to pay attention so that you know when your order is called?

It takes everything in me to not rub my hand across my face. I hate this part of the job. I am forced to push my shoulders back and paste on a smile as I play the cheerful barista, while customers treat me like I am a piece of furniture. But my bills don't pay themselves, and my tuition doesn't vanish into thin air, never to be heard from again. So here I am, at Brewed Beginnings, pouring coffee and trying to keep my shitty thoughts to myself.

"Anything else?" I ask, making myself sound more cheerful than I feel as I hand over the drink.

The woman, scrolling through her phone, mumbles something about extra napkins, and once I give them to her, she hurries off without a thank you.

That doesn't surprise me. If I had a penny for every time someone didn't acknowledge the act of service I'd just given them, I'd be a millionaire. It doesn't make it less annoying, however.

I take a deep breath, counting to three in my head. Patience, Hailey. You need to have patience.

But who am I kidding? This is just another day of me slinging overpriced caffeine to sleep-deprived students. One of the few silver linings about this gig is the free drinks I can consume while I'm here. To be honest, it's the only thing keeping me from quitting.

I scan the room as students and professors shuffle in. Some are bleary-eyed and yawning because of the early hour. The constant hum of conversation fills the café, broken only by the occasional laugh or loud sip. Everyone here looks as exhausted as I feel. Welcome to life as a college student.

As the morning rush at Brewed Beginnings continues, I slip into a rhythm that's equal parts robotic and resentful. Is it normal to be irritated this early in the morning? No, but I am, even though I do my best to hide everything behind a pleasant mask. Each "Thank you" and "Have a nice day" I offer is as automated as the espresso machine hissing beside me. Thankfully, both of us are working well today.

"Skinny vanilla latte!" My voice cuts through the hum of conversations that surround me, but it's met with the same vacant stares and slow reactions. "Skinny vanilla latte is ready!"

When I get the same reaction, I'm tempted to snap. How hard is it to listen for your order? Is it time for us to ask for people's names with their order?

A guy in a black Crestwood University jacket finally looks up. I notice the earbuds in his ears and the surprised expression on his face. He reaches for his headphones, unplugging himself from the music-infused bubble he'd placed himself in. With a quick nod and a mumbled,

"Thanks," he rushes out of the coffee shop. At least he said thank you.

A woman approaches the counter, and I turn my gaze toward her. I offer her a very fake smile. "How can I help you?"

"A large mocha," she says. I nod and write the order on the cup. A strand of my wavy brown hair falls out of my messy bun. I brush it aside with a huff.

"Next!" I call out as I wrap up another order. I'm more than ready to take the next customer.

A student strolls up to the counter and carefully examines the menu for a long time. Then she looks up at me and speaks. "Caramel macchiato, please," she whispers, and her voice is so low that I question whether I heard her.

"Size?" I ask, already reaching for a cup. She answers, and I write her order on the cup before handing it off to my coworker, Ben, who is standing at the espresso machine. I keep taking orders and making drinks because the line looks as if it is never going to end. While doing this, I think about what I'll need to do in my classes today. It's an endless cycle that plays on a loop in my mind as I try to talk myself into embracing what has already started off as a busy day.

The line dwindles, giving me a moment of relaxation. I lean against the counter, taking a second to scan the café. Students are leaning over their laptops, homework and other papers tossed on tables, and the occasional burst of laughter fills the air. It all feels familiar and captures college life at Crestwood University.

The school is in the heart of Crestwood, Virginia, and is home to the Crestwood Red Wolves. Although the university was built after the town was founded, you'd think it was the other way around. The campus itself is stunning with its manicured grounds and picturesque buildings. While most of the things we could ever need can be found somewhere in the vicinity, our college administration encourages us to go into town and patronize local businesses.

Speaking of businesses, things are slowing down at Brewed Beginnings, and I sigh before I glance at the clock on the wall. It's time for my break, but first, I should find Marc, my manager.

I scan the area for him, but I grow irritated when I don't spot him. Despite my dislike for him, he is someone I must deal with while working here. And right now, he is standing between me and another cup of coffee.

Seeing that Marc is nowhere to be found, I turn my attention to Ben and Thomas, who also work several of these morning shifts with me during the week. "Hey guys, I'm going to take my break now."

Ben looks up and gives me a quick nod. "Excellent. I'll take mine when you're back."

I untie the back of my apron as I walk over to the espresso machine and start on my drink. My fingers work on autopilot, handling the espresso machine as I brew my usual pick-me-up. The steam wand hisses as the rich aroma of the coffee grounds wraps around me like a source of comfort, one I'd grown used to after only a few days of working here. I decide that a latte will satisfy me right now.

Once I finish making the drink, I step from behind the counter, holding the cup close to me. I head toward the corner of the coffee shop that has become my usual hangout on my breaks and when I stop in during a non-work shift. The small nook, with an old table and chair, provides an excellent opportunity for people-watching, which is what I usually do when not engrossed in my phone.

I whip off my apron, which gets caught on my messy bun just before I set my drink down on the table in front of me. Sitting in the chair, I close my eyes and breathe. Away from the counter, this is my time to recharge, even if only for a few minutes. I open my eyes and as I take a sip of my latte, my gaze drifts around my workplace.

Brewed Beginning's exterior has a charming red brick façade and large, welcoming windows. The interior show-cases its warm, rustic charm because of its exposed wooden beams and soft lighting that casts a lovely glow over the room. Local art decorates the walls, adding splashes of color and character to the space. The shop's success, in part, stems from the aesthetic it presents. That's not including how good our coffee tastes, the speed that we get people in and out of here, and our convenient location right on campus.

"Hailey."

I hold back a groan that threatens to fall from my lips. Of course, Marc finds me right now as I'm trying to enjoy my break. I place my cup down, plaster on a fake smile, and give him my full and undivided attention. I'm willing to bet money that whatever he wants to say could wait until after my break is over.

"What can I do for you?" I ask, clenching my fists because it's the only thing I can do to avoid rolling my eyes or showing any other sign of frustration.

"Restock cups and lids and clear tables at your earliest convenience," he says with unnecessary harshness.

I glance at the stacks of cups and lids and raise an eyebrow. I shift my gaze to the tables that have been cleaned. The only ones that are dirty are the ones where customers are currently sitting. I resist the urge to point out that "when I have a moment" means after my break, since I'm pretty sure he's aware. But I simply nod in acknowledgment of his request.

I look up and find Marc staring at me as if he's expecting me to have a different reaction. His perpetual frown is permanently etched on his face, and if anyone else looked at me like that, it would be creepy. The 'scowl of death' gives him an unapproachable appearance. Because of this, most of my coworkers are intimidated by him.

But me? I couldn't care less about what he thinks of me, and I refuse to kiss his ass. I assume he hates me but can't fire me because I'm one of his most efficient and reliable employees. Plus, corporate might give him hell if he fires me for no valid reason.

My eyes land on Thomas and Ben, who aren't doing too much of anything at the moment. If he wants to have something done immediately, he has plenty of choices without bothering me.

"Do you remember what you said to me when you were desperate for me to hire you?"

I remember it because he brings it up every time he knows he's stepping out of line. "Yes. I said that I can handle anything you threw my way."

That day, just a little over three years ago, had been the worst and best day of my life. The best thing is that I'd gotten a job and could supplement the scholarships I'd earned, the loans I'd taken out, and the money Dad had to put up to pay for school. I must maintain my grades and job or find another one to remain at Crestwood.

Not to mention, he has no issue with reminding me about how disastrous my first week at Brewed Beginnings was because I had barely any training and they threw me into the proverbial fire. He'd been on the brink of firing me several times then, but I begged him to let me keep this job. Now, he holds it over me every chance he gets.

"Well?"

I'm drawn back to the man in front of me. Assuming

that he wants me to actually say the words, I put us both out of our misery so that he'll leave me alone. "Got it. I'll do it after I'm off my break," I reply, knowing better than to argue with him. Telling him that I understand what he wants me to do is fine, but I can't resist adding the last part in.

"Get it done quickly and watch the attitude." With that, he turns on his heel and walks away.

Thank fuck.

With my manager out of earshot, I exhale deeply. The tension I feel every time I have to interact with him melts away. I finish my coffee, check my phone, and return to work. The rest of the morning shift passes in a blur. Getting what I need to get done before I leave is the only thing on my mind.

As the clock inches toward eleven, I can see the light at the end of the tunnel. My early morning shift is coming to an end, and I have about an hour before I need to head to class.

Just as I'm about to walk toward the counter to begin the process of leaving for the day, Jade Samuels, my best friend and roommate, breezes in with a grin on her face. Her golden-brown skin shines as she brushes her dark brown curls off her shoulder and walks over to me.

Before she can speak, I ask, "What are you doing here?"

The words leave my mouth a bit more harshly than I intended, but she should be used to me by now. The expression on her face doesn't indicate that she took offense to anything I said.

"I left my last class early and came to see if you wanted to grab lunch. Then we can walk across campus to our next classes. I think they're both in the same building."

Her coming here is sweet, yet unsurprising. She's always been this nice, spontaneous person since we ended up in the same dorm building our freshmen year. I swear she's the reason I survived that year, and I don't know what my life would be without her.

Well, it would be a lot less bright, that's for sure.

"That's a great idea. I need to finish a few things before we leave."

She gives me a small nod and I finish up the minor tasks I need to complete before I leave for the day. I debate whether it's worth grabbing a small pastry from the coffee shop instead of stopping somewhere else on campus to sit down and eat.

No. We have enough time to eat, and I need to focus on taking some time out for myself instead of rushing to do or attend to the next thing.

I take my apron off for the last time today and go to the backroom to grab my things. Once I double-check that I have everything I came in with, I walk back up to the front and find Jade standing as she places her bookbag on her back.

As we walk out of Brewed Beginnings, Jade leans in and says, "You look like you're tired."

I snort. "What college student isn't tired?"

It's the truth, but my answer is a way to get her off my case about my workload. We all must do what it takes to achieve our goals, and I'm doing my best with what I have. As seniors this year, we have a lot to think about regarding our future. I don't want anything to deter me from doing something with my future environmental science degree.

"You know what I mean. You're too preoccupied with work and school to enjoy yourself. One of these days, I'm going to get you to do something spontaneous and fun just for the hell of it. Mark my words."

"I do spontaneous things." Well, I do sometimes. Or rarely.

"Like what?"

"Binge-watch reality television shows," I say.

Jade lets out a short laugh as she loops her arm through mine. "You preplan that too and I sometimes watch them with you. Doesn't count."

"Touché."

"Hey, it's not like I'm going to recommend we go skydiving or something."

"If you did, I don't know if we can be friends anymore."

Jade looks at me with her mouth open. "Hey! That's not nice to even joke about."

The corner of my mouth twitches upward for a second. "Okay, I won't say that again. Ever. Regardless, I'll believe that you'll get me to do something spontaneous when I see it."

And that isn't a lie. I've come to embrace my work ethic and the time I put into getting things done. It doesn't leave much time for me to have impromptu adventures.

Memories of finding my mother's side of the closet empty after returning home from school and the silence that followed are something I won't ever forget. Although my dad and I adjusted to our new normal, I was forever scarred and changed. Since then, every decision, every action, was a step toward maintaining stability, ensuring I would never find myself in that position of loneliness again.

And that is the story I'm sticking with.

2

LEVI

I can't help but stare at the pair of discarded red lace panties, confused by their presence. I don't think I'm the reason why they are on the floor, especially since I only just opened the door. However, it wouldn't surprise me. After all, it wouldn't be the first time it's happened.

The bass coming from the speakers pounds in my chest as I step over the discarded garment. I allow the noise and energy of the party to wash over me. Laughing voices, shouts, and the clink of beer bottles fill the entire house. I'm sure the noise can be heard halfway down the street with how loud this party is rocking.

"Levi! Dude!" Wilder Blake shouts near my ear as his hand lands on my shoulder. It doesn't take much to see that he is living up to his name. He pulls me into the room, and I'm greeted by the rest of my teammates from the Crestwood Red Wolves hockey team. I grin and exchange one-armed bro hugs with the guys. Their slaps on the back and shouts of "Let's go, Cap!" only force the smile on my face to grow wider.

We're all riding the high that comes with our win today. I'm truly happy right now, but I know it's temporary.

I reach over and snag a beer off the counter across from Wilder. I pop the top and take a swig. The bitter taste is almost like heaven on my tongue. I swear the only thing that tastes better is pussy on my—

The thought pauses in my mind as my gaze lands on Mya, who's standing with her friends on the other side of the room. Or is her name Monica? Her eyes are on me as if I'm the only person in the room. When she tosses her hair over her shoulder and looks away, I raise an eyebrow. It's all part of this game she likes to play, and I only indulge her when I'm bored.

However, right now, I'm not in the mood. Why did I even bother leaving my apartment?

I take another sip of my beer and it goes down easy. Almost too easy.

It takes a second for me to confirm with myself that her name is indeed Mya. I freeze up as she leans in close, her hand running along my chest. "Wanna get out of here?"

I pause, then give her my most charming smile. Her finger trails down my body toward my pants. I'm curious about how far she'll go, and when she grabs my dick through my jeans, I snag her wrist. "As tempting as that sounds, I can't leave my teammates hanging."

Mya pouts as she shifts her gaze from my hand that is holding onto her back to my eyes. "You sure? We could have some real fun, just the two of us."

"Next time," I say, though I know it's an empty promise.

Mya rolls her eyes and walks away from me. Looks like she knows my words are a lie too. It is easy to see her disappointment even with her back turned to me. I watch her go back to her friends, briefly considering chasing after her, but I stop myself. I'm prepared to be the villain tonight. Any other night, I would be more than willing, but tonight, I'm not in the mood.

I rub the back of my neck as I scan the room. The living room fits perfectly in what you could imagine is your typical off-campus house. I'm supposed to feel as if I'm in my element here. This isn't the first time that I've partied here, but it is the first time that I've felt that I was better off staying at my place.

As the party continues to rage, my gaze drifts across the room until I find Asher Bennett, my best friend and teammate, chatting with a bunch of people by the keg. I'm willing to bet he's talking about our win tonight. Knox

Sanchez is quietly in the corner, talking to a girl that I vaguely remember seeing around campus. Even though Wilder is in another room, I can hear his laugh over the music. The guy's a walking party no matter where he goes.

Then there's Blaise Dalton, standing slightly apart from everyone else. He, like me, is watching the scene before him. Unlike me, I notice he is amused by the sight before him.

But I feel nothing. I know I'm just going through the motions, partaking in an act I've perfected over the years.

My phone buzzes in my pocket. I don't bother looking because I know who it is. He's a big part of the reason I'm on edge right now.

"Who wants to play a round?"

I turn my attention toward the voice and find Wilder standing in the doorway. He's pointing over his shoulder, and I shift my body until I see the beer pong table behind him. That will give me something to do to pass the time until I've stayed long enough that it wouldn't look awkward for me to leave. I nod my head in acknowledgment, letting him know I will join him. Two other guys who I've seen around campus before joining us at the table in the back.

"I'm Seth and this is Rob," Seth says as he holds out his hand for me to shake. His words are slightly slurred, and I wonder how much he's had to drink before we met.

"Levi and Wilder," I say as I gesture to Wilder before we set up the game.

When the game begins, I wait for my competitiveness to kick in, but it doesn't. Inside, I feel nothing although I don't show it. I'm still playing the role I'm supposed to play, yet I can't help but feel like a fraud.

I grab a ping-pong ball and take my position. Focusing on the red Solo cup down on the table, I tune out the rest of the world and shoot. The ball arches perfectly through the air before landing with a soft plop.

"Drink," I say with a smirk. Wilder gives me a high five while Seth takes a sip of his beer.

My phone vibrates again in my pocket. I know I should answer, but I don't want to talk to my father right now. I can already predict how the conversation will go and I don't want it to put me in a worse mood. I press one of the buttons on the side of my phone, sending the call to voicemail without bothering to pull it out of my pocket.

"Hey, Levi, heads up!"

I snap back to the present as the ping-pong ball comes flying toward me. I catch it easily, falling back into the rhythm of the game. The mindless activity is a welcome distraction.

As I move to take my next shot, I feel a hand clap on my shoulder. It's Asher. "Excellent shot, bro," he says with a grin. "You need to drink more."

"That's not a bad idea," I reply. I allow myself to relax slightly.

"How about we switch things up a bit? How about a shot instead of a drink?" Asher asks.

That causes Wilder to do a double take. "I've been waiting for someone to say that all night."

I raise an eyebrow at Asher's suggestion. While he parties as much as the rest of us, I usually don't expect him to be the ringleader of the shenanigans.

Asher grins, clearly enjoying all of this. "Well, Wilder, looks like you're in luck."

I watch as Asher leaves the room but quickly returns with a bottle of premium tequila, judging by the label and small plastic cups. This isn't what we usually drink, but then again, this isn't shaping up to be a regular night.

Wilder's eyes light up like a kid in a candy store. "Now this is what you meant when you said we're partying hard tonight!" he exclaims.

I turn to our beer pong competition, Seth and Rob, and ask, "Are you guys in?" I gesture to Asher, who is now slightly shaking the bottle.

Seth replies, "Fuck yeah, man." Rob nods and places the ball in his hand down on the table.

Continuing our game after taking shots of tequila is going to be an interesting endeavor. Maybe this evening will be interesting after all.

As if Asher grabbing the bottle of tequila was a bat signal, the other guys come in and bring a bigger crowd with them. He lines up plastic shot glasses as if he's some sort of pro bartender at some high-end club versus the guy that usually has to be convinced to party harder.

He fills each glass, and I can't help but stare at the

clear liquid shimmering under the low lights. Everyone waits until Asher finishes pouring the liquor before grabbing their own cups.

Wilder raises his shot and says, "To bad decisions."

We all raise our drinks, clinking them together. "To bad decisions," we repeat, and I can't help but grin. I raise an eyebrow before bringing the plastic to my lips.

As the sharp, warm burn of the tequila slides down my throat, I shake my head and let it warm my body. It is delicious and exactly what I need to distract myself from thinking temporarily. I put the cup down and run a hand down my face. Focusing on this beer pong game is going to be a challenge, but it makes things more interesting.

I chase my shot of tequila with some beer before I glare at the red Solo cups staring me down. There is no way the fuckers in front of me are going to win this game. "Are you guys ready to play again?"

I can see that the tequila is hitting them more than me. I glance at Wilder out of the corner of my eye, and either he has the best poker face I've ever seen, or the tequila has barely affected him. When the two dudes in front of us give us a small nod, I snatch the ping-pong ball from the table and move to aim.

The ball leaves my fingers, soaring through the air in a perfect arc before landing gracefully in one of Seth and Rob's cups. A collective gasp leaves everyone's lips before a loud round of applause erupts.

The urge to be cocky is strong, but I do my best to hide

my smirk as I watch the opposing team exchange wary glances. Their eyes narrow and I can feel the shift in the energy in the room. This is beginning to feel like a battle instead of a friendly game of pong.

As I reach for my cup of beer, I catch sight of Wilder grinning mischievously. He extends his arm, pointing at our opponents' side of the table. "Looks like there's only one cup left on their side. Let's wrap this up right now, shall we?"

That does little to soothe the tension that is growing between us and the other team, but I am not surprised. It's the same attitude that Wilder brings with him to the rink and that helps us win so many games.

His words have the exact opposite reaction on the crowd as their cheers seem to bounce off the walls, reminding me of what it feels like to step out onto the ice.

But before we can continue what will surely be a win for us, a voice breaks through the noise. It's one of the opposing players and I can read the anger on his face.

"Hold on a damn minute. You haven't won yet," he says, his eyes blazing with the kind of fire that could only be the result of tequila and a bruised ego. "We've got one cup left, which means we're still in this game."

The room grows slightly quieter as the tension goes up another notch. I watch as he adjusts his stance, takes a deep breath, and then tosses the ping-pong ball. The room holds its collective breath as the ball defies gravity for a moment before it clatters against our side of the table and bounces off into no-man's-land.

A chorus of disappointed groans fills the room from the people that wanted them to win, but Wilder and I just exchange knowing looks. It's our turn again, thank fuck.

I lean over to Wilder and mutter under my breath, "Finish this."

He gives me a quick nod and then grabs the ball. He moves it between his fingers before he launches it through the air. It arcs perfectly, and with a small splash, nails it right in their last cup. And just like that, we clinch the win.

Wilder's shot causes the room to erupt like a volcano of cheers and applause. As the defeated team hangs their heads in tipsy acknowledgment of their loss, Asher strolls over to the table once more with a new bottle of tequila. Soon we're taking shots again, and I begin to feel more relaxed.

The room buzzes as the crowd around us continues to celebrate. Their laughter sounds as if it's bouncing off the walls, but not everyone is happy.

I look over and my eyes find Seth, who is slowly turning red. He looks to not be taking the celebrations too well. Before I can react, he stumbles and slams his palm against the worn wood of the beer pong table, causing several cups to jump, spilling some of the liquid that is still in them.

I watch as he steps up to Wilder, but Wilder doesn't move an inch. I'm mentally preparing to jump in if it comes to it. I know Wilder can handle himself and the right thing for me to do as captain would be to set the right example. However, there's no way I'm going to watch one of my teammates get into a fight and not act.

"This isn't over," Seth says.

I momentarily feel like we've gotten transferred into a B-rated action flick.

Wilder cocks an eyebrow as if he's amused by the sight in front of him. He looks unbothered even though I know the tequila must be affecting him by now. "It's just a game, man. Let it go."

Wilder is right, but that might not have been the best move. His just a game comment only adds fuel to the fire. I watch as Seth's hands clench into fists at his sides. The crowd senses the change in the air as laughter fades and the whispers increase. People start moving away from the table and toward the walls and exits, and I can't blame them at all.

As if sensing something is about to happen, Asher's hand hesitates over the bottle's cap. His eyes dart between Wilder and the pissed off guy, calculating what he should do.

"Don't give me that bullshit," Seth says, inching closer to Wilder and invading his personal space. I already know where this is going to go, and I can already see myself having to explain this to Coach in the morning.

Before I can process anything, anger flashes on Seth's face just before he shoves Wilder with both hands. Wilder stumbles back but regains his balance before I make my move.

I jump into action, sliding between Wilder and the other guy to prevent things from escalating further. "Hey!" I shout. "Fucking cool it! It's supposed to be a fun night for all of us."

Rob joins him now, and I predict that this is going to get ugly fast. I can see from my peripheral that some of our teammates move toward us too, showing that we aren't alone either.

The music has been turned down, probably by someone who wants to get a front-row seat to the drama. I'm trying to think of what to say next in order to defuse the tension drifting between our two groups, but I come up empty. That is unlike me, but this is an unusual night.

But I need to find a solution before fists get thrown. I glance over at Asher, and he gives me a small nod, alerting me that he has my back.

I clear my throat and speak once more. "We were here to play a friendly game and have a good time. It would be wrong to have this end on a shitty note."

Despite my attempts to mediate the situation, my words mean nothing.

"Stay out of this," Seth says. I get a whiff of his breath and it is both the least pleasant thing I've smelled in a while and a mixture of different alcohols. It triggers something within me and makes me wonder how much he's had to drink tonight. His friend takes several steps closer to Wilder, making it clear what they are gearing up for.

Wilder's stance shifts subtly, feet spreading to better distribute his weight as he prepares himself for a fight. "Back the fuck down or you'll regret it."

That warning only further escalates the situation. With a noise I can't quite describe, Seth lunges toward Wilder before I can do anything, but thankfully, Wilder's reflexes are sharp. As if he hasn't taken even a single shot of tequila, Wilder shifts to his left and counters with a swift uppercut that startles Seth.

I'm in motion before I fully register what's happening, grabbing Rob's arm to make sure he can't jump into the fight as well. The crowd backs away even further in an attempt to avoid getting harmed in the fight, but staying nearby enough to watch what is going on.

Seth's fist flies toward Wilder, but before it can connect, Knox and Blaise appear, grabbing Seth's arms and pulling him away. Asher stands between them while I grab Rob. We manage to break them apart, but not before Seth has a split lip.

Rob fights against my grip, but there's no way I'm letting him go. The only thing that is preventing us from getting into an all-out brawl with them is us not wanting to lose our ability to play our next game.

With the situation finally under control, I take the lead

once more. "Alright, the party's over for you two. Let's get them out of here."

If any of the assholes want to say something, they know better at this point. I can hear the guy I'm holding mumbling under his breath, but he says nothing as we escort him and his friend to the front door. Blaise opens it and we shove them out of the house without further incident. Knox makes sure the door is securely closed behind them.

"Fuckin' A," Knox mutters, rubbing the back of his neck. I'm willing to swear that I heard a collective sigh of relief once the door clicked shut.

"Back to our regularly scheduled programming, then?" Blaise suggests with a half-smile, trying to lighten the mood.

"Yeah, let's forget about all of... that," Wilder agrees. I can see a small bruise forming under his chin, but the other guy looked far worse for wear. "Anyone up for more drinks and shots?"

"Already on it," Asher chimes in and I watch as he heads toward the kitchen to grab what he needs to pour more shots.

Soon I'm standing there with another shot filled to the brim, and I take it all in one swift motion. The feeling of the burning liquid sliding down my throat will never get old. The mixture of it and the adrenaline coursing through my veins because of the fight should have me feeling as if I'm floating on cloud nine.

But I'm not.

As my gaze lands on my friends and teammates that have gathered here tonight, I've never felt more alone.

3

HAILEY

Early the next morning, my phone's alarm sounds loudly at five a.m., and it takes me a second before I manage to turn the shrilling noise off. I understand the point of having an alarm is to alert you about something, but can't they make the sounds more pleasing to the ear?

I lay in bed for a second before I force myself to move. I somehow manage to drag myself into the shower and get ready for the day. While doing all this, I'm glad I don't make too much noise. The last thing I want to do is wake Jade up because that would make me an asshole. No one else deserves to be up at this ungodly hour.

After completing what I need to get done, I grab my bag and walk out the front door, making sure to close it behind me as silently as I can. The brisk morning air brushes against my face, aiding in my attempt to wake myself up. The campus is still asleep as I make my way toward Brewed Beginnings. The silence that surrounds me is only broken by the occasional bird chirping in the distance. While it is quicker for me to drive, walking to work is usually peaceful and I enjoy doing it.

As I approach the coffee shop, I notice the lights are already on which means either my manager or coworkers are there. I pray to myself it's the latter because if it's Marc, he's only going to annoy me.

The chime above the door at Brewed Beginnings café sounds as I push the door open. Thankfully, I see Ben and not Marc. I'm already counting it as meaning that today will be a good day because things could be so much worse.

"Morning, Hailey," Ben says from behind the counter. He briefly looks up at me before turning his attention back to restocking supplies.

"Hey," I reply as I head to the back room to put my things down. Once I've done that, I walk back to the front while tying my apron behind my back. "Is Marc here?"

"Not yet. Wouldn't be surprised if he doesn't get here until after we open."

That wasn't uncommon. While Marc was supposed to help open when he had the morning shift, he often came in late because he couldn't be bothered to do his job properly. It is one of the many issues I have with him. Most of them I have to suck up because I need to keep this job until I graduate.

"Let's hope the espresso machine doesn't feel like being a complete dick today."

Ben chuckles, and as if on cue, the grinder whirrs to life. The scent of freshly ground coffee beans fills the air.

I join Ben behind the counter, my hands instinctively reaching for a small cup that I then place under the spout before I adjust the settings on the espresso machine. With a few taps, I change the settings slightly and watch as rich, honey-colored espresso flows into the ceramic mug.

I drink the liquid as if it's a shot and it feels like one as well. The drink forces me to shake my head once and then twice. The cobwebs in my brain, left over from sleeping and having to wake up this early in the morning, are now long gone.

As I continue checking off the tasks that I need to get done, Ben arranges pastries into the glass case and my stomach growls in response to seeing the golden croissants he sets out. I mentally kick myself for not remembering to grab a protein bar before I left my apartment.

A glance at the clock confirms we're only seconds from opening. The chime from the bells above the door announces the arrival of our first customers, and I take a second to suck in a deep breath. This is just another regular shift, and I can make it through it.

While I'm cashing a customer out, another man comes up to me with a cup in his hand. I fixed his drink moments ago, so I'm confused as to why he's standing here. Once I'm done, I turn to address him.

"Hi, what can I help you with?"

He doesn't miss a beat, thrusting his cup forward. "This isn't what I ordered."

I take the cup, resisting the urge to throw it at him because I know the drink is correct. Instead, I say, "I'm sorry for the mix-up. Let me make you a new one."

As I set about correcting his order, I think about how I didn't act on my intrusive thoughts and dump the drink on his head. That's got to be growth, right?

With the corrected drink in hand, I return to the angry man in question. "Here you go, exactly as you ordered."

He takes a sip, nods, and walks away without another word. I'm not irritated by him showing no manners because I'm happy he's gone.

My shift proceeds as normal after that even with Marc making his entrance. He only manages to grunt as he walks past Ben and me, and I consider it a win. Some of the orders I have memorized because several of the regulars come in at their usual time, making things slightly easier than the morning rush.

As I hand out drinks and do my best to keep something resembling a smile on my face, I notice a lull in the crowd. As I wipe down the counter during a small reprieve from customers, my gaze falls on the door as the chime sounds once more.

I'd be lying if I said that I didn't recognize the person who just walked into Brewed Beginnings. Levi Jamison. All-star athlete and hockey captain of the Crestwood Red

Wolves. I wish I could pretend that I don't know him, but it would be a lie given Jade's friendship with Wilder. Not to mention his face is plastered on one of the walls leading to the gym where I occasionally work out. Although Levi and I haven't ever talked, both his and the hockey team's reputation precedes him. Their antics are well-known throughout the school.

Of course he's sporting bed hair that looks messy but perfect at the same time. I'm willing to bet he just rolled out of some girl's bed and decided today is the day that he would stroll into this café. He's dressed in jeans and a t-shirt, but still manages to look put together. I look down and shake my head once. I open my eyes and keep wiping the same spot although I'm pretty sure it was cleaned twenty seconds ago.

When I've cleaned the same spot for the fifth time, I glance up again and notice several patrons who were enjoying their drinks and snacks in the café are now watching Levi as he makes his way toward me. He doesn't notice or care, and I can't help but think it's because he's used to the attention.

When he's several feet from the counter, I put the cleaning supplies away. When I stand up straight, our eyes lock, and I'm slightly taken back by how blue his are. He gives me an award-winning smile and I raise an eyebrow in response.

"Hey." My annoyance is apparent to me, but I'm not sure if he senses it. Not that it matters. "What can I get you?" Deep down, he's just another customer I have to deal with before I can move on with my day.

He continues to stare at me for a moment and I can't help but wonder why. Then he finally responds, "Give me the strongest thing you've got, thanks." His voice is rough, matching the just-woke-up look he's sporting.

"Coming right up," I say, turning to the espresso machine.

"How was your night?"

The question throws me off guard. I pause before I look over my shoulder. Shock that he's trying to make conversation with me clouds my brain for a second. Then I say the thing that I was holding back. However, I should have kept to myself. "Obviously, not as rough as yours."

It's the last thing I should have said given that Marc is somewhere around here, looking for a reason to fire me. I don't need a customer to report me for being an asshole. Panic sets in as I desperately try to think of a way to salvage the situation.

But instead of getting angry or offended, the man in front of me simply smirks. "What gives you that impression?"

He's... enjoying this?

I gesture toward his appearance. "You look like you rolled out of bed and threw on whatever clothes you could grab to get here."

Levi's hand makes its way to his head as he pulls on his very dark brown strands, but he doesn't look embarrassed by my summary of his appearance. Instead, his hand drops from his hair as his smirk widens into a grin. I'm willing to bet his smile can charm the pants off anyone he meets. He leans casually against the counter, his elbows resting on the surface as if he owns the space. It only irritates me further.

"I like to think of it as an effortlessly stylish look," he replies with confidence, but the arrogance I expect to see in his gaze isn't there. "Not everyone can pull it off."

And he is right. Not everyone can manage to look so casual yet put together at the same time. Levi, however, does so with ease. And he knows it.

"Listen, I don't usually do this, but I was wondering if you wanted to—"

I cut him off. "Are you flirting with me? Getting ready to ask me out?"

"Is there something wrong with that?"

Levi looks confused by what I've said, and I don't blame him. However, I want to end this now before it can even begin. "You're flirting with me and, in my humble opinion, it's too early for it. Is this the norm for you? Doesn't it get exhausting? Regardless, I'm not interested." The words come out sharper than I intend, but I don't care. Chances of him ever speaking to me again are slim anyway.

Any other girl on campus would probably be losing her shit at what I'd just done, and what I said wasn't the complete truth. Levi is hot and I will admit to myself that the attention is nice, but I don't want to have to deal with it or him.

To my surprise, Levi laughs, and I'm lost because I don't think anything I said was funny. "I guess it's part of my charm. Can't turn it off."

I hate that I don't have a ready-made response for him, so I turn to focus on getting him his coffee as quickly as possible. The last thing I need, besides talking to him, is for him to create a line and add another tally to the list of things Marc could get pissed at me about.

But Levi doesn't let me get away that easily.

"So," he continues, breaking my concentration once more. "I take it you're not much of a morning person."

I glance up at him briefly as I slide the drink across the counter. "What gave it away? The scowl or the sarcasm?"

"Both are pretty telling," he replies as he picks up the cup. "But your coffee-making skills are unaffected."

I fold my arms across my chest. "How would you know? You haven't tasted it."

He brings the mug to his lips, his eyes still locked on mine. "I don't need to taste it to know. I have complete faith in your abilities to awaken all of my senses."

A deep sigh falls from my lips because I'm slightly impressed. This guy is as good off the ice as he is on it. No wonder he has a fan club that can fill the entire shop.

Levi takes a sip, maintaining eye contact as if challenging me. "See? Excellent," he says, and I can feel my cheeks heating slightly.

"Thanks," I respond dryly, hoping that he'll take the hint that this conversation is over.

The chime above the door rings again, drawing my attention away from the situation at hand. A group of three girls walks in, their eyes lighting up when they spot Levi at the counter. He doesn't glance their way, though I can tell by their hushed giggles and not-so-subtle pointing that they're talking about him.

That has to be annoying.

"Oh look, your fan club is here," I mutter under my breath.

Levi's gaze flickers toward them for a moment before returning to me. I can already guess what he's going to say based on the smile on his lips. "Jealous?"

I snort in response and roll my eyes. "In your dreams."

Much to my annoyance, his grin only grows wider. As the three girls approach the counter, their voices get louder and more excited. I cringe inwardly as they giggle like high schoolers who have a crush on a big-name celebrity. Heck, maybe they are just out of high school so that explains their reaction.

Then again, I can't say I blame them given how our college and this town worships the ground our athletes walk on. This isn't to take away from the hard work that goes into being able to perform at such a high level, but the spectacle that is forming around him is a lot to take in. I can't imagine living life like this every day.

"Oh my God, Levi," one of them squeals, "we were just

talking about you!"

They close in around him, invading his personal space. It's as if I'm not standing there trying to do my job. Then again, while he's temporarily distracted, now is the perfect time to sneak away and do something else.

Levi chuckles softly, seeming more amused than annoyed. "And what were you girls discussing about me, huh?"

The girl blushes brightly. "Well... we were talking about how amazing you were during last night's game."

One of the other girls steps forward and says, "Would it be weird to ask you for a photo?"

"No, but we should step out of line so we don't continue to disrupt Hailey."

I pause. It didn't take a rocket scientist to realize he'd read my name from my name tag, but having him say my name surprises me, nonetheless. Having him consider how this affects my ability to do my job is shocking as well.

The newly formed group steps out of my line and I walk over to help Ben finish up another customer's order. I pour it into a to-go cup and push it in the direction where the customer is standing. I look around to see if anyone else needs something but come up empty. As I'm about to turn around to see if I can help Ben some more, Levi steps away from girls and appears in front of me once more.

"Apologies for that and thanks for my drink."

"Why are you apologizing?" The question falls from my lips, and I wish I could take it back. Instead of looking at him, I make myself look busy by ringing up his order.

"Because I stepped away and interrupted the conversation we were having."

That causes me to look up at him briefly. "We were barely talking."

"I disagree. We were getting to know each other a little bit," he teases.

"Hailey."

The sound of my name stops any response I'm going to make. A curse word sits on the tip of my tongue, but I hold it back because I know it will not do me a bit of good.

Having Marc come out now should be considered a blessing, but who knows how long he's been watching me interact with Levi. Speaking of which, Levi's gaze lands on Marc, but his expression is unreadable.

However, the look on Marc's face is quite clear. The stern expression is directed right at me, and I know I've given him enough ammunition to berate me in front of everyone. "What are you doing, Hailey?"

"She's talking to me. I had some questions about the menu, and she cleared them up for me. I apologize for holding up the line."

I glance at Levi out of the corner of my eye, wondering why he decided to jump in front of the firing squad. I want to question him more about what he did, but I know better than to do that right now.

The look on Marc's face softens; I know Levi's charm is working its magic. He studies the man of the hour for a moment before he says, "You look familiar."

"Levi is on Crestwood's hockey team," I interject softly, still not knowing what to make of Levi.

Marc's face lights up as recognition hits. "I should have known. I've seen your face on posters around campus, but never fully paid attention. Congrats on the win last night."

Who knew Marc was a hockey fan? I surely didn't, but I also didn't try to get to know him either.

"Thanks." Levi's attention turns to me. "I need to head out. It was great meeting you."

Although he could have been talking to both of us with that sentence, Levi's eyes are trained on me. I refuse to give into the urge to look away even though it feels as if he is staring into the depths of my soul.

"Come back to Brewed Beginnings anytime," Marc chimes in, breaking the stare down Levi and I are having.

Levi nods politely at Marc and then focuses back on me. "I will, and I'll bring my teammates with me." His gaze lingers for a moment longer before he turns to leave.

"Get back to work, Hailey," Marc says before he, too, turns and walks away.

I stand there, somewhat stunned at what has just occurred. With a slight shake of my head, I force myself to get back to work because that is what I'm here to do.

4

HAILEY

I watch the stream of light coming from the bright afternoon sun dance along the whiteboard at the front of the classroom, I find myself struggling to maintain focus on anything else.

The only other thing keeping me somewhat focused is the pen in my hand. I lightly tap my pen against my notebook as I listen to my professor. He's talking about green spaces and how they can have a positive impact on mental health. It is a topic I'm normally passionate about and while I'm attempting to take notes, my mind isn't fully here.

At least I'm smart enough not to take my laptop out of my bag because it would only distract me further.

My eyes drift down to look at what I'd already written from today's lesson. My neat penmanship shows I've at least been listening somewhat, and if I get called out for my daydreaming, I at least have something to say.

As my professor continues to talk about the importance of trees and parks, my mind wanders off into its own little world. It's a place where I can replay the events that happened this morning at Brewed Beginnings on repeat without judgment.

As much as it irritates me, Levi's actions toward Marc are living rent free in my head. It is so silly for me to overthink this, especially since Levi is a complete stranger and everything I know about him I'm not a fan of.

Including the fact that he plays hockey. Well that's more so because hockey and sports aren't my thing.

Why am I even thinking about this? It was a fleeting moment and chances are, given how many students are on Crestwood's campus, I probably will not see him again.

Yet nothing could remove the encounter from my mind.

As I pack up my things, I can't help but be excited about the project. I debate whether I should mention something to Professor Klein after class. However, there are a few people waiting to speak to her so now probably isn't a great idea.

Instead, I leave and head to the library until I need to go back to the coffee shop. However, this time, it won't be to work a shift.

I get lost in studying and time passes by quickly, and

before I know it, it's time for me to return to Brewed Beginnings.

As I walk through the front door, I confirm I'm the first one there. It's what I prefer to have happen because it helps show that I'm committed to this organization.

I wave to another person I sometimes work with, Jenna, and say a silent thank you because Marc isn't here. Then I move along to transform one corner of the coffee shop into a space fit for our meeting.

Tiredness begins to make its way into my body as I rearrange tables and chairs into some semblance of order. Marc allows me to put up a sign to direct people to where chess club meets, and I make sure it is up. Once I'm finished setting up, members start trickling in. I swallow how I want to react and try to be as friendly as I can muster.

"Yo," I say when I glance up and see Jeff, a longtime member of the club.

Jeff raises an eyebrow.

"Well good evening to you too," he says, plopping his backpack down. "Having a shitty day?"

"Isn't that every day?" I snap. "But no. Just tired and wish I would have taken a nap between the end of class and our meeting."

"I hear that."

I take a deep breath to steady myself as I see a few new faces walk into Brewed Beginnings and head in our direction. Time to put on my game face and make sure the smile I'm wearing doesn't look completely fake.

"Hello and welcome to chess club," I say as I approach them. "I'm Hailey, president of the club. I've already set up some boards and you can sit at any table where there is one. We've got clocks for timing games if you wish to use them. I'll also be teaching some of the basics over here. There's coffee and snacks on the counter. If you have any questions, please let me know."

I give them a thin smile, hoping to keep our interactions short and to the point. The less I have to say, the better. I glance at the display case that still has pastries and other treats. I make a mental note that I should get a brownie because it's my favorite item that Brewed Beginnings sells, and I haven't eaten since this morning.

Once the new members have settled in, I quickly realize no one wants to be taught the basics, much to my relief. I retreat to the counter and chit chat with Jenna as she grabs me a pastry. It will not settle my stomach for long, but at least I have food in my body. I take one last look around the room, making sure that no one needs anything, before deciding it's time for my own game.

I find an empty table and set up a chessboard for myself. Playing by myself has always given me an opportunity to unwind, and after today, I desperately need it.

As I sit there moving both sets of pieces, I fall into a rhythm. Each move is a silent conversation with myself, a strategic dance in a way that helps clear my mind. The clink of the pieces as they touch the board is therapeutic, the familiar patterns of the game comforting.

While I don't mind having an opponent, there is something about playing by myself that I absolutely love. Each move gives me time to reflect and process my feelings, giving me the opportunity to settle the thoughts in my mind.

At least somewhat.

Although I'm aware of my surroundings, it all fades into the background. Time slows down as I stare at the board in front of me. The pawn in my hand gives me something to roll between my fingers while I think about my next move.

I carefully set down the pawn, having finally decided on my next move. As I reached for my knight, the tension I've apparently been holding in my shoulders lessens. I take a moment and look up to see if anyone is looking over at me, needing my attention, but everyone is focused on what move they need to make next.

Perfect.

I shift my attention back to the chessboard, studying the arrangement of pieces. I have many options for my next move with my knight, each with advantages and disadvantages to consider. But one thing is obvious. Here, in this moment, it is just me and the game.

Finally, I make my decision. With a soft clink, I set down the knight, taking the other color's bishop. I lean back and survey how things have changed on the board.

There is still more that needs to be done before I can wrap this up. I quickly finish the game and rise from my chair, stretching my muscles in the process. With a heavy sigh, I know it's time to socialize once more.

I carefully pack up the chess set, buying myself more time before I need to start my rounds. After convincing myself that going up to order a drink and a brownie from Jenna would only prolong the inevitable, I begin to make my way around the room.

I fold my arms across my chest as I make my way around the room, scanning the various games in progress. I'm slightly impressed with how focused everyone is. Many people join a club on campus because it'll look good on their résumé when they need to show extracurriculars. It is one of the most annoying fucking things. At least the people that are here tonight seem interested in the game.

As I make my way around the section of the coffee shop that we're using, I take in the sight of the various chess games in progress. At one table, I notice Jeff and Liza, his opponent, locked in an intense match that requires a lot of concentration. Both of their kings are under threat and while I can see pathways for either one of them to choose, I keep my mouth shut so they can figure them out on their own.

In the back corner, I notice Camden, someone who joined chess club around the same time I did, is patiently guiding a new guy through the basic openings. The new dude is listening intently to his instructions and will be better for it if he retains the knowledge Camden's giving him.

Once I've checked in on everyone, I stand between two tables near the center of our section. I clear my throat and announce in a loud, clear voice, "Hey! There are some decent games going on. We've got about five more minutes before we need to stop these matches. After that, take a breather, grab a drink, do whatever you need to do. But be quick about it. We're switching partners and starting a new round of matches ASAP."

Low murmurs start up again as everyone returns to their games. I pull out my phone to check to see if I have any messages, and I find one from my father.

> Dad: Just checking in because I haven't heard from you in a while. Hope everything is going well.

As I reread the text, a sharp pang of guilt slices through me. My mind races as I try to remember the last time I spoke to my father—could it have been a week ago? Maybe two? How could I have let that much time go by without at least saying hello?

I shouldn't have to wait for him to message me in order for me to consider calling him. Especially after all we've been through.

My fingers fly across my phone screen as I type up a response that reads like nothing more than a shitty excuse and press send.

> Me: Hi. Everything is going fine. Sorry
> I've been busy, but I can call later tonight
> if you're free.

I switch it to vibrate so I'm alerted when he sends me something back. I then stick my phone back into my pocket, forcing my mind away from my guilt and back on chess for the time being.

Nothing on my face gives away the emotions I feel churning inside of me. It's a look I've perfected and comes in extremely handy, especially when I don't want people to ask questions or get into my business. Having a resting bitch face is really useful when the only thing you want is to be left alone.

After walking around a couple more times, I glance up at the clock. Seeing how much time has passed, I say, "Okay, that's it."

The chess club members finish up their games and set up the chessboards so they will be ready for the next players to begin. I say nothing as several people stand and walk around while others chat with one another.

Instead of interacting with people, I stand off to the side and watch. Deep down, I know I should be doing the same thing, but I can't bring myself to do so. I'd rather sit on the sidelines and people watch as I debate with myself about how the rest of this meeting is going to go.

At least that is my plan until I notice Jeff walking toward me out of the corner of my eye.

"Are you planning on playing anyone this next round?" he asks.

I fight the urge to sigh. It is nothing against him personally, I just don't want to be bothered. I glance at him before staring straight ahead again. "Nope."

"How about you and I play against one another?" he suggests, taking a small step into my personal space.

I consider moving away but decide the best course of action is for me to stand still, holding my ground. Is there a chance I'm the only one seeing it this way? Yes, but it doesn't change my response.

I think about his proposal before asking, "Are you sure it's something you want to do?"

My question isn't meant for me to come off as being an asshole, but it is true, and he knows it. After all, I'm one of the best players, if not the best player, here.

"I could use the practice to get better."

That was a good point. "If that's what you want, then so be it."

I step away from Jeff as I realize that the break is over, and people are waiting around for me to give the next instructions.

"Okay, we're going to discuss a little bit of strategy before starting the next round of timed matches. These aren't going to be anything like rapid or blitz chess, so if the match isn't over by the end of our club meeting, that's fine. Any questions?"

Seeing none, I continue speaking. "Let's talk about one of the most fundamental strategies in chess: controlling the center of the board." I walk up to a chessboard and point to the squares e4, d4, e5, and d5.

I move a pawn to e4, then to d4, demonstrating what I'm trying to explain. "Controlling these central squares gives your pieces more room to move. Your pieces can move around more easily, giving you more options so you're not just acting on defense against your opponent. It's a more offensive strategy and gives you more opportunities to attack."

I go through a demonstration and explain my point. Several people ask questions and I answer quickly. Once that portion of the meeting is complete, we all pick a seat and get ready to begin our next matches.

"Are you ready?" Jeff asks me.

"Yep," I say in response. I set the timer and then we get to work.

Since I'm sitting on the side with the white pieces, I make the first move—advancing my king's pawn two spaces. Jeff mirrors what I've done on his side of the board. We continue exchanging moves, both aiming to control the center as I had demonstrated earlier. I have to admit, Jeff proves himself a worthy opponent, countering each attempt I make to gain the upper hand.

I gain a slight advantage when I manage to exchange

my bishop for one of Jeff's knights, but he responds aggressively, putting my king in danger. I have to think carefully to find a way out without losing too much ground.

Just as I'm about to force a draw, he makes a careless move, giving me an opening to checkmate him in three moves. I consider showing him the sequence but decide it's something I can explain after the match is over. Instead, I take his queen with my knight, leaving his king defenseless.

"Checkmate," I say, sliding my knight into place and sticking out my hand. He stares at my hand for a moment, stunned, before he reaches across the board and shakes it. "That was a close match."

"Yeah, it was," he says with a grin. "I'm getting better."

"You are," I respond. "It was really good. Let me show you the mistake you made."

I reorganize the pieces as we had them before and show him the move he made and how I was able to use it to get the win. He nods along as he watches, hopefully understanding what I'm trying to showcase here.

Our discussion is interrupted by the timer going off, signaling the end of this round of matches. I help Jeff clean up our board before standing up to address the room. "Great job today, everyone. If we can all help by cleaning any messes that we created, that would be great and won't piss off the manager here. We'll meet at the same time next week."

I'm kind of impressed with the number of people that stayed behind to clean things up, making my life easier. As the last members leave the coffee shop, I let out a long exhale as I sink into a chair.

I'm done for the night.

"Do you need anything?"

I look over and find Jenna staring at me before I shake my head. "Nah. I'm going to head out for the night."

"Sounds good."

I take a deep breath and stand up. Time to go home and recharge for another day. I leave Brewed Beginnings and walk back to my apartment, checking my phone and finding that I don't have any missed calls or text messages.

Unexpectedly, loneliness creeps in because the one person that is always there for me hasn't returned my text.

5

LEVI

What the hell am I doing?

It's all I can think about when the smell of coffee slams into me as I pull open the front door of Brewed Beginnings. I'm greeted with the sound of the bell above the door, one that I'm beginning to wonder, if I come in here enough times, will I start to hear it in my dreams. After all, this is the second time I've been here in three days, so I'm convinced it is bound to happen.

I hear Asher yawn as I hold the door open for him. There is no doubt in my mind that if he could get away with it, he'd strangle me right now.

"Why are we here again?" The exhaustion and annoyance in his voice is apparent.

"To get some coffee," I answer matter-of-factly as if

he'd asked the worst question in the world. Why else would most people go to a coffee shop?

Asher might have responded to me, but I don't hear him. All of my attention is on finding the person who, for the last couple of days, has played a starring role in the movie I keep playing in my mind. I look around and smile when I find the beautiful girl standing behind the counter with a black apron tied around her waist. Her long brown hair is in a bun on the top of her head and, right now, there is nothing I wouldn't give for the opportunity to run my hands through it.

Hailey doesn't bother glancing up from the steam wand hissing in her hands, but maybe she didn't hear the chime near the door. She's too focused on what looks to be a latte of some sort that she's making for a customer. There's a permanent crease between her eyebrows as if every coffee order is a personal attack on her peace of mind. But it's clear she takes pride in her work because, I swear, she's the most efficient worker here.

"I'm going to order something. Do you want anything? I'm buying."

Asher slowly turns his head toward me. "No, but I want to deck you for forcing me to wake up early just to come here before practice."

I wince slightly because I do feel bad about waking him up this early. But we usually travel to practice together, and there was no way I was missing an opportunity to see the girl who has caught my attention if I didn't have to.

My eyes follow Hailey as she finishes up the latte order and rings the customer up. I wonder if she's always this intense or if it's the pressure of the morning rush getting to her.

"Next!" Hailey calls out in a bored voice without looking up.

I debate getting into the line, but it would mean that I would have to wait even longer for a chance to talk to her. When I reach my decision, I know it's not right, but my patience is wearing thin.

"Can you get in line for me? I'll meet you at the front." Before Asher can protest, I walk away with only one destination in my sights.

My gaze is fixed on Hailey as I approach, but she still doesn't look up. She's scribbling on a cup, clearly focusing on the job at hand and not the distraction that is about to land in her lap.

I lean against the counter, clearing my throat loudly. "Good morning, Hailey."

Her head jerks up, eyes widening in surprise. "Uh, hi. There's a line, you know." She briefly gestures to the queue of people.

"Oh, I know. I'm not ordering yet. I wanted to come say hi." I don't tell her I'm doing this because it allows me to talk to her longer than I would be able to if I just waited in line for her to take my order. "How's your day going?"

Her hazel eyes meet mine. "Same stuff, different day," she shoots back without missing a beat.

"Rough crowd today?" I ask, and I eagerly await her response.

"If by rough, you mean they want coffee and they want it now, then yes. Do I have to remind you again that there is a line, and you need to be in it?"

"Ah, but you handle it with such grace," I say, ignoring what she said about me skipping the line. Instead, I lean forward on my elbows, trying to catch her eye. "You're like the barista equivalent of a ballet dancer. With zero cheer or happiness."

"Flattery will get you your coffee, but not any faster, especially if you're trying to skip a bunch of people to get served first. I don't care who you are or what team you play for," she responds, though the corner of her mouth twitches.

Warmth spreads through me because I almost got her to smile. "Fair enough." I chuckle, tilting my head to catch her eye again. Her smart-ass answers are funny and make me want to know what's beyond the sarcasm she likes to toss around.

But that isn't the only thing keeping me captivated. Hailey turns around and my eyes are instantly drawn to her body. The apron she has on does its best to hide her curves, but as soon as her back is to me, I notice the way the yoga pants she decided to wear today are molded to her ass as though made specifically for her.

It is too early for me to be staring at her body like this. I need to focus on hockey practice that is occurring in less than an hour, but I can't tear my eyes away.

What I wish I had a front-row seat to is her breasts, but they are hidden beneath her shirt and the apron. Perhaps one day I will be lucky enough to see and caress them, but for now, my imagination will have to be enough.

By the time she turns back around, my gaze is focused back on her face, leaving her none the wiser about the thoughts I'm having about her.

"By the way, I wouldn't use my status to skip the line. I'd use it to find out more about you."

She snorts and rolls her eyes. "Good to know. I'll file that away for never gonna happen."

"That sounds like a challenge to me." I run a hand through my hair as I enjoy the banter between us.

She shakes her head and although I'm sure she would never admit it, there's a hint of amusement in her eyes. It's the first time I've seen her look at me with anything other than annoyance, and it makes me feel oddly victorious and happy. This back-and-forth with her feels fresh and new, as if it is something I've been missing and didn't know it. I like this feeling.

Hailey waves another customer forward, but her attention is still firmly on me. "You know, I'm not even sure why you're here."

"Oh?" I say as I wait for her to expound on her point.

Hailey stops what she's doing and looks me right in

the eye before she says, "Based on my very limited interactions with you, I'm convinced you don't even need any coffee. You have enough energy in the morning to power the sun."

I can't help but chuckle. "I've been told that a time or two."

As I wait for her to respond, I have to bite my tongue from appearing overly excited. I want to extend this moment of casual banter with Hailey, but deep down, I know this isn't the time or place. But there is an ease in our conversation that's different from last time, and I find myself wanting to linger in it.

As Hailey is about to say something, one of her coworkers calls out to her from the other end of the counter. "Hailey, can you give me a hand here?"

She glances over her shoulder, a hint of annoyance flickering across her face. "Sure, just a sec, Ben." She then turns back to me, but now her face shows complete indifference. "Duty calls."

I nod, choosing to mask up my disappointment with a shrug. "Understandably."

As Hailey walks away to assist her coworker, I notice Asher, who is a few people away from me in line, looking amused. He raises an eyebrow at me, but I know he's enjoying watching me interact with the barista that has caught my eye.

"So, what the hell was that all about, huh?" Asher

nudges me, his smirk widening. "She was the reason you wanted to come here before practice."

I try to brush it off with a laugh. "The coffee's good here. That's all."

Asher laughs, clearly amused. "Sure, dude, it's all about the coffee. Nothing to do with the barista making you lose whatever cool points you had."

"Whatever, Ash," I reply, trying to hide the smile that is threatening to appear on my lips. He's not really wrong, but I'm not about to admit it.

He leans closer, lowering his voice a bit. "Look, I don't know if I've ever seen you shift your routine or schedule for anyone, and clearly, she's caught your eye. If you're into her, just go for it."

"You make that sound so easy," I say as I glance back at Hailey, who's now sharing a laugh with her coworker. She's back at her register and Asher and I are two people away from being at the front of the line. "I barely know her."

"That hasn't stopped you from taking any other girl back to your place and fu—"

I roll my eyes and interrupt him before he can finish his sentence. "Listen, it's not that simple. I can't play it like I usually would."

"Why?"

I cross my arms over my chest, preparing to explain. "Because I'm not sure if she likes me." I make sure to whisper the entire sentence because the last thing I need is for anyone to overhear what we're talking about.

"Based on what I saw, I would say ninety percent no, ten percent yes."

"I don't mind those odds because it's not a zero."

Silence follows instead of a response from Asher, which is something I hadn't been expecting. Before I can question him about it, it's our turn to place our order, with no one else but Hailey.

Her hazel eyes land on me first before darting to Asher and then back to me. "So you do know how to stand in line."

"Well, he knows how to force someone else to stand in line for him," Asher chimes in as if she is talking to him. He sticks his hand out and says, "Asher. I'm his best friend and one of his teammates."

"Hailey," she says as she does the same. I'm not sure why I'm somewhat surprised she returned the gesture, but I am. With a sigh, she asks, "What can I get you?"

As Hailey leans forward slightly to hear my order over the chatter in the café, I can't help but mirror her actions, allowing me to get closer to her if only for a few seconds. It's then that I smell something vanilla and citrusy. It's cutting through the smell of coffee, and I find it intoxicating.

A piece of hair falls out of her bun. I watch as she quickly tucks it behind her ear before her gaze narrows at me.

"Can I get an Americano? Make it a large because it's going to be a long day."

Hailey nods and it seems she's fighting to not give a more colorful response before saying, "I can only imagine how much energy you're going to have now."

"Wouldn't you like to know," I say, unfazed by her dry tone. "Gotta stay alert for practice, classes, and for your comebacks."

Hailey's expression doesn't change much, but I catch a small smirk as she starts pouring coffee into a to-go cup. "I hardly call what we are doing sparring."

"Maybe sparring isn't the right word. How about flirting?"

She scoffs. "I thought we talked about this yesterday, never mind that that's the complete opposite of sparring."

As she hands me my coffee, I take a moment to study her, trying to capture her reaction to my comment. She's unfazed, but there's a spark in her eyes that wasn't there before. I glance at the display of food to my left before looking back at her. It is when I decide to lighten the mood a bit. "Quick question. Asher and I were debating what the best snack for studying is. A blueberry muffin or a chocolate chip cookie. Which would you prefer?"

Hailey looks startled for a second before she catches herself expressing an emotion. "You guys really have nothing better to do than debate snacks?"

"It's a matter of survival," I reply without missing a beat. I can feel Asher staring me down out of the corner of my eye, probably wondering if I've lost my mind. It's not my fault that there is food staring me right in the face. Plus, it gives me a way to keep our conversation going while still keeping it about the coffee shop.

"How about an actual meal?"

Asher laughs from behind me, apparently catching on to what I'm doing. "That's not the fun or sugar rush we're looking for."

She sighs again. "Well, if it's sugar you want, the muffins are your best bet. But don't blame me if you're feeling like shit after a sugar crash."

I grin, happy to have gotten her to continue our conversation. "Noted. I'll take a blueberry muffin as well. Thanks."

Hailey reaches for a blueberry muffin from the display and takes a moment to place it into a small paper bag. The paper rustles as she rolls the opening down then closes it before passing the bag across the counter toward me.

I hand her my credit card and quietly wait for her as she rings me up. Once she's done, she passes my card back to me.

"Good luck with whatever you're planning to do after ingesting all that caffeine and sugar."

While there are a million and one things I could have said, I decide expressing my gratitude is the easiest. "Thanks, Hailey."

Her eyes meet mine for a split second before she turns away. I stuff my card into my pocket and grab the coffee and muffin before walking out of the shop with Asher trailing behind me.

As Asher and I walk to the door, he clears his throat. "Man, she doesn't give an inch, does she?"

"Nope," I say, stealing a last glance at her before I push open the front door with my shoulder. Hailey is already attending to another customer. "Makes it all the more interesting though."

"I can see why you're developing an appreciation for coffee now."

I know where he's going with this, and I'm not going to have it. "Watch it, dude. Let's focus on hockey now, shall we?"

All Asher does is laugh and shake his head in response. There is no doubt in my mind that the next opportunity he gets, he's going to give me shit for this.

6

LEVI

Later that day, I jerk my head to the left as an ear-piercing sound forces me to slow down. The shrill pitch of Coach Aaron Johnson's whistle pierces through the air, signaling the end of another grueling practice session.

"Good work today, team!" he screams and claps his hands twice. "See you at our next practice."

With the loud blast of the whistle still ringing in my ears, I linger behind as my teammates begin to make their way off the ice. Skating over to Coach Johnson, I wait for him to acknowledge me before I start to speak. "Coach, do you mind if I stay out a little longer? Just want a few extra minutes on the ice."

He gives me a look, scanning my face as if he's trying to figure out the best solution to a problem, before he nods. "Alright. But don't overdo it. Remember, we've got a big game this weekend. We need you."

"Thanks. I won't be out here very long," I say.

As I turn back to the ice, Asher skates up beside me. "Everything good?"

"Yeah, I just need to clear my head," I reply. "I'll catch up with you later."

Asher gives me a supportive clap on the shoulder before joining the rest of the team heading off the ice.

As the heavy metal door leading to the locker room closes, the sound echoes throughout the empty rink. There is a finality to it all that goes beyond it announcing that my coach and teammates have left.

It brings a sense of peace and relief as I have a moment to myself. No more pressure or distractions, just me and the ice.

Finally.

The only thing I can hear is the sound of my skates moving against the ice. Skating is second nature to me. My body moves with ease; every turn, every motion perfected through years of hard work and dedication. It's almost as easy to do this as it is for me to breathe. There's nothing that beats the feel of the wind as it whips across my face as I fly around the rink.

The emptiness of the rink is both haunting and liberating. Being away from Coach, who is normally watching my every move, and my teammates, who are looking for me to also be the leader they deserve, I find a rare moment of peace. Right now, I can just be, and that is perfectly alright with me.

I push myself to move faster, letting the chill of the rink fill my lungs. The cool air feels wonderful to the frustration that's been present within me. Every time I step out onto the ice with the team, the weight of my father's expectations and his desire for me to be the best rests on my shoulders, weighing me down. When I'm out here alone, it's as if I can shake off him and the critics that are watching my every move, effectively silencing them.

However, they can't be silent forever. I'm willing to bet my father is calling me right now to check in on how everything went because he knows what time practice ends. That's one headache I don't want to deal with right now.

Instead, I close my eyes for a second, trusting my body to know the ice like the back of my hand. Some will consider it a dangerous move, but I don't care. The thrill of it sends adrenaline coursing through my veins, but it's not the same as what I feel every time I step out on the ice to play a game.

But it doesn't matter right now. I open my eyes as I complete another lap around the rink.

As I glide, my mind begins to wander away from my father and the shitty relationship I have with him to Hailey. Her image appears in my mind, and for the life of me, I can't understand why. She and I have only seen each other a couple of times, but I can't get her out of my head.

There's something about her that unnerves me, but I can't figure out what or how she's doing it. This is all while she seemingly couldn't care less if I combusted into flames right in front of her. Yet the intrigue is still there, and that's both exciting and frustrating.

I round the net and come to a sharp halt, spraying ice in an arc. I exhale and look up at the empty stands. In a few days, they'll once again be filled with roaring fans, and there is nothing like the feeling of knowing all of those people are there to watch you kick ass.

But for now, it's me and no one else.

A puck lies abandoned at center ice. I skate over to it and give it a half-hearted tap with my stick. It slides across the ice before I chase after it and line it up for a shot. I slap it hard toward the goal.

It hits the post with a loud ping, bouncing back toward me. I have to admit, I'm happy that miss happened now and not during a game.

I pause for a second to line up another shot, and a voice slices through the air, ruining my focus.

"Jamison! Are you planning to make a day of it?" Coach Johnson's voice booms across the rink, forcing me from my thoughts. "Don't you have a class to head to or something?"

I look up at the clock and then at Coach Johnson. I didn't realize how much time had passed. "Uh yeah. I'm coming now, Coach!" I say back. I'm slightly embarrassed

Coach found me deep in my own thoughts, but at least he doesn't know what I was thinking about.

I know I should probably get off the ice as quickly as possible, but I can't resist the urge to give the puck another hard smack. This time, it's a release of pent-up frustration and anger, directed at my father.

The sound of it hitting the boards reverberates through the rink, matching the intensity of my emotions. I dash over to pick up the puck and quickly skate toward the exit where Coach Johnson is waiting for me.

Once I'm off the ice, I quickly put my skate guards on and gather my things. I meet Coach Johnson near the doorway to the way to the locker rooms, where he is leaning against the doorframe with arms crossed. The look on his face is impossible to read, but that's not unusual for him.

"Everything good, Jamison?" Coach Johnson asks. His gaze is focused on me as if he's trying to peer into my soul. "You seem a bit off."

I nod, even though I'm feeling anything but okay. "I'm fine, Coach. I only wanted another moment to skate, you know?"

He thinks about my response for a moment longer than is comfortable before he unfolds his arms. "Okay. We can't have you losing focus if we can prevent it. You're one of our best players. But also keep in mind hockey isn't everything. Having balance is important. Try finding another hobby or something to give you a small break to come back refreshed."

"I know and that's a good idea," I reply. I'm not sure if he believes me, but at least he doesn't ask any other questions.

Coach Johnson's hand lands on my shoulder pad before he steps to the side to walk into his office. "Get to class then."

"Will do. I'll see you later." I continue walking to the door that leads to our locker room.

"And Jamison?" He pauses when I look back at him. "If there's anything you need to talk about... you know where to find me."

"Thanks." I give him a short nod and continue on my way to my locker.

"Damn it," I mutter to myself. I don't know why I'm surprised he seemed to catch on to my lie when he's been coaching for decades at this point, but I am. Then again, maybe it is wishful thinking on my part.

I shrug off the conversation with Coach Johnson as I reach my locker. It's as if I'm working on autopilot while I'm opening the lock. It's a little eerie to be in here by myself. I'm used to being around my teammates, but their chatter and noises have now been replaced by the quiet hum of overhead fluorescent lights and the distant roar of a Zamboni cleaning the ice for the next practice.

I strip off my gear, each piece hitting the bench closest to me with a thud. My skates are the last to come off and I make sure to set them down gently before tucking them away in my bag.

Once I'm showered and back in the clothes I arrived here in, I stuff everything else into my duffel bag. I shove the bag onto my shoulder before heading outside.

The air is crisp outside, reminding me that I should have brought a hoodie with me. It is the one thing I'm definitely going to grab when I get home. The walk back to my apartment is a short one, and as I'm walking through my front door, my phone buzzes in my pocket. I snatch the phone from its resting place and glance at the phone screen: Dad.

I hesitate for a moment. I've been avoiding his calls for a while and maybe now is the time to answer to get him off my back for a bit. Because if I don't, he'll keep calling until he reaches me. Then it might escalate into something bigger. I let out a heavy sigh before swiping to answer the call and put it on speaker.

"Hey, Dad," I say, trying to sound upbeat as I toss my bag on the floor and close my front door.

"Levi, how are you?" my dad replies. His voice is stern but not unkind, but there is time for him to shift to that. "I wanted to check in and see how you're handling everything with the season starting up again."

I wander into my kitchen and grab a glass from the cabinet. "I'm doing alright; just finished up practice actually."

"Good, good," he says. There's a pause and I can

picture him nodding on the other end. "Now listen, your coach mentioned he wants to see more leadership from you this year. As captain, you have to set the example."

I clench my jaw, filling my glass with water from the fridge. Of course Coach Johnson called my dad. They've been friendly for years, but I wouldn't call them friends.

"I know, Dad. And I'm ready for it, I promise." I take a long drink to calm down, hoping he'll leave it at that.

"Are you really though? Because if you're not, you'll miss out on crucial opportunities," he continues to press. "This is your time to step up and show everyone you're the best of the best. It's what Caleb would have done and was on the way to doing."

And there it is. Any time hockey comes up, he finds a way to loop it back to my older brother, Caleb. Hockey prodigy, killed in a car accident three years ago. I grip the edge of the counter until my knuckles turn white.

"I know, Dad. But I'm not Caleb." My voice comes out strained, barely above a whisper. Deep down, I know where every call from my father about hockey is going to lead, but it's still like a knife to the heart when Caleb is brought up. I wish for once he could see me as me, not an inferior replacement for the son he lost.

An uncomfortable silence passes between us before he responds. "You have the potential, Levi. You always have. But you need to push harder. That's what I've always tried to instill in you."

He's telling the truth about that. With how many

hours he works, Caleb, Mom, and I barely saw him unless it was him finding a way to attend one of our hockey games. I can't even remember the last time we went on a family vacation with all of us. Definitely not since Caleb died.

I shake my head in an attempt to remove the memories. "I understand and realize it more than you know." It is time to end this, or he'll further ruin my mindset. "Listen, I should get going because I have class, but I'll talk to you later, okay?"

"That's fine. We can talk about some of your strategies for the year and—"

"Bye, Dad," I say as I end the call, happy to have remained slightly unscathed.

It's as if he never hears anything I say, but that's the norm. He loves to push me to live up to the expectations that were set for my brother, and then he gets disappointed when I don't meet them although they are unrealistic anyway. It's exhausting, time consuming, and is just another thing I don't need to have shoved into my face constantly.

I finish my water and set the empty glass in the sink with more force than necessary. The glass clatters loudly against the metal basin and I shake my head as the sound rings in my ears for a couple of seconds.

Walking into my bedroom, I grab the hoodie I should have brought with me this morning before going back into the kitchen. I check the time and curse to myself. I have to be out of my apartment in a couple of minutes in order to arrive at class on time.

I run a hand through my hair as I try to ignore the feelings I have as a result of the conversation with my father. I know my dad means well in his own way. He wants me to be the best version of myself. But constantly comparing me to Caleb only makes me feel inadequate.

Growing up, Caleb was the golden child because he was talented, driven, and charming. Everyone loved him, especially my dad. They were always so close, bonding over hockey at the rink. Caleb was also my role model and the reason I got into hockey. I love hockey, but it was definitely Caleb's thing before it was mine. I started playing to have something in common with him and to seek my father's approval.

When Caleb died, it gutted our family. My parents were never the same. While the light in Mom's eyes dimmed, my father became more invested in me and my hockey playing. He started pushing me harder as if he was trying to keep Caleb's memory alive through me. And that, to me, is unfair.

I grab my backpack and sling it over my shoulder. I quickly make sure I have everything I need for the classes I have today and leave my apartment, forcing myself to leave the thoughts I have about my home life there as well.

7

HAILEY

There are several things I prefer to do on a Saturday morning.

Sleeping in for as long as I can.

Eating whatever I want.

Binge watching reality television shows.

Reading a book on my never-ending TBR.

Not being at Brewed Beginnings if Marc is there.

One thing that is definitely not on the list? Darting across campus with Jade for a scavenger hunt.

I swallow my annoyance as I walk up to the place where we're supposed to meet to start the festivities. Because I'm running a little late, Jade decided to meet me at the quad because she's too excited about this. I don't fight her on this because it gives me some time to myself to mentally prepare for whatever the hell is going to be thrown at me.

I use my hand to block the sun as I get closer to the quad. It's easy to find where we are supposed to be due to the colorful balloons that are tied on the lampposts and the table with a rainbow-colored sign labeled *Scavenger Hunt* taped to the front of it.

It is also easy to find Jade.

Her bright red shirt makes her easy to spot but it's her energy that puts the spotlight on her. I can't help but smirk because of how happy she looks right now. She will never admit this, but she's literally bouncing on the balls of her feet. I'm not sure if I've ever seen anyone do that besides being caught in a cold environment, but it is the best way I can describe what she is doing.

In her left hand, I assume she's holding the list of things we need to find, and in her right, she has her phone. She's probably this close to calling me because I'm not here five minutes early.

Jade spins around and when her gaze lands on me, I see her visibly breathe a sigh of relief. "Hailey! You're just in time!"

I give her a small smile even though this is the last thing I want to do. My feet drag my body the last couple of yards toward her and I stick my hands into the back pockets of my jeans. "Great. Wouldn't miss this for the world," I reply with a hint of sarcasm.

Jade, who I'm sure is intentionally ignoring my lack of enthusiasm, claps her hands, forcing her phone and the pieces of paper to come together. She looks down for a moment before sticking her phone into her pocket, probably because she didn't need to call me and ask where I am. Once it is safely put away, she waves the white pieces of paper in my face once, and the only thing I can think of is that it's a white flag signaling my defeat. This is really what I'm going to be doing this Saturday morning.

"So I've been strategizing about this since last night," Jade says, and I'm not at all surprised. She hands me a copy of our scavenger quest, and I hold back the sigh I want to let loose as it touches my fingers. With her focus back on the piece of paper in her hand, she says, "What do you think? Should we split up or stick together?"

I shrug. "Let's stick together for now," I say decisively. "There might come a point where we have to split up, but I'd rather do this with you."

It is also my way of ensuring that I won't decide to say fuck this and go back to our apartment.

"The whistle should blow in a few minutes and then we can start," she says.

I nod. "Well, since they gave us the list early, why don't we write down some of the answers we might know to the clues and head there first?"

Her face lights up before she looks back down at the list. "That's a great idea! See, you're getting into this."

I don't know about that, but at least she thinks I am.

"Also," Jade pauses for a second, "depending on which clues we figure out, we should list the answers by their locations. That way we aren't running across campus unnecessarily."

This is all unnecessary, but I can see her point. "That's a good idea. Excellent strategizing," I say as I pull out my phone. Together, we find ourselves staring down at the scavenger hunt list. The first clue reads:

"Head to the hub where minds meet and ideas spark, near the silent guardian that stands tall even in the dark. You'll hear no ticking, but its stance is grand, close to the realm of knowledge, where projects are planned."

The clue sounds ridiculous, but the campus library with a gigantic clock sculpture in front of it flashes in my mind.

"That's gotta be the Ramsey Library," I mutter, typing the answer into my phone.

"Exactly what I was thinking!"

Without waiting for me to say anything else, she starts reading the next clue out loud. We figure out the answers to a few more clues and several we might know but aren't completely sure about. I send Jade a quick text with the information I've typed out just before the sound of a whistle cuts through the morning air. It makes both of us pause for a few seconds before everyone, including ourselves, disperses in every which direction.

"Go!" Jade almost screams, grabbing my arm and pulling me toward Ramsey Library. We end up jogging lightly and reach the library within minutes. She pulls out her phone once more and snaps a picture, providing the proof we need to show that we've completed this task.

"What's another clue we've already solved?" I rush out before I can lose my breath. I'm in decent shape but having to jog unexpectedly didn't bode well for me.

She grins at me like she knows exactly what's going through my head and flips over to the next page. "'Where creativity and the great outdoors merge. Look up, look down, where these elements play, and uncover the beauty that is here to stay.' We said that was the community garden murals."

"Yes, that's right," I reply with more enthusiasm than I was anticipating. It's as if my competitive streak has decided to make itself known, and now I want to do well in this event. Sometimes being an overachiever has its advantages. "Let's head over there."

We set off again, but this time we walk fast instead of jogging. As we approach the community garden murals, a beautifully vibrant kaleidoscope of color comes into view. The garden displays an array of colors due to the organic produce and plants here. It's only a matter of time before the colder weather hits and a lot of this colorfulness will be missing. However, that is when the murals on the wall overlooking the garden will become a more prominent feature. Each piece of art reflects student and campus life. They range from bold, graffiti-style pieces to peaceful landscapes that all fit together in this space. Outside of helping to plant some of the produce here, I'm realizing I never come over here to enjoy this part of campus.

Jade is quick with her phone again, taking pictures of the murals and the garden. I find myself staring at the artwork for a few seconds too long before Jade nudges me.

"Look," Jade says softly, pointing to one particular section of the mural where a beautiful sunset flows into a portrait of a former professor who passed away a few months ago.

We spend another minute admiring the murals, but we know time is of the essence and we have to continue the scavenger hunt. I glance away from the wall and toward the path that leads out of the garden and spot a familiar figure up ahead. Broad shoulders, messy dark hair, wearing a backward cap...

"Wilder!" Jade calls out, waving.

The man in question turns around at the sound of his name and his face breaks into a smile when he sees us. His eyes linger on Jade a bit longer than they should before he says, "Hey! What are you doing here?"

Jade answers for the both of us. "We're doing a campus-wide scavenger hunt. What's your excuse?"

"Just finished wrapping up breakfast. Why don't I walk with you guys while you continue searching? I could use the exercise to get the digestion going."

Part of me wants to call him out on his bullshit, but I let it go. First, I'm surprised to see him out and about this early on a Saturday morning. If I had to guess, I would have thought he'd been up partying late last night with his teammates. The things Crestwood's hockey team is rumored to get up to were legendary at this point, and I have no problem believing it is worse than we all know.

But hey, they keep winning and bringing more attention and money to the school, so who cares, right? At least that is the approach the school's administration takes.

Jade shares a look with me, and when I give her a small nod, she grins. "That's a great idea. We'd love to have you join us."

Finding Wilder at the community gardens, though unexpected, doesn't delay us much. He falls into step alongside us, occasionally glancing over at Jade as we walk. At least I hope it's occasionally because I will not be held responsible if he trips over his own feet due his attention being centered on the woman standing between us.

"So, where to next?" he asks casually, his hands tucked into the pockets of his well-worn jeans.

Jade stares down at the piece of paper and reads off the next clue. "Where java flows and laptops glow, in the heart of campus life's ebb and flow. Seek the spot where the wired and weary find their brew, your next location lies in plain view."

"Brewed Beginnings!" I exclaim. It is probably the most enthusiasm I've shown all day, but that doesn't mean I'm actually excited to be going there. I'm happy I was able to figure out another clue. We hadn't gotten to that one earlier, so I didn't expect it to be on our list.

"Yep," Jade confirms with a smile. "It makes sense for it to be on the list. How fitting is it that we're going to go to your job and you're wearing a chess club shirt?"

I have a few clothes that allow me to rep the club I'm president of and I don't mind wearing them. They are comfortable and it helps me get the word out about chess club without having to talk to people.

Wilder gives me a curious look and then his eyes widen slightly. He snatches his phone out of his pocket and his fingers begin flying across his screen. I look at Jade who shrugs, but something in the pit of my stomach tells me that I might know what this is all about.

The scene that is unfolding before me isn't a coincidence, and I can't stop the words that fall out of my mouth. "Wilder, is everything okay?"

"Yeah," he says without looking up from his phone. Maybe I am going to be responsible for him falling on his face after all.

"Are you sure?" Jade chimes in this time. I'm happy she's also reading this situation as odd even though she doesn't know everything I do.

Wilder glances up from his phone with a smirk on his face. "Everything's good," he says casually. "Had to send a quick text."

He tucks his phone back into his pocket as we continue walking. I want to press him further, to call out the convenient timing of all of this and ask who he was texting. But I hold my tongue for now.

We reach Brewed Beginnings a few minutes later. The coffee shop is busy, with people sitting at tables with their laptops open as the clue described. Jade snaps photos with her phone of the sign as Wilder clears his throat.

"So, you must really like chess to be a part of the club and to wear their gear."

This is the most awkward shit, but Jade saves me from saying something that would make me sound like an asshole. "She's not just a part of the club. She's the president of it."

"It's not a big deal," I mumble, feeling suddenly self-conscious about Jade's praise. I'm not embarrassed about my position, or anything related to chess club, but I don't like too much attention being put on me.

"Are you kidding? That's cool," Wilder says, sounding genuinely impressed. "Maybe Jade and I will stop by sometime."

Jade snorts. "How are you dragging me into this?" She then turns to look at me. "No offense, Hailey."

"None taken," I answer automatically. I get what she's saying. If Jade was interested in chess, she could come with me at any point. It isn't her thing, and I respect that, but it almost feels comical how Wilder is trying to invite both her and himself along to a club meeting.

"I don't do much outside of hockey so going to a chess

club meeting will be something else to do, that's all," he says.

But it doesn't feel like that's all. However, in the interest of time, I say, "We can table this discussion for another time because we have a scavenger hunt to finish."

"Hailey's right," Jade says. "We've already lost some time standing here instead of moving onto the next clue."

Excellent. I need to get this scavenger hunt done quickly so I can get away from Wilder. I can't stop thinking about who he was texting and how it is most likely Levi. It could also be a group chat, which is more concerning.

"Okay. Well, what's the next clue?" Wilder asks.

While I can pull the list of clues out, I wait for Jade to do so, and the three of us read over the next set of clues as we decide which location might be the next one we need to visit.

The rest of our time together goes by quickly. The conversation between the three of us is easy even with the thoughts in my mind swirling at a million miles an hour. After completing our photo scavenger hunt, we finally make it back to the quad where we began. While we didn't come in first place, I can admit going around campus was fun for the most part.

Wilder is the first to break the silence. "Well, that was fun, but I should probably get going though. I have to do a couple of things, and I told some of the guys on the team I'd meet up with them."

"Oh, okay," Jade replies. "It was cool of you to join us. I'll talk to you later?"

"For sure," Wilder says. "Have a good rest of your day!"

He gives us a little wave before turning and walking across the quad.

I wait until he's out of earshot before turning to Jade. "Was it just me, or was Wilder acting kind of weird?" To be honest, I don't really know if this is weird for him because I don't hang out with him all that much, and I want to get Jade's feedback on the situation.

Jade frowns. "What do you mean?"

"I thought it was odd that he pulled out his phone to text someone as soon as you told him about my working at Brewed Beginnings and being president of the chess club."

Out of nowhere, my phone buzzes in my pocket, shifting my attention completely. I pull it out and glance at the screen and find a text from my dad.

Dad: Sweetheart, do you want to go out to lunch? I was thinking Riverstone Grill.

Me: Sure, let me know what day and time you're thinking.

Jade's question cuts through my thought process. "Everything okay?"

"Yeah, it's my dad. He wants to do lunch," I say after putting my phone back in my pocket.

Jade glances at Wilder for a moment as he walks away

before turning back to me. "I don't know, but I can try to get it out of him if you want me to."

I think about her proposal for a second before I shake my head. "Nah, I'll let it go."

Who am I kidding? That is a lie. I'm still going to be wondering exactly what Wilder might have told Levi or the rest of the team, especially if it's about me. Although I'm curious about what is going on, there is absolutely no way I'm letting Levi Jamison into my life.

8

LEVI

A monstrous yawn escapes my lips, one I'm pretty sure is long enough to set a world record. The urge to turn over and go back to sleep is strong. I rub the sleep away from my eyes as I roll out of bed.

Am I tired? No, but my energy only gets kickstarted after I've thrown some water on my face.

Living alone has its perks. Not being woken up by a roommate for one. Another perk? Being able to leave your apartment in any state you desire. While I usually do my best to maintain some sort of order in here, I've been slacking off this week. For now, the messiness has to wait until after I've met my basic needs for the day.

I stretch as I step over my shit strewn on the floor in order to get to the bathroom. I flick on the light and squint against the brightness. My dark brown hair is sticking up at odd angles and another yawn falls out of my mouth.

With a heavy sigh, I turn on the showerhead and wait for the water to warm up. When it reaches the temperature I like, I take off the only thing I wore to sleep last night, my boxers, and toss them in the direction of my laundry basket. I make a mental note to do laundry today before I run out of clean underwear.

As I step under the spray, I let the warm water start working its magic, washing away the grogginess from sleep. I rest my arm against the coolness of the tile and close my eyes. I slow my breathing down as I try to relax under the water droplets, and the longer I stand here, the more I start to feel human.

When I open them again, I reach for my soap and begin to wash myself, each movement boosting my alertness. Within seconds, I have enough energy to power the sun.

As I replay Hailey's words, it forces an image of her into my mind, but let's be honest, she's not too far from my thoughts since the moment I first saw her.

Did I think she was beautiful? That is an understatement. I knew she was gorgeous the moment I laid eyes on her even though I was half-asleep. But the way she has no issue with trading fire with fire draws me into her as well. She challenges me under the guise of not being able to stand me, but I've seen hints of a smile playing on her lips when she thinks I don't see it.

I run my hand through my hair just before it makes its way down to my morning wood. I give myself a few light strokes, feeling the slickness from the soap and water coating my fingers. It feels nice but I know it won't be enough.

When I can't resist any longer, I give in to pleasure. Letting out a soft moan, I grip myself a little tighter. I move up and down as I think about her face and how I want to make those hazel eyes of hers roll into the back of her head.

I close my eyes as my hips start to rock forward, moving in sync with the motion of my hand. All I can picture is her naked in this shower with water cascading down her body as I take her against the wall after my mouth has its fill of her pussy.

The image alone has me ready to explode, but I force myself to slow down before it's all over. This fantasy can't end too soon, because right now, it's all I have. I think about her nails digging into my back as she moans out my name...

"Fuck," I growl, unable to stop myself any longer. My cock shoots out cum all over the shower tiles, and I'm left breathless. I lean against the wall, panting heavily while letting the water wash away the evidence of my masturbation session. I can't remember the last time I've done that.

Leaning against the cool tile, I close my eyes and try to catch my breath. After a moment, I push myself from the wall, removing the haze from what just happened from my brain. I finish up my shower, scrubbing away the last of the soap and the tiles that ended up being on the receiving end of my load. I turn off the water and reach for my towel.

Wrapping it around my waist, I step out onto the bath-mat. As I wipe the fog off the mirror with my hand, I catch my reflection, but I barely see myself. Despite my orgasm, Hailey's image is still in my mind, almost taunting in a way. I shake my head, as if physically trying to rid myself of the distraction she's become, but I'm lying to myself.

I make my way back into the bedroom and I start by tossing aside piles of clothes—some clean, some that will end up in the laundry basket that was already overflowing —until I find a pair of boxers, sweatpants, and a t-shirt.

I put my clothes on and walk straight for the kitchen. I grab a glass to pour my orange juice in and open the fridge. I decide on a quick breakfast sandwich, with the plan to find something else to eat if that isn't filling enough.

After I get the eggs sizzling in the pan and the bacon is cooking in the oven, my phone makes a sound, alerting me that I've received a text message. Although the urge to pick up my phone is there, I decide to finish cooking my breakfast sandwich first before checking it. There's a chance I might get distracted, and burning my food or my apartment down isn't exactly in the cards for today.

During the time I'm preparing breakfast, my ringtone plays several more times. The only reason I don't think it is an emergency is because whoever it is didn't try to call me too.

Once I proudly assemble my sandwich, the golden egg yolk sitting perfectly atop the crispy bacon and cheese in between a bagel, I finally give in to my curiosity. I wipe my hands on a paper towel and grab my phone from where I'd plugged it in the night before in my living room. I sit down on my couch and watch as my phone's screen lights up with a barrage of notifications, but it's the texts from Wilder to our hockey group chat that force me to raise an eyebrow.

Group Chat: Ice Kings

Wilder: Hey, Cap! You up yet?

Wilder: You can't still be sleeping now. You're wasting daylight.

There is an assortment of emoji included with the text messages and I shake my head.

Knox: There's nothing wrong with sleeping in, especially on a Saturday. Stop blowing up our phones.

Wilder: Then mute me, dude.

Knox: Don't tempt me with a good time.

Asher: I just want to know what all of this is about.

> Wilder: Guess who I bumped into this morning?

> Knox: Our campus is huge. It could be anyone.

> Wilder: Fine, I'll put you out of your misery. Hailey, the barista from Brewed Beginnings.

I briefly see red. *How the hell did he end up with her?*

> Blaise: Wait, isn't that the girl Asher said Levi's been low-key obsessing over?

I swear that is the most words I've ever seen Blaise type in one of our chats. It is time to put an end to my silence.

> Me: Obsessing? Seriously, Blaise?

> Blaise: Don't shoot the messenger.

> Asher: Told you he has it bad. How did this all happen?

> Wilder: Apparently, she's besties with Jade, and they were doing this scavenger hunt thing around campus. Got to spend some time chatting with her.

I wait for him to continue typing or for anyone else to send a message, but no one does. I know what they are waiting for me to do, and I hate that I'm about to give into it, but I want to know.

Me: Well... what did she say?

Wilder: I knew you would want to know. She was chill and we talked mostly about the hunt, but I did find out she is the current president of Crestwood's chess club.

Chess? That's interesting. I take a bite of my sandwich and wonder what I can do with that information.

I'm no stranger to the world of chess. My grandfather taught me how to play when Caleb and I were children, but it's been quite a while since I have played. Hockey consumes the majority of my time and doesn't leave much room for anything else.

Wait a minute.

I stand from my couch, suddenly motivated by this trip down memory lane. I step over the laundry that I've yet to pick up and go back into my bedroom. I dig through the top drawer of my dresser, where I toss things I can't bring myself to throw away but have no immediate use for. My hand finds the item I want—an old, slightly faded photograph of a much younger me and Caleb sitting at a wooden chessboard. Our eyes are focused on the board in front of us as our grandfather is standing to my right, pointing at one of the pieces. We all look happy.

A wave of nostalgia causes a smile to form on my face. I can't believe I forgot about this moment until now. While I don't remember everything about that day, I remember being proud of myself as I was catching onto the rules and how you have to move some of the pieces.

I go back into the living room and place the picture on the coffee table before picking up my phone once more. A couple of text messages are waiting for me.

> Knox: So now we know what Levi's going to be doing for the next hour. Trying to find out when and where the chess club meets.

> Asher: Yep. He's probably at his place right now trying to plan his future chess matches right this second.

> Me: Funny, assholes. Let's not act like I can't see the things you're writing about me, okay?

> Wilder: And here I was, just about to start on the chess puns. Don't ruin our fun.

I chuckle and silence my phone. The teasing isn't bothering me, and I know there is more where that came from, but I now want to enjoy my food in peace.

I take another bite of my sandwich and my gaze lands on the economics textbook that I need to open.

There's an entire chapter on Keynesian multipliers that I need to read by Monday. Because nothing says relaxing weekend or peace like economic theory.

This isn't to say that I don't like economics. I do, and it's one of the foundations I need to study in order to complete my business major. Given that it is the weekend, and we don't have a game or practice today, today is the perfect day to catch up on everything else I've neglected.

But my mind is still about as far away from econ or cleaning as it can get. Because the only thing my thoughts want to do is figure out a way that I get to know Hailey better.

And that way might just be through chess.

9

HAILEY

I push open the heavy oak door of the Riverstone Grill in a hurry; its hinges letting out a small groan. The smell of sizzling steaks and wood smoke hits me, taking me back to the meals I've enjoyed here with Jade on occasion. I walk up to the podium and wait for the hostess to give me a smile as a greeting.

"Table for Reed," I tell the hostess. She nods, picks up a menu, and gestures for me to follow her. We make our way through the restaurant, and I spot my father sitting at a table by the window, lost in thought.

Even from a distance, I can see the kindness in his soft hazel eyes, eyes that mirror my own, along with his salt-and-pepper hair that is swept off his face. He's dressed in his usual button-down shirt and dark jeans, a style he's worn for as long as I can remember. As if he senses someone is watching him, he looks over at me when I'm a few feet away from him.

"Hailey!" Dad's face splits into a grin as wide as the river that gave this restaurant its name. He stands, his chair scraping lightly against the hardwood floor, and sweeps me up in one of those hugs that manages to be both awkward and heartwarming at the same time.

"Hey, Dad." I return his smile with a small one of my own, settling into the chair across from him. "Sorry I'm late. I had to submit an assignment before coming here."

"It's not a problem," he says. "How's everything? School? Friends?"

"School's good. Professors are still assigning homework like it's going out of fashion, hence my tardiness," I reply, picking up the leather-bound menu and scanning it without really seeing the words. "Friends are... friends. Can't complain."

He nods knowingly. "Ah, the joys of college. Makes you appreciate the weekends even more, doesn't it?" He takes a sip from the glass of water on the table, but his gaze remains on me.

"Yeah, weekends are sacred. Gives me an opportunity to catch up and sleep."

We're approached by a waitress with a warm smile and a tablet. "Hello and welcome to Riverstone Grill. Can I start you off with something to drink?" she asks.

"I'll have a water." I pause for a moment and then add, "Actually, add a slice of lemon, please."

"Make that two," Dad says.

"Excellent. And do you need a little more time to decide what you would like to eat?" After Dad and I nod, the hostess replies, "Great. I'll get you those waters and I'll be right back."

The waitress leaves and we're left to think about what we would like to eat. Once I decide what I want, I look at Dad as he scans his menu. I can't help but notice Dad has shadows under his eyes that weren't there the last time I saw him.

"Everything okay with you, Dad? You look tired." The words slip out before I can stop them. I know it's a result of me being partially concerned and feeling guilty for not checking in on him more.

He shakes his head before he says, "I'm fine, sweetheart."

I want to press further because there's something behind his casual dismissal that feels off. But we're here to catch up and enjoy each other's company, not dwell on anything too serious. At least not yet.

I decide to let it slide for the moment and change topics. "So, have you been to any interesting places lately? Any new hiking trails?"

Dad's eyes light up, the tiredness momentarily forgotten. Hiking is something we tend to do together, more so before I left for college. "Actually, yes. I discovered this beautiful trail about an hour away from here. Not many people know about it, so there wasn't too much foot traffic when I was there. The trail is a rather easy hike as well."

"That sounds great. Maybe I could join you next time?"

"I'd like that," he replies with a nod and then adds with a raise of his brow, "Would give us a chance to spend some more quality time together."

I playfully roll my eyes, but the guilt is still there. "You're hilarious."

He chuckles just before he sobers up and pats my hand. "On a serious note, I feel like I rarely hear from you, kiddo. I'm trying to give you space as you continue to grow and become your own woman, but I miss you."

Our conversation is interrupted by our waitress returning. She sets down the glasses with a gentle clink, the lemon slices bobbing slightly as she does so. She also brings some warm rolls I can't wait to dig into.

"Here you are," she says warmly. "Are we ready to order or do we need a few more minutes?"

I glance at Dad, and he gives me a nod, indicating he's ready to place his order. "I think we're ready," I reply, closing the menu. "I'll have the grilled chicken salad, please."

"And for you, sir?" The waitress turns to my father.

"I'll go with the rib eye steak, medium-rare, and the baked potato on the side. Oh, and could you bring some extra sour cream?"

I'm surprised Dad ordered it given the price it is listed

at. We usually do our best to not spend too much money, especially with me in college. I don't say a word, but the look on my face must have given me away because Dad turns his attention to me.

"Are you sure that's what you want? This is my treat by the way."

"Yes. I'll keep the grilled chicken salad," I say as I hand over my menu and watch my father do the same.

"Of course. I'll get those orders in for you right away." The waitress collects our menus and walks away.

Silence falls between us as I take a sip of water and take a bite from one of the rolls. Dad is studying me again, his expression thoughtful, but he doesn't say a word.

Once I'm done chewing, I speak first. "Back to our conversation. I know I haven't been talking to you as much as I should be, and I promise to be better."

"Thanks, but also don't feel as if I'm pressuring you to call your old man every day. I would just like to hear from you more to make sure you're okay."

"Of course. That makes complete and total sense."

A moment of silence passes between us, the weight of our words lingering in the air between us. It's not an uncomfortable quiet, but I'm grateful when Dad's light laugh breaks it.

"You know, I've been thinking about getting a dog," he says.

"Wait, what? A dog? Since when are you a dog

person?" I ask. Surprise is an understatement because I've never heard Dad mention anything about dogs.

He shrugs, a small smile playing on his lips. "I thought it might be nice to have some company around the house. Plus, it would give me an excuse to get outside more, even when I don't feel like hiking."

"Any particular breed in mind?"

"Well," he replies as he lightly taps a finger on the table. "I've been looking at some rescue sites. I don't know which breed or age for that matter, but I figured I'd know the right one when I see it. A lot of older dogs need loving homes, and I've been thinking why not?"

"That's great, Dad." My heart swells at the thought of him opening his home and heart to a furry friend. "If you want me to come with you when you go and visit a shelter, I can do that too."

His face lights up in almost the same way it had when I arrived. "That'd be wonderful," he replies.

We continue talking about potential dog names and what adjustments he might need to make to our home to make a dog the most comfortable. Then our conversation shifts through other lighthearted topics and shared memories, and I start to feel more connected to him than I have in a while.

Our waitress returns and places our dishes before us. We eat mostly in silence, and once again, it's a comfortable one. The food is absolutely delicious, and I can tell by the way Dad is licking his lips, he's thinking the same.

As we finish dinner, Dad looks over at me and asks, "Do you want something for dessert as well?"

I shake my head immediately. There is no way I can fit another ounce of food into my body right now. With a heavy breath, I lean back in my chair, patting my full stomach. Dad smiles at my exaggerated gesture and takes a final sip of his water. Once he places the glass down, he looks back at me and every hair on my body stands at attention because of the look on his face.

"Hailey, there's something else I wanted to tell you."

"What's up?" I ask quietly.

His hands fold together on the table as he leans forward slightly. "I've been doing a lot of thinking," he starts and clears his throat before he continues. "About us, about our family... and where we are in life. This kind of goes hand in hand with my thinking about getting a dog, but it's not quite the same."

I nod encouragingly, thankful that this doesn't sound like he's sick or anything like that. However, I'm still unsure of what he's about to say.

"And I've realized that, well, it's been quite some time since your mother left." He stops to gather his thoughts. "I've spent these years focused on you and work, and I have no regrets. Rebuilding our lives when it was just you and me was hard, but now, it's something I would never change."

I can feel a knot forming in my stomach. Dad rarely, if ever, talks about Mom leaving. It's like an unspoken agreement between us—a chapter that has already been written in a book that is shut and put on a shelf to collect dust.

"But lately," he goes on, his eyes now holding mine, "I think it might be time for me to start considering the idea of dating again."

The words hang in the air between us. I blink several times as I process them, and I'm not completely sure why it's so hard for the words to sink in. My father, the man who seemed perpetually content with his routine, is thinking about dating again.

Dating.

And here I am, thinking the strangest thing he's going to say tonight is about wanting a dog.

The concept is so strange when applied to him that it takes me a moment to find my voice.

"Dating?" I repeat as if I don't understand him.

He nods slowly. "Yes, dating."

"It's been years, Dad. You deserve happiness... someone to share your life with." But even as I say those words, there's something in the back of my mind that speaks up. It's concerned about change and the fear that comes along with it.

"Sweetheart, I haven't made a decision yet. And this doesn't change anything between us," he reassures me.

I manage a small smile despite the swirl of emotions within me. "I know it doesn't," I reply softly. "And I want you to be happy."

The silence that follows is not the same comfortable one we had while eating. Or maybe I'm assuming it's not because I'm not sure what to think.

Dad reaches across the table, his fingers brushing mine. "I wanted you to know first before I made any steps. I don't want to blindside you with any of this."

All I can do is nod.

We stay like that for a few moments, and when our waitress comes by again, it jolts us back to the present.

"Is everything alright? Can I get you anything else?"

"No, we're good, but can I get the check?"

Once Dad takes care of the bill, we leave the restaurant and walk toward where our cars are parked next to each other. That was intentional on my part.

The afternoon breeze is gentle, playing with the strands of my hair that have fallen out of my bun.

"I'm sorry for catching you off guard with what I said back there. I wasn't sure how to bring it up."

"It's completely fine. I just wasn't expecting it." When we stop at my car, I turn back to him and say, "I meant everything I said back there. I want you to be happy."

"Thanks, honey."

I watch him unlock his car door before turning toward mine. "Text me to let me know when you get back to campus, okay?" he asks.

"Of course. And drive safe."

"You too."

As I climb into my car and close the door, I'm happy to

be somewhat shut off from the world once more. Why does it feel like everything is changing when nothing really has?

I start the engine but don't pull out immediately. Instead, I sit there for a moment longer and let myself think about what Dad said. About him dating again.

For some reason, my mind drifts back to memories of him being there for every event that I had as a child, even before my mother took off. The thought of someone else standing beside him at future events is both warming and chilling at the same time.

I'm happy for him; I am. He deserves to find someone who makes him laugh and feel loved in ways that go beyond what I can offer as his daughter. But a part of me is still reeling from what Mom did and feels like it's losing something all over again.

Dad's words repeat in my head—this doesn't change anything between us—and I hold onto them as I finally pull out of the parking spot and drive back to campus.

By the time I park in my apartment building's parking lot and kill the engine, I'm ready for a much-needed nap. With a quiet sigh, I rest my forehead against the steering wheel, allowing myself a moment to just be before leaving the comfort of my car and closing the rest of the world off once I shut my front door behind me.

10

LEVI

I'm not sure if I've ever been more tired in my life.

Having both hockey practice and a mandatory presentation that I needed to attend is brutal. I feel as if I can fall asleep standing up without any trouble and that's unusual for me.

I'm almost in a trance as I'm walking across the quad to get back to my car. A few people that I don't recognize wave to me, and it takes all of my energy to wave back to them. Must maintain the image I've created because coming across as rude could easily make waves for me at school and on the internet.

After I finish waving at the last of them, I realize something is very different here.

The campus quad is alive in a way I'd never seen before. Strings of fairy lights dance between the trees, casting a soft glow on the faces of students who lounge on the grass. There are food trucks lined up on the street nearby, and I find myself wondering how the hell I didn't know this was happening.

At the center of it all is a makeshift stage, where a local band is belting out their covers of today's pop hits.

I'm vibing along with the music, allowing the rhythm to draw me in. I'm exhausted and only plan on staying here for a minute more when something—or rather, someone—catches my eye.

Like a moth to a flame, my eyes are drawn to Hailey sitting on a blanket in the grass. It seems as if she, too, is entranced by the music, but there's something different about her. Whereas I'm used to her sharp wit and her being completely focused when she is at work, here she looks... lost.

What put that look on her face?

I shake my head, trying to shake the fatigue that is clouding my mind in case I'm imagining it, but I soon realize this is all real. During the times I've interacted with her, Hailey has been so put together, with an armor that seems meant to protect her from the rest of the world. But now I see a crack in the mask she shows to the outside world. She seems vulnerable and out of her element, and I want to know more.

I hover around the periphery of the crowd, watching as Hailey brushes a stray lock of hair behind her ear when it falls out of her messy bun. Is she looking for someone? The thought makes me frown. Why do I even care?

I want to walk over there and ask her if there is anything I can do to help her, but another part of me doesn't think Hailey would want me intruding. I'm torn between acting on instinct and respecting what she might want.

The band switches to a slower tune that the lead singer announces is "Invisible String" by Taylor Swift, but I knew it before he uttered a word. I may have played Folklore on repeat in the months following my brother's death because it provided relief. The lyrics he is singing are what help me make up my mind. Before I know it, I'm walking through the crowd to get to her.

"Hey," I say as I approach, making sure that she can hear me over the music while keeping my voice casual despite feeling anything but.

Hailey's eyes pop open. She's startled by my appearance but just as quickly as the shock appeared on her face, her expression changes to one of indifference. "Levi Jamison, hanging out with the general population? Now I've seen everything."

"It does sometimes happen," I say before laughing. Brewed Beginnings has become a regular pit stop for me because it gives me an opportunity to see and chat with her, however brief. But unlike when we usually talk there, her words don't have the same bite. It's obvious to me something else is at play. I debate with myself for a split second before I ask, "Mind if I join you?"

For a moment she hesitates, probably weighing the pros and cons, but then she scoots over slightly on the blanket she brought with her.

"I don't mind," she replies. I can't help but feel surprised that she's letting me do this.

Just like that, I'm beside her. For the first time, I can see the flecks of green in her hazel eyes, all the more reason why I find them stunning. However, I don't voice that thought. Instead, we sit quietly next to each other, enjoying the music.

After a couple of minutes, I finally break the figurative ice. "Do you come to events like these often?" I ask. The words sound lame to my ears, but they get the job done.

She shakes her head. "No... this is actually my first time. Came here because Jade is trying to get me to step outside of the box I've put myself in, apparently. Trying new things."

That somewhat surprises me, but I decide not to voice that opinion. This is a delicate situation. I'm not sure if she's letting me in at all, but I don't want to risk it if she is.

"Also, I'm usually too busy," she adds, as if needing to further justify why this is the first time.

"I get it," I reply with a nod. "I haven't been to one before because I'm usually too exhausted from practice and class."

Her lips twitch but they don't form a full smile. There's

plenty of time for that to happen, however. "The life of the star hockey captain at Crestwood University," she says. The tone of her voice has a bit of her usual sarcasm and I'm happy about it.

"Yeah, well." I rub the back of my neck. "Sometimes it's not all it's cracked up to be."

She turns her head to look at me, and our eyes lock for a moment. "I can imagine."

It's not something I want to get into right now, much like I'm sure she doesn't want to explain to me what is wrong in her life. I leave her comment hanging in the air and allow the music to speak to us until I find something else I can ask her.

"Do you like this song?" It's another silly question, but this one is an attempt at getting our conversation to focus on something neutral.

"It's okay," she admits with a shrug. "I preferred the last song they played."

I nod. "Yeah, that one had a good beat to it."

I watch as her foot starts tapping against the grass unconsciously, and I can't help but mirror the action. Our movements sync for a brief second before she notices and stops abruptly.

"So how's hockey going?" she says out of nowhere.

I tilt my head to look at her, somewhat confused. Not so much by the question, but the fact that she's the one asking. "Pretty good, I can't complain. Why? Planning to come to one of my games?" The question slips out before I can think it through. It is bolder than I intended it to be, but I can't take it back.

I need to expect the unexpected when it comes to her. Her bluntness is something I don't usually have to deal with. It's refreshing, but I also love the way she challenges me. She's not about to kiss my ass, but I also need to defend the sport I love. "Hockey is not just about aggression, you know. There's a lot of skill, strategy, and—"

"Grace?" she interrupts with an eyebrow raised, clearly not buying it.

"Exactly, grace. You might be surprised by the amount of grace it takes to do what I do."

Hailey's skepticism is written all over her face. "I'll take your word for it." She shifts her gaze back to the musicians and I can feel the barrier between us growing once more, and I'm stuck wondering whether I want to push my luck further or not.

My eagerness soon wins out. "What's stopping you from coming to a game?"

"Sports aren't really my thing."

"Might be something adventurous for you to check out. Like this," I gesture to the local band we've been listening to.

"Would you get me tickets so that I can sit as close to the sidelines as possible?"

I can't help but chuckle. "Sidelines? We call it rinkside or the boards."

Hailey holds her hands out in front of her. "Oh... but

see what I mean? I don't know the first thing about hockey outside of it involving ice, a puck, and a hockey stick. But there's more to my reluctance than that."

"Tell me. I want to know." I really do.

I'm prepared for a sarcastic response, the usual from her. What I get, however, is once again, something I'm not expecting. Hailey turns her head slowly to look at me and something flashes through her eyes that I can't quite explain. "The hoopla that surrounds all of it. I'm sure you realize how popular you are. Don't deny it."

That last sentence falls out of her mouth when she sees me getting ready to speak to defend myself.

"You and I live in completely different worlds that just happened to collide when you walked into Brewed Beginnings that day."

I chew on her words for a moment, but I'm not sure I completely agree with them. We're both students at Crestwood. While I might not be in the same clubs and have the same interests that she does, we still attend the same school, and I'm sure we have other things that connect us. "Excuse my ignorance, but I don't understand what you mean."

Hailey's lips part as if she's about to speak, then close again. She gathers her thoughts before her gaze meets mine once more. "You're in the spotlight. People love you and they celebrate every goal you make and every game you win. That's your world."

"And what's yours?"

She leans her head back and looks up at the sky as if it holds the answer to my question. "My world? It's quieter. It's learning about the ways to protect the environment, shifts at the coffee shop, and running the chess club."

I don't let on that I already know she is president of the chess club. That piece of information has been sitting in my pocket since Wilder told me about it. Now the more I talk to her, the more a plan is forming in my head about how best to use it.

I nod as I get what she's saying. "I see your point, but maybe our worlds aren't so different."

"Maybe or maybe not." She stretches her hands over her head and says, "Listen I have to go. Long day ahead tomorrow."

I watch as Hailey stands up and I follow suit to help her gather her belongings. Once we're done, she starts to walk away before I call out.

"Wait. Did you drive here? Let me walk you to your car." It's the gentlemanly thing to do, after all.

"I didn't drive because my apartment isn't too far from here," she gestures behind her. "Thanks for the offer, but I'm good."

"Okay then. Good night, Hailey."

"Night, Levi." And she turns and walks away.

I'm left staring after her for a moment before I head to my car to drive home. While I'm still tired, the time I spent with Hailey energized me in a way I can't describe. Having her let me in, ever so slightly, felt wonderful, and lets me know I haven't been imagining our chemistry.

Chatting with her helped me come up with a plan for how to show Hailey that she and I aren't that much different after all.

11

HAILEY

A couple of days later, I'm sitting at a table on the main floor of Ramsey Library, with both Jade's and my things spread out across it. We both needed a break from our apartment, so we chose the library as the place to do our homework today. Instead of working on one of the quiet floors, we pick the main floor because we can at least talk softly here.

"Seriously, how do these equations even make sense?" Jade grumbles, her curly hair bouncing as she shakes her head. She squints at the calculus problems before her as if that will help.

"Because some masochist centuries ago thought this would be an excellent form of fun," I toss out as I tap my pencil on the open textbook.

Jade laughs before she says, "Before we attempt to get

back to work, did you have any more details about the event you want to pull together at Gran's retirement home? Do you need anything from me?"

I rub a hand against my face as I think about the chess event I've been planning for the residents at Oak Terrace, Jade's grandmother's retirement community. "I think it's coming together?"

"You don't sound confident."

"Look, I think it's a great chance for us to connect with the community outside of Crestwood's campus. It's just a little more work than I thought it would be, which is being added to my already busy schedule." I bite my lip before I continue. "I did have a call with the activities director, and we have the main common room booked so there's that."

"You, my friend, are a force of nature. If anyone can pull this off, it's you."

I chuckle, despite the mild panic that has risen in my chest. "What would I do without your unwavering faith in me?"

"Crash and burn?"

I roll my eyes as she continues to speak.

"But seriously, Hailey, if you need help with organizing or setting up, just say the word. Gran's already excited about the chess night. She keeps bragging to her friends that she's going to win every match she plays."

"That's adorable. And I'll take you up on that offer. You might regret it later."

Jade tucks a curl behind her ear. "Never. Not when it comes to this. Anyway, sorry to distract you. We should probably get back to work."

I nod in agreement, and she turns her attention back to her math problem and I turn back to the textbook that is open in front of me. I've read over the same paragraph three times and still haven't retained any of the information I'm supposed to.

All because my thoughts keep drifting back to a certain someone and us hanging out briefly a couple of nights ago. I close my eyes and sigh as if the physical motion can remove the thoughts I keep having about him. It's all Levi's fault, really. Not having to see him would make things so much easier, but he is determined not to let that be the case.

All of the times he's now come into Brewed Beginnings have been in the back of my mind even when I've done my best not to think about him. I didn't think much of it before, but then seeing him at the concert on the quad, it is like he threw me off-kilter. To think that the only reason I attended the event is because Jade thought it would be another way for me to do something out of my comfort zone and then, of course, I ran into him there as well.

Jade clearing her throat brings me out of my thoughts. "Earth to Hailey," she says, making sure to elongate the 'ey' in my name.

I blink several times before my eyes focus on her. "Sorry, just thinking."

"About the chess night?"

"No," I confess with another sigh. "About Levi."

After the concert, I knew I had to come clean. Jade now knows everything there is to know about what has happened between Levi and me. When she tosses her pencil down, I know that calculus is long forgotten now. "Oh? What about him? Is it about the fact that he likes you and you're fighting your attraction to him?"

"Jade..."

"Then what was it?"

"The whole concert thing and—" I stop talking immediately when Jade's eyes widen, and she shakes her head so hard that I wonder if it's going to fall off her body. "Are you okay?"

"Yeah, but you'll never believe who just walked into the library."

My eyes shut involuntarily. It can't be who I think it is.

I open my eyes and slowly turn around. I find the man of the hour standing near the entrance of the library.

Levi runs a hand through his dark brown hair as he walks into the main area of the building.

His shirt, a simple gray tee, and black hoodie that looks soft to the touch, cling perfectly across his broad shoulders and chest, almost hiding the physique that has been crafted from the rink and the gym. He finishes the look off with a pair of dark jeans and white sneakers. Even from here, I swear I catch his piercing blue eyes scanning the room, looking for who knows what.

Jade leans forward and whispers, "What the hell is he doing here?"

I turn my head to look at her again and whisper back, "Maybe he's like us and wants to study here?" Although I didn't have a highly favorable opinion of him, my response made the utmost sense.

"But he's obviously looking for someone."

"I can't help with that issue."

I know that I should resist the urge to turn back around in his direction, but in this instance, I'm weak because I turn my head around again to find him. Of course, that is when he spots us, or, more accurately, he spots me. His eyebrows shoot up briefly before his mouth curves into a smile.

Fuck. I think he was looking for me.

As he walks over, I turn to look back at Jade and glare. To be honest, I don't know why I'm glaring at her. Maybe her asking me what I was thinking about and me admitting that I was thinking about Levi caused him to materialize.

So all of this is her fault. I'm just kidding. Kind of.

When he finally reaches us, I can't help but notice a subtle scent that I've never noticed before. It is woodsy and mixed with something else I can't quite figure out. Whatever it is, suits him and smells incredible.

I glance back at Jade and find her looking from Levi to

me and back to Levi and then back to me. Her eyes continue to dance between the two of us because she knows something is up. Even if I hadn't talked to her about Levi previously, I know she would see right through my bullshit now.

Levi gives us both a brief nod before his eyes settle on me. "Hey," he says casually, as if we bump into each other in the library every day. He keeps his voice somewhat low because of where we are. "Hope I'm not interrupting."

I speak before Jade has an opportunity to. "If I said you were, would that make you leave?" There. That comment felt normal.

Levi chuckles, a deep sound that does something strange to my stomach, but I refuse to think about it. "Maybe, but then I wouldn't be able to ask for your help. That is a missed opportunity for me," he says.

Out of the corner of my eye, I notice Jade sits up straighter, as if Levi has her full and undivided attention. "Help with what?" she asks before I have a chance to throw out my comeback. The tone of her voice suggests she finds this entire interaction far more amusing than I do.

"Coach wants me to find another activity, and I thought another sport wouldn't be wise," Levi admits with a casual shrug, as if it's no big deal.

"Oh? And what does any of this have to do with me?"

"Well, I've chosen to learn chess and apparently, since

you're president of the chess club, you're the best person to teach me."

I blink at him, taken aback by the request. Him deciding to learn chess is random given all of the activities you can do at Crestwood University.

"Absolutely not."

Levi's expression falters for a moment before he recovers. "Why not?"

"Because I don't tutor people and I'm super busy."

I can see the challenge in Levi's eyes before he utters a word. "That's not what's on the chess club's home page on the school website."

"Maybe I'm not the one who's giving the tutoring lessons."

"There's a photo underneath it that looks as if you're teaching someone with a chessboard in front of you. Your email is also listed there as the point of contact."

Fuck.

Jade's grin widens and she taps my hand gently. "He's got you there and would you look at that," she whispers loudly enough for both of us to hear. "Levi Jamison needs the expertise of Hailey Reed. You should feel honored."

"Extremely," I mutter dryly, still trying to process what the hell all of this is. "If I were to do it, what would I get out of this?" Why am I even thinking about doing this?

Levi leans against the table, one corner of his mouth tipping up. "What do you want in exchange?"

I cross my arms and consider him for a moment. Normally I would have sent him away immediately, but the new situation intrigues me, despite myself. I glance at Jade, who is barely holding herself together as she watches us.

Then an idea forms in my head. "If I do this, our schedules will have to line up to where this doesn't become a burden to me, and I want your help with putting together a chess event at Oak Terrace."

There's a chance that with his hockey schedule this won't work, and I'm banking on it. It might be the only way I can convince him this is something that I can't do. But having an extra set of hands to help with the senior citizens event at Oak Terrace wouldn't be the worst thing in the world either.

Levi's eyes narrow as if he's considering my proposal, and then I see when the proverbial light bulb turns on above his head. "I would need to double-check my schedule, but how about we exchange numbers and I'll shoot you a text when I have it?"

"Or you can send an email to the email address on the chess club's website."

Jade's snort is so loud that it causes several other people who are sitting nearby to look over at us. She shakes her head and quickly looks back down at her textbook.

"Texting would be easier."

I hate that I have to agree with him because it is easier. I roll my eyes and say, "Fine. Let's exchange numbers."

Levi pulls out his phone, and I recite my number for him to enter. He texts me so I'll have his.

"Got it," he says. "I'll be in touch about my schedule. It might be a couple of days because our game is tomorrow. Thanks for agreeing to do this. I know it's random, but I appreciate the help."

His sincerity catches me off guard. I just nod in response.

"See you around," Levi says with a small wave. He turns and makes his way out of the library.

Once he's gone, Jade's eyes widen, and her hands fly to the top of her head before they plop down on the table. "Well, that was an interesting turn of events," she whispers.

"You're telling me. He didn't even bother to stay here to do work."

"That's because he obviously came in here to find you."

I turn to look at her, my eyes narrowing slightly. "Did you know he was going to come here?"

Jade shakes her head. "No, but I'm not upset because I just got to witness THAT."

"Okay, okay. We have work to do so get your mind off Levi and this chess thing."

"Fine. But I want an update as soon as he sends you a

text. And I'll refrain from saying all of the things I actually want to say about what I just saw... for now."

"Great," is all I can say because I don't want to egg Jade on any further. I can already see the wheels in her head turning as she's conjuring up silly scenarios about how Levi and I are going to be together.

She couldn't be more wrong.

12

LEVI

The locker room is about as chaotic as you'd think it would be on game day. Nerves are running rampant as we suit up in our hockey gear.

Much like every game, today is about getting out there and doing the best we can. It also means having to see my father for the first time since I got back to school. It's the last thing I want to deal with. A loud shout draws me out of my thoughts, and I turn to see what is going on.

"Hey, watch it!" Knox snaps as Wilder playfully shoves him, nearly causing a crash into Blaise, who's taping his stick, lost in his own world.

"Relax, it's just pregame jitters," I say, trying to cut the tension because there's a chance this could escalate. Knox shoots me a look but doesn't say a word.

"Or it's Wilder being an ass," Asher chimes in from across the room.

"Someone's gotta keep you on your toes," Wilder replies, bumping fists with Asher before eyeing me. "Right, Cap?"

I can't help but chuckle at the antics. "Yeah, someone's gotta do it," I reply, pulling on the last of my equipment. "But keep in mind that someone better not rack up penalties before the game even begins."

I catch Asher's eye and nod—our silent signal that it's time to come together. The whole hockey team moves into place in the center of the locker room.

Coach Johnson walks up to us and starts his pregame speech. "Alright, each of you has prepared for this moment. You've bled, sweat, and pushed past your limits to be right here, right now."

He pauses for a moment, letting his words sink in as he looks at each and every one of us. "We are going to go out there and play smart and tough."

Coach runs through some last-minute strategies and guidance before going through tactical strategies for each position before he wraps up his talk.

"When you step out on the ice today," Coach Johnson's voice softens slightly, "remember why you play this game. Remember who you play for—your family watching you proudly from those stands, your coaches who've seen something great in each of you, and most importantly," he places a firm hand over his heart then extends it toward us all, "play for yourselves and each other."

Coach's words hang in the air, and he looks over at me and gives me a single nod. It is my turn to speak.

I step forward, feeling the weight of the captain's "C" on my chest. "Alright, listen up." My voice isn't as stern as Coach's, but I think I'm doing a pretty good job. "You heard Coach Johnson's words. Today's is about showing everyone what we're made of out there."

I look around at the faces of my team and I can't help but feel as if we're going out there to battle on the ice. Each one of these men is a brother-in-arms, and I will do everything I can to help them.

"We grinded hard for this moment. This opportunity. Remember those drills that had us ready to collapse? I'm pretty sure I heard Blaise sobbing uncontrollably," I continue with a wry smile. My joke draws a few chuckles from the group because that has never happened. "The sprints that had us ready to throw the towel in? They were done to prepare us for now."

I pause, willing to bet everyone in the room can feel the physical and mental anguish that flew through our bodies during those grueling practices. "When we hit the ice in just a few short minutes, we leave everything out there."

"And yes," I acknowledge with a glance toward Wilder from his earlier antics, "we keep each other on our toes. We challenge each other because we know that's how we improve and get better. But more than anything else, we have faith and trust in one another."

The room nods in unison, and I wait a few seconds before I continue.

"We're more than just a team, we're family." I let the word roll off my tongue. Family is a concept that means different things to each one of us because of our different experiences in life yet somehow unites us all. "So, let's go show them what this family can do! On three, Red Wolves! One. Two. Three."

"Red Wolves!"

Our shout is followed by an uproar from my team-mates. The energy is bursting at the seams. Everyone is amped up and ready to go. The pregame jitters are still there, but I prefer them to be.

If they aren't, then I don't love this sport anymore and I'll need to find something else to enjoy.

Our team leaves the locker room and goes through the tunnel. The air is cold and crisp, and every step I take reminds me it's that much closer to game time.

I lead the team onto the rink and just before we begin our warm-ups, I look out into the crowd. As I expected ahead of time, I find my father sitting in the stands. But I am surprised to see my mother here as well.

For most people, it isn't an issue to have their parents at their sporting event, ready to cheer them on. But for me, it's different. I wish neither of them were here. I'd have told them to stay home if I could have. Mom isn't nearly as bad as Dad, but that doesn't change the fact that this is the last thing I want.

Dad's face barely hides his anticipation while Mom looks somewhat indifferent, almost numb to it all. When she spots me looking over at them, however, she gives me a small smile and wave. I do the same back and as she prepares to tap my father, I turn away.

I push their images aside along with any thoughts that threaten to distract me from the game. I can't let their presence here get to me or else it's going to throw me off my game.

The warm-up starts with some light skating around our half of the rink. Asher joins me on a few laps, but he doesn't say a word. Words aren't needed. We've done this routine together so many times that it will be stitched in our memories for eternity.

Knox catches up with us and is the first to speak. "Ready to beat their asses?" he asks casually, as if we're just discussing plans for the next party that is going to be thrown.

"Always," I reply.

As we begin drills, they, too, feel like they are ingrained in my brain. It's muscle memory at this point, and that's how it should be.

Coach Johnson blows his whistle signaling for us to gather around him one final time before the match officially begins. After that, we break off and take our positions as the starting lineup is announced. I wait for the announcer to say my name, and as soon as he does, it is followed by cheers that send even more adrenaline through my body.

The referee signals to us that it's time for a face-off.

I skate to the center circle, and I swear I can feel every eye in the crowd on me. Opposite me, my counterpart mirrors my stance, our eyes locked on the puck in the referee's hand. It's as if time slows down for just a moment.

As I crouch, the referee's hand hovers over the ice and everything else fades because the only thing that matters is the puck and my opponent.

Before I can blink, the black disk drops to the ice and that is all I can see.

It's game time.

With a swift flick of my stick, I direct the puck toward Asher. The game is in motion and our team moves as if we're in sync with one another.

We have no issue with dominating from our first possession. In the stands, I can feel the electricity coming from the crowd, and it grows with each goal we score. It fuels me, and I'm sure the rest of my teammates feel the same.

As the game continues, I steal a glance at my parents again during a brief moment that I'm on the bench. They're on their feet now, my mom is clapping along with the rest of the fans, but I can't say the same for my father. He's turning slightly red from yelling. It's easy for me to guess that he's probably yelling about the things he feels I'm doing wrong and what I need to do in order for me to be better in his eyes.

Same shit. Different day.

I look over at Coach Johnson's face as it breaks into a rare grin. At this point, if we're winning and he's happy, that's all that matters.

The game continues until the final buzzer blows. The crowd is still on their feet as we celebrate winning our game. I slow down and circle the rink, relief flowing through my veins. Everything has paid off as we can add the first win to our season.

And it feels so damn good.

The players from both teams join us on the rink and we line up to shake hands and thank each other for a good game. The handshakes are quick and I'm willing to bet each player is trying to calm down from the high that comes with playing this game. There will be time later to start thinking about what went right and what went wrong during this match.

When all of my duties on the ice are complete, I skate off toward the exit leading directly to the locker rooms. Coach Johnson finds me and puts a firm hand on my shoulder.

"Good work out there," he says.

I nod, happy about the compliment. "Thanks, Coach."

"Don't forget you have to meet with the media in a little bit."

"I won't forget."

In the locker room, the energy is contagious. Everyone is happy, and I'm willing to bet some of the chatter I'm hearing around me has to do with a party or two that will be happening in celebration. Asher slaps my back as he passes by toward his locker.

"Excellent work," he says.

"It was all a team effort," I reply with a grin because it's true. It truly was and I couldn't be prouder of how we did.

I remove my gear and take a few minutes to catch my breath. The evening winds down as the interviews with local and national media outlets conclude. While I don't mind the actual act of being interviewed, having to answer the same questions over and over again becomes repetitive after a while.

Once that is done, I'm finally able to be back with the team. I listen to Coach Johnson's wrap up of our performance before hitting the showers. Later, while exiting the arena in street clothes with my duffel bag slung over my shoulder, I spot my parents waiting outside with fans that want to see us leave.

This confrontation is something I should have anticipated after seeing them in the stands tonight, but I didn't. While I wish I could just walk away from them, I know it isn't the right way to go about this, especially since my mother hasn't done anything wrong.

Taking in a deep breath, I make my way over to where they're standing. I can see my mother's eyes light up, her smile warm and genuine. My father, however, has an all-too-familiar look on his face and I know he's about to dissect my performance.

"Great game tonight, honey!" my mother exclaims as she pulls me into a tight hug. I return the embrace.

"Thanks, Mom," I say.

My father clears his throat, and I turn to face him.

"You did alright," he offers with a small nod. "But there were moments where your focus obviously wasn't there."

"Dad, please. Can we just be happy about tonight? We won the game and that's what matters right now."

My father pauses, looking taken aback by my interruption even though he should have been expecting it. I usually stop him before he can do too much damage with his words, but that doesn't mean the anticipation of being criticized doesn't cut me up inside.

"But you know there's always room for improvement and we should discuss this while it's still fresh," he says.

"I know, Dad. I just... not tonight."

"Very well," he says, but I know this is only a temporary truce. "We can talk strategy some other time. Maybe I'll call you tomorrow?"

As if I don't already have a coach, teammates, and other staffers that I can talk strategy with. But at least he isn't going to say another word about it tonight. At least I can be happy about that. Small talk between my mother and me is what fills the silence until we reach my car. We say our goodbyes and I promise to call Mom later in the week.

A curt nod is all I get from my father.

After they walk away, I sit in my car for a moment before I snatch my phone from my pocket. I stare at Hailey's number for a moment before my fingers fly across the screen. I'd been sitting on information about my schedule since this morning and now is the perfect time to let her know.

I need a little pick-me-up, and sending her a text is the perfect way to do it.

Once I read over my message, I press send and toss my phone into the passenger's seat. The further away it is from me, the less likely I will have the urge to check it while I'm driving home.

Now, I only have to wait for her response.

13

HAILEY

With a deep sigh, I unlock the door to the small on-campus apartment I share with Jade. The quietness that greets me is surprising, but I know it won't last too long because I have no doubt in my mind that Jade is home.

Our small living area is a mixture of both of our tastes. Jade has a love for color whereas I love keeping things simple and minimalistic to a certain extent. The thought of sinking into our gray couch filled with a bunch of different colored cushions is calling to me, but I know as soon as Jade sees me, that pipe dream will be over.

Instead, I walk over to Jade's room and find her door slightly open. I push it further and am greeted with a burst of color and energy as I find her sitting in a pile of clothes. She tucks a piece of her hair behind her ear and looks up at me. I shake my head at the big grin she gives me.

"About time you got home. You need to start getting ready!"

I bite back the sigh I know is coming. I wish I could forget about the party, but Jade has been reminding me nonstop about it through text messages for the last couple of hours, making it impossible for it to not be at the front of my mind. "I guess I do."

"It's gonna be epic!" Jade continues, rifling through the clothes on the floor. "We can drink, dance, and who knows who's going to be out there tonight. Hell, maybe you'll get some dick."

I narrow my gaze at her but don't say a word.

A sly grin forms on Jade's lips. "I'm kidding... unless that's something you actually want to do. I hope you're excited."

"Thrilled," I deadpan, making sure my tone reflects how I feel.

Jade rolls her eyes dramatically. "Oh, lighten up, Hailey. We're gonna have a blast, I promise." When I don't reply again, I watch as her eyes scan my face in an attempt to read it. She knows parties aren't my thing, and I wonder if she's starting to feel guilty about pushing me to go.

"You're not going to flake on me, are you?" she finally asks. The excitement in her voice is tamer.

I hesitate before answering. Jade's enthusiasm is hard to resist, but having her shift gears and sound disappointed in me hits a different button. Parties aren't my scene. They're Jade's domain. But I made a promise, and I intend to keep it. It is a great opportunity for my best friend and me to hang out together.

"No, I'm not."

"Tell you what," she says. "If you get overwhelmed and want to leave early, just say the word and we'll come back home. Deal?"

Having an easy out makes the idea less dreadful. "Deal. Let me go change," I concede, managing a small smile.

Jade beams at me before looking down at the mess she's made. "If you need something to wear, I probably have something in this pile of... stuff." She gestures to the things on the floor.

"I'll let you know," I say as I head out of her room and into my own.

My room is the complete opposite of hers. Everything is in its rightful place, organized in such a way that it makes it easy for me to start with a clear mind each day and to end the day with a sense of calm. Well, most of the time anyway.

As I'm taking my phone out of my pocket, my eyes land on a text notification I should have been expecting, but yet I hadn't been.

> Levi: Hey, Hailey. Here are the blocks of time I'm free for chess lessons. Do any of these times work for you?

I must be in denial. I truly didn't anticipate him reaching out to me, but here we are. For some reason, I can't think of what to say back to him even though it should be an easy response.

No. I'm not going to worry about this now. I need to focus on going out with Jade.

As I put my phone down, I decide it won't hurt to take a quick shower. I hurry into the bathroom and turn on the showerhead. While I wait for the water to warm up, I strip out of the clothes I wore to Brewed Beginnings and redo the messy bun I'd thrown my hair into. I don't have any time to wash my hair, and to be honest, it is the last thing I want to do.

Once I step into the shower and pull the shower curtain to stop any water from getting out, I close my eyes and just breathe. The stress of the day slips away as I try to silence my thoughts.

The warm water falls down my body, soothing my tired muscles. I stretch my limbs as the steam fills the bathroom. This is the best idea I've had all day. I reach over to grab a bottle sitting on a small shelf in the shower. The familiar scent of my body wash fills the room as I pour the liquid onto my loofah.

In the back of my mind, I know I can't spend as much time as I want to in here because Jade is waiting for me. With that thought, I start the dreaded process of wrapping up my shower and soon I find myself wrapping a towel around my body as I stare into a mirror that is more than just a little fogged. I lean back to turn on the fan to help clear out the steam in case Jade wants to use this mirror to do her hair and makeup.

I dry myself off and throw my robe on before walking back into my room. There I find Jade waiting on me.

"You know, I was just going to tell you I have no idea what in the hell to wear tonight."

"And I could sense that, which is why I'm here. I have several options. Would you prefer to wear a dress or jeans?"

"Jeans," I say without a second thought. Having to put on a dress in addition to *partying* tonight isn't the vibe I want at all.

"So I'm thinking a sparkly top would work, but I need to find a pair of dark-colored jeans." She tosses the shirt at me and walks over to my closet. While she is looking through my pants, I stare at the top in my hands.

I'm watching the way the shirt's silver material shimmers in my hands when Jade gasps. I look up and see her holding up a little black dress. "Why have I never seen you wear this before?"

I shrug, taking the dress from her. "Never had the opportunity. Plus, it shows more skin than I'm usually comfortable with."

"Damn, because you'll look stunning in it." Jade grabs the fabric, forcing me to hold the dress against my body. "See? All the guys will be drooling over you."

I make a face. "Drooling guys is not my goal here."

"I know... I know," Jade says as she goes back to searching through my things. I let out a deep breath when she finds the pants she wants and gives them to me.

I quickly get dressed before walking over to my mirror. The outfit looks great, and I have to admit the top shows that I've put some effort into this look. I tell myself I'm going to wear my leather jacket with this to tone it down a bit.

"Are you going to wear your hair down tonight?"

I turn my head to look at Jade before I say, "No. I don't want it getting in the way of anything."

Jade nods. "Then maybe we can find some earrings that won't clash too much with what you have on. I'll grab something from my room."

I touch my earlobes. "Or I can just wear the earrings I have on."

"That works too."

I don't want to cause a big fuss over this adventure that I hope is short-lived. We sit in silence as I redo my hair, deciding that instead of a messy bun, something a little different would be nice. I put it in a low bun and make sure that my stray hairs lay flat. I add a light coating of makeup, including a more natural colored lip because of the busyness of the shirt.

I watch Jade approach the mirror out of the corner of my eye, and she says, "You look amazing. We're going to have a great time tonight. To be honest, we'll probably be laughing at some of the things people are going to do because they are too drunk to think straight."

I raise an eyebrow. "Are you sure you're not going to be one of those drunk people?"

"Me? Never!" Jade laughs.

We both know she's full of shit. Jade has had some wild nights, and I've witnessed several of them. One night in particular pops up in my mind because I made her a quick sandwich before tucking her into bed so she could sleep off the alcohol she'd consumed.

"Whatever you're thinking, we don't need to bring it up again," she says before looking down at her own clothes. "Anyway, I need to change. I'll meet you in the living room?"

"Yeah. I'll be there in a minute."

Jade exits the room, leaving me alone with my thoughts. I glance at myself in the mirror one last time and pull down the shirt. The motion is about giving my hands something to do versus fixing the placement of the shirt. After telling myself for the millionth time that tonight is about stepping out of my comfort zone, I snatch my crossbody bag off my desk and head to the living room.

My stomach growls as I flop down on the couch. Getting something in my system takes priority over drinking. I debate whether it makes sense to fix something quickly I can snack on or convince Jade to stop somewhere to eat before we go to the party. Before I can reach a decision, Jade walks out of the room in a sparkly blue dress that, given what I'm also wearing, fits with her personality and closet.

"So, what's the plan for tonight?" I ask, as I sit up and move my purse from my lap. "Are we going straight to the party or grabbing something to eat first?"

Jade flips her hair over her shoulder to get it off her neck. "I was thinking we could grab something to eat at Marco's."

I'm glad we are on the same page. "Sounds good to me."

Marco's is a place I've been to quite a few times, and I can't help but picture it in my mind. A burger from there is calling my name, plus, I just got paid so treating myself isn't a crime.

"Ready to head out?" Jade asks.

I walk over to our front door and open it. "After you."

Once we are outside, the evening air whips across my face, but it isn't too bad. I look over at Jade because she left our apartment without a coat or jacket and has on a short dress. "Are you cold?"

"Nope."

I can't help but wonder if we develop a second skin when it comes to wearing cute outfits when it's chilly outside. Maybe that's something that can be someone else's senior thesis.

We chat quietly as we make our way through the

streets of Crestwood until we see the sign indicating that Marco's is only a couple of buildings away.

Jade holds the door open for me as we enter the space. We are greeted by the sound of people chatting mixed with the aroma of delicious food. At Marco's, you are allowed to seat yourself, so we find a table in the corner and settle in.

"So, what are you getting?" Jade asks, flipping through the menu even though she knows it by heart.

"Their burger. I knew what I wanted as soon as you mentioned coming here," I answer. For the life of me, I'm unable to resist the thought of the juicy, flavor-packed meal that Marco's is known for. "What about you?"

"Same," she says with a grin. "Can't go wrong with a classic."

Once we place our orders, we talk about the latest things that have happened to us. I wonder if I should fill Jade in about Levi's text message, but there isn't much of a point. Plus, the last thing I want is for someone to overhear us talking and suspect that there's something going on when there isn't.

The burgers arrive, perfectly cooked, and we waste no time before we dig in. Our conversation ceases to exist because the only thing we can focus on is the delicious food in front of us.

As we finish our meal, the door to Marco's swings open, drawing my attention away from my dinner plate. In walks Wilder, and after running into him at the scavenger hunt a while ago, I'm beginning to wonder if he's following us.

"Hey, Jade!" Wilder greets her before waving at me. I am not sure if he remembers my name or not, and I'm not offended about it. I prefer it this way because it draws less attention to me.

He turns his attention back to Jade, whose face lights up. "Wilder! I didn't expect to see you here."

"I decided to do takeout and came here."

All three of us chat for a couple of minutes, and when the discussion shifts to hockey, it takes everything in me not to squirm. For obvious reasons, whenever hockey is mentioned, I think of Levi.

Abruptly, Wilder's attention shifts to his phone, which I hear vibrating in his pocket. He glances at the screen, and then nods.

"I should go grab my food. It has been good seeing both of you."

"Likewise," I reply.

He and Jade share a smile before he nods at both of us and walks up to the front counter. Jade and I remain silent as we watch Wilder grab his food and walk out of Marco's.

I get ready to say something about their interaction before Jade interrupts me.

"You're done right?" She claps her hands together. "Let's get the check so that we can go party!"

14

HAILEY

"This is such a bad idea."

Although I can't see her face, I can feel Jade rolling her eyes at my statement. After all, it is the fifteenth time I've said those words since we left her room.

The moment I step into the off-campus house, I want to go back home and do literally anything else. I immediately regret agreeing to this, but for some reason, I can't tell Jade no. So I'm here at a college party because it is her idea of fun, and she thinks I need to let loose.

As I navigate through the living room turned dance floor, the bass pounds in my chest like a hammer. I try to keep up with Jade as I push past a cluster of laughing students. If I'm being honest with myself, I feel like an outsider even though here it's kind of hard to be. The room is a circus of students caught up in themselves and lost in the buzz of alcohol.

I wish I had said no.

My inner voice is drowned out by the thumping beat that surrounds me. I've never felt at home at these wild college parties. To me, they're nothing but a noisy pit of chaos and a waste of time when there is never enough time in the day. I don't judge anyone who loves attending parties, but it just isn't my scene.

Just as I consider making a quick escape, a guy in a fraternity sweatshirt barrels into me. His drink sloshes over the rim of his red Solo cup and I just manage to miss getting soaked in beer. However, the beer that has fallen on my hand needs to be cleaned up as soon as possible.

"Watch it!" I snap, the annoyance evident in my voice.

He barely acknowledges the near collision. I hear something fall from his lips—perhaps mumbling an apology—before he vanishes into the crowd. With a roll of my eyes and a sigh, I make my way toward the kitchen, hoping to salvage what's left of my dignity and get this beer off me with some paper towels.

Somehow, Jade hears my outburst over the loud music because she turns around with a confused look on her face. "Are you alright?"

I nod. "Some asshole almost soaked me in beer, but I'm okay. I did get some on my hand though so I'm hoping to wipe it off."

Jade rolls her eyes. "How hard is it to be a decent person in this world?"

"I ask myself the same question daily. I'm going to find the kitchen and I'll catch up with you."

"Are you sure?"

I nod once more. "Yes, because it'll only take me a second. I'll catch up with you. Don't leave without me."

Jade squeezes my non-wet hand before I walk away and try to find the kitchen. As I find a hallway, I pass a couple practically devouring each other's faces, almost blocking the doorway. I shove myself past them and I hope the minor inconvenience that I caused by pushing them ruined their night. Is that rude? Sure, but I'm feeling a little petty so it's whatever.

In the kitchen, there are several guys and girls taking shots and cheering. They are standing near the sink, so I change directions to grab some paper towels and wipe my hand. While it would have been nice to actually wash my hands, I don't want to bring attention to myself.

I toss the paper towels in the trash just as I'm planning my escape route back to Jade. I hope she is somewhere near where I left her in the living room or else it will be hell trying to find her. I turn to leave the kitchen when the noises surrounding me dips. It feels like the universe is deciding now is the time to turn things down a notch, giving me some space to breathe.

But it only lasts for a second.

That's when I spot him. Of course, Levi is here. Why

should I be surprised that he's here? The team is known for their hard-partying ways and he's not the exception. However, he is standing in a corner of the room all alone. He's staring out the window like he's lost in another world, far away from here. It's weird seeing him in this state. The confidence and charm that normally radiates from every pore of his body isn't there. What's in its place, I can't fully describe.

Everything in me is yelling to let him be, but curiosity has me taking one step after the other toward him. We're not friends, even though he might beg to differ, but right now, he's the only familiar face I see. Not to mention, seeing Mr. Hockey Captain looking as thrilled to be here as I feel is kind of refreshing.

Misery really does love company.

"Levi?" I say softly.

When he turns to look at me, a small smile appears on his lips. "Hey, Hailey. Fancy seeing you here."

The text message he sent me earlier today is now at the forefront of my mind.

Damn it. I hadn't been expecting to see him tonight and now this is awkward.

"I got your text message. I was going to respond but got distracted by all of this." I gesture to my outfit for... whatever reason.

"I get it," he says as he studies my body.

His reaction flusters me. I feel slightly guilty about not responding promptly, but there is nothing I can do about it now. The awkwardness I'm feeling is outshined by the look on his face. There is no doubt in my mind that there is something going on with him. "This isn't really your scene either, huh?"

Levi leans back against the wall and shakes his head. "Nah, not tonight. Sometimes all of this is too much."

I nod because I understand where he is coming from. "The noise, the people pretending to have a great time... it gets overwhelming."

He glances around before his gaze lands back on me. "I think they are having a good time, if I'm being honest. We're just the two losers sitting in the corner watching them."

I snort and Levi raises an eyebrow at me as if he's confused by my reaction. I brush off his reaction and ask, "Do you ever get tired of it?"

"The party scene?"

I nod once, knowing that is more than enough to clarify what I mean. Awkwardness starts to rear its ugly head as I realize this is the longest I've been in Levi's presence without exchanging any snappy comments with him.

"All the time," he admits. I'm surprised he's being honest. I open my mouth to speak, but he continues. "But it's not just here. It's on the ice, in class... I'm always on, if that makes sense? I'm always supposed to be Levi Jamison, the hockey captain of the Crestwood Red Wolves. But sometimes, I just want to be Levi, you know?"

"Yeah, I can see that," I reply. It's not something I experience on a regular basis because no one really knows who I am outside of serving them at Brewed Beginnings and chess club. But there has to be a certain amount of pressure that is put on a person when they are living in the public eye, even if it is just at Crestwood University.

Levi chuckles, the sound is warm and genuine. "You know, that's one of the things I like about you. You're real, no pretense."

The compliment catches me off guard and I find myself staring up at him, wide-eyed. "Thanks?"

"Don't look so horrified that I gave you a compliment."

"I'm not horrified. I just didn't think you had it in you to compliment anyone that isn't yourself. Stop it." There. The truce is over, and everything is back to normal.

"I will when you actually want me to stop paying you compliments."

"I've told you I don't want—"

Levi leans into me, noting the shift in the air between us. "And we both know it's bullshit. You enjoy this little tug-of-war game that we play just as much as I do."

My brain refuses to cooperate given the intensity of his stare. I can sense the change between us and I'm not sure how I feel about it. Our back-and-forth is something I look forward to when he stops into Brewed Beginnings even though I wouldn't admit it out loud. But this here is something different. Completely different.

My comeback dies on my lips as my eyes meet his. There's a challenge there, a silent invitation to acknowledge the unspoken tension between us. I know it has always been there and I've ignored it because this can't happen.

I swallow hard in an effort to regain my composure. Finally, I'm able to form words. "You think you've got me all figured out, right?"

"Maybe not all figured out. But I'm willing to take my time and learn."

His words hang in the air, mostly because I'm not sure how to react and Levi is waiting to see what I will do with that information. Before either of us can say anything else, a loud voice interrupts us.

"Levi! There you are!"

We both jump away from each other as if we were caught doing something wrong. I turn toward the source of the voice and see Asher, one of Levi's teammates. He stands there with a beer in his hand and a smirk on his face that says he thinks he knows what he interrupted.

Levi and I step back from one another, pretending like nothing happened. Levi stands up straight and crosses his arms over his chest while I take a few more steps back, creating even more space between us.

Asher doesn't seem fazed at all and continues talking as if nothing is wrong, "Hey, dude, where have you been? Come on, let's go play some pool in the basement."

Levi glances at Asher before his attention is shifted back to me. "Yeah sure, let's go."

But he doesn't move. It's like he is waiting for me to say

or do something first, and I am eager to get out of this situation as soon as possible.

"I need to head back to Jade."

With a small dip of his head, Levi walks away without another word or glance in my direction and I do the same.

I find myself weaving through the crowd as soon as I reach the hallway. There are more people here than when I came in, but I can't focus on what is happening before me. All my mind wants to do is replay my conversation with Levi.

I snatch my phone out of my pocket and quickly send a text to Levi with my schedule. After seeing him in person, I figure there's no point in waiting any longer. When I make a promise, I intend to keep it.

Once I've pocketed my phone, I continue on my mission to find my best friend. I'm so caught up in thinking about Levi that I almost miss Jade who isn't in the living room anymore and is instead standing near the front door.

"There you are!" she exclaims. "Ready to go? I'm not really feeling this party like I thought it would be."

"Yeah," I say as I look over my shoulder and glance at the kitchen once more. "More than ready."

I zip up the jacket I never got a chance to take off as we leave the party and step out into the cool night. I can't deny leaving the noise and chaos behind me is a relief. But I also can't stop thinking about Levi.

15

HAILEY

He's late.

I don't know why I'm surprised that he is. Being late for our first chess session isn't the best way to make a good impression. Unfortunately, my initial thoughts about him seem to be correct.

If he has an issue, texting me about it would be the right thing to do. Communication is key and he's now wasting my time.

During the time I've been waiting for him, I set up the chessboard, ordered a decaf coffee and a brownie, and I've been reading.

There are a few reasons why I'm not completely annoyed by this. First, I have my homework assignment that is due at the end of the week done already. If I didn't have it done, I would have just gotten up and left and probably never spoken to him again.

Second, he's lucky I've been keeping myself preoccupied with a book that has been on my TBR for way too long. I began reading the book today and now I'm halfway through chapter thirteen, where one of the heroine's love interests has already asked her out on a date. The cute cover on this book is hiding a multitude of dirty things and no one is the wiser unless they are reading over my shoulder.

Third, I have one of the best brownies on the planet keeping me somewhat happy. Emphasis on somewhat.

Just as I'm sticking another piece of the chocolatey goodness into my mouth, the bell above the front door of Brewed Beginnings jingles. I shift my gaze, taking me out of the fictional world I'd been in, forcing me back to the present day where I still have to deal with someone who didn't have the common decency to tell me something came up and he would be delayed.

And it is him.

Levi rushes in and spots me almost immediately. He runs a hand through his hair as he walks over to me quickly.

"Hailey, I'm so sorry," Levi says, breathlessly, as he reaches the table where I'm still seated. "Practice ran over, and Coach wouldn't let us off the ice until we got the drill right."

How can someone who looks as if he ran all the way here still look hot and put together? It is another talent he has, I'm sure.

I roll my eyes but close my book with a soft thud, marking my spot with a bookmark I'd thrown in my bookbag a week ago. "It's fine."

"No, it's not. I should have texted; this is all on me."

His admission forces me to look up at him. Did he really own up to this being his fault? And here I thought tonight wouldn't have any surprises, and he is already proving me wrong.

Levi sits down at the chair across from me and begins fumbling with his backpack. I narrow my eyes, trying to figure out what he's trying to do or get. Just as I'm about to ask, he presents me with a white box tied with a delicate purple ribbon. I blink in surprise and stare at it like I've never seen a box before in my life.

"What's this?"

Levi shrugs. "It was a thank-you-for-doing-this-for-me gift, but now I guess it's doubling as an I'm-sorry-for-being-late-and-not-letting-you-know gift."

"Alrighty then..." My voice trails off as I reach for the box and gently pull the ribbon loose. It falls away gracefully, as if in slow motion, adding to the suspense. With a careful lift of the lid, twelve purple roses greet me. My mouth drops open in surprise because this is the last thing I expected to see. Apparently, the surprises are determined to keep on coming.

"These are Ecuadorian roses. They're preserved," Levi explains. "I saw that you were reading an environmental science book the other day and thought you might appreciate them. They don't need water or much care, and they should last at least a year. Figured it was perfect for a college student... and now I need to stop rambling."

Is Levi nervous?

I glance up at him then, caught off guard by his thoughtfulness. A small smile tugs at my lips as I touch one of the petals. I'm still confused as to why he decided to buy me flowers of all things. We've already come to an agreement about what he is going to do in exchange for my doing this, so this is extra.

"They're beautiful," I admit but try to maintain control of my emotions. Before I know it, I'll be swooning at the sight of him like the thousands of people on this campus and around the country. "Thank you."

Levi watches me for a second before he says, "You're welcome. I'm glad you like them."

"Wow... Seriously, thank you," I say again. I place the box on the book I was reading and that draws Levi's attention to it.

"What are ya reading there?"

I look at the book and then back at him before my eyes settle on the book again. He doesn't know what he's walking into by asking that question. "A romance novel."

Levi leans forward. "Oh yeah? What's it about?"

"Are you sure you want to know?" I ask, giving him an out. "I won't be offended if you're just blowing smoke up my ass."

"I really want to know, Hailey."

I move aside the white box, sit back, and fold my arms across my chest. "Fine. It's a spicy romance where the heroine has multiple love interests. But the cover is cute, right?"

Levi stares at me for a moment, I'm sure he's trying to process what I just threw out there. It is as if a switch goes off and I watch as his blue eyes darken slightly. "Is that something you're into?"

I tilt my head, considering the implied meaning behind his words before deciding to keep the conversation on lighter ground. "It's fiction. Pure escapism." I put the roses carefully back down on the book, praying that the sudden heat I feel on my cheeks isn't making what I'm thinking obvious. "I do like reading about it, however."

He nods, a playful smirk appears on his face. "Right, of course. An escape from real life."

The mood shifts back as I clear my throat and say, "Shall we get started on learning about chess?"

"I'm ready when you are."

I slide the romance novel and the roses to the side and gesture to the board.

"Okay," I start, pointing to the polished figures. "These are your pieces, sometimes referred to as chessmen. Pawns are up front. They're your front line, essentially. Knights are next; they move in an L shape, so keep that in mind. Bishops move across the board diagonally." I demonstrate each movement with a gentle touch on the pieces, watching Levi nod along as he memorizes their paths. "Then you have the rook," I say, pausing to point at the piece that resembles a small tower.

Levi nods along and then he says, "The rook."

"Yes, it moves straight ahead or side to side—not diagonally," I explain. "Think of it as being your castle, your stronghold on the board. It can be one of the most powerful pieces, especially toward the endgame."

He's silent for a moment as his gaze switches between the board and me. "So, it can be the backbone of my strategy," he says out loud, but it doesn't seem as if he's talking directly to me.

However, I can't deal with awkwardly sitting here, so I decide to respond. "That's one way to put it," I reply, intrigued by the fact that he is taking this seriously.

"Alright, Rook, what's next?"

And then he has to ruin the good thoughts I was having about him.

I roll my eyes at the nickname, deciding this time to let it slide. "The queen," I continue, picking up the most versatile piece on the board. "She's powerful—can move in any direction and as far as she wants, as long as she's not blocked."

"I've seen that piece before. And this is your king?" He brushes his finger against the piece.

I nod. "The whole game revolves around him. Once he's in checkmate, the game is over regardless of how many other pieces are left on the board."

"Protect him at all costs."

"Exactly."

We start a mock game where I explain each move and tactic. Levi surprises me with his quick grasp of chess strategy. During the game, he asks thoughtful questions. I also find us discussing some of our likes and dislikes, all the while keeping chess as our main priority.

"So, what got you into hockey in the first place?"

He glances up at me for a moment. "My older brother. He played. I idolized him, and wanted to be just like him."

I notice the change in his mood, but I don't press. "Sounds like he was a big influence on you."

"Yeah, he was everything I wanted to be." Levi's smile is bittersweet, his gaze drifting away for a moment before refocusing on the game. "What about you? Why chess?"

The shift in topic feels natural though I sense there's more he's not saying, but I don't want to pry. Instead, I find myself sharing my passion for chess and the environment.

"Chess was actually my dad's thing first," I explain. "When I was younger, he taught me the basics and it was a way for us to bond together. I swear, we'd play in the living room for hours, just the two of us. And I fell in love with it. When I go home, Dad and I still play together."

"That's really nice, having that connection with your dad," he says.

I nod, suddenly feeling self-conscious under his stare. Clearing my throat, I redirect my attention back to the board. "So, I think you've got the basics down. I'm impressed."

"I never thought I would hear you utter those words to me, Rook."

"Okay, stop calling me that," I demand.

He shrugs but doesn't say anything further.

All I can do is stare at him through a narrowed gaze. "Why don't we try a real game?"

Levi grins, rolling up the sleeves of his hoodie. "You're on. I think I can handle this."

I raise an eyebrow and begin resetting the board. "Alright, Let's see what you've retained and what we need to work on for next time."

With a nod, I make my first move, the King's Pawn Opening. Levi watches intently, his hand hovering over his own pieces before he mirrors my move. The game progresses, with both of us losing pieces, him more so than me. His strategy is pretty good, but I end up victorious.

"Good game," Levi says, shaking my hand across the table. His palm is warm and calloused against mine.

"You too, not bad for your first real match," I reply.

"I have an excellent teacher."

I feel my cheeks flush at the unexpected compliment. There's no denying they're red now. "Well, you were a quick study," I say, tucking a strand of hair that has fallen out of my bun behind my ear self-consciously.

"Thanks again for taking the time to do this. I know you're busy."

"It's no problem, really. I don't mind teaching someone, especially when they are eager to learn."

We don't say anything else as we clean up the mess we made. I end up locking the chess set up with the others that I keep here for chess club. As I'm walking back to where Levi is, he taps two fingers on the table and says, "Since it's dark now, how about I walk you home?"

It's weird that I've gone from thinking that Levi is an egotistical jock, when he's showing me that he's anything but. There is much more to him, but I'm not willing to admit that to him. "Thanks, but no thanks. I drove here so it's not an issue."

"I can make sure you get to your car safely then. I also drove here, which helped me not be later than I already was."

I hesitate for a second. It's silly because I'm perfectly capable of walking myself to my car. Yet there's something sweet about his offer. With a slight shake of my head, I say, "Alright, please walk me to my car."

As we leave Brewed Beginnings, the night air is a small shock to my system given how much chillier it is since I entered.

Levi and I walk in comfortable silence. At least for me, it's because I'm not sure what else to say. I'm not sure why Levi's being quiet.

As we reach my car, I unlock it, putting my things in the passenger's seat before walking over to the driver's side. Turning to face Levi, I extend my hand.

"Thank you for walking me to my car and for the flowers," I say sincerely.

He takes my hand in his and shakes it firmly. "No need to thank me. And I'm not going to thank you again for the lessons because while I'm grateful, I'll be repeating myself for the seventh time at this point."

I let go of his hand and unlock my car door. As I slip into the driver's seat, I hear him call out, "See you around?"

"Yeah," I reply, starting the engine. "See you around, Levi."

16

HAILEY

I have a smile on my face.

And it's the strangest feeling.

This isn't to say that I don't smile at all. I simply prefer to keep my smiles reserved because it's the best way to keep from having to talk to people. It works, which is why I continue to do it.

But right now, I couldn't remove the smile off my face if I tried. I'm not sure how to feel about it.

What I do know is that it has everything to do with Levi.

Fuck.

My grip on my steering wheel tightens as I think about it. Thankfully, I'm almost back at my apartment and then I can think without having to worry about whether I'll get into an accident or not.

Soon, I find a parking space not too far away from the entrance of my apartment building and I kill the engine. The silence I'm in is still way too loud as my gaze lands on the white box that he gave me. It's a whole different layer to this puzzle that I don't want to get into right now.

I unlock my car door and make sure to grab all of my things so I can avoid having to go around to the passenger's side door. Once my car is locked, I quickly make my way through the entrance of my building and unlock the front door of my apartment.

"Hey, H," Jade says as soon as I walk across the threshold. She's sitting on the living room couch watching a movie. However, as soon as I close the door behind me, she turns her body so she's giving me all of her attention. "What's with the box?"

"Why don't you look at it," I say as I hand it to her because there is no point in playing dumb. I turn my back to her as I take off my shoes and jacket. As I'm putting them in their rightful places, I hear a squeal come from the living area.

"Who gave you flowers?" She pauses after her question before she continues. "Was it—"

"Levi?" I ask, cutting her off. "Yes, those are from him."

"You've got to be shitting me."

"I'm not and before you jump off the deep end, he told me those are thank you flowers for teaching him how to play chess."

Jade jumps off the couch and says, "You know that's such a lie. It's complete and utter bullshit." I throw a side eye her way, but she keeps talking. "I'm willing to bet money that him giving you those flowers has nothing to do with him wanting to say thank you."

"Those were his words, not mine."

Jade rolls her eyes, obviously not believing a word of it. "You and I both know Levi Jamison didn't need to buy you flowers just to say thanks for chess lessons."

"I think you're reading too much into this," I reply, trying to brush off what she is implying. But given how much I overthink things, I'm going to think of one million possibilities as to why he did buy them until I find the right one.

"You're seriously telling me you don't see it?" She waves the flowers in the air as if they were evidence in a trial. "Come on, Hailey. When was the last time someone got you flowers just because?"

I bite my lip, not wanting to acknowledge it would have been my dad years ago.

Jade places the flowers on the coffee table carefully before making her way over to me and gently squeezing my shoulder. She softens her tone, maybe sensing my discomfort. "Look, all I'm saying is that maybe it doesn't hurt to see where all of this goes."

"There's nowhere to go because nothing's going on, J. Anyway, what were you watching—"

"Hailey Reed, queen of the chessboard and deflection," Jade accuses, but her tone is light, teasing.

Who needs enemies when you have friends like this? This time she's on the receiving end of my eye roll. "Why can't a guy give a girl flowers without an agenda? He literally said they were a thank-you gift." I am talking more to myself than to Jade. "Why are you making this more complicated?"

"Because we're human and this is complicated," she fires back immediately. "And that guy isn't just *a guy*. Levi Jamison is Crestwood's hockey god—"

"I don't care about his status," I cut in sharply, surprising myself. Why am I defending him?

Thankfully, Jade doesn't pick up on my snarkiness. Or if she does, she doesn't call me out on it. "Oh, I know you don't," she says, dragging out the words in a singsong voice. "But there's no denying that the hockey captain has got you overthinking everything, and that's something you try to avoid doing."

"Yeah, because it takes up too much brain power to sit here debating this. I have other things I need to worry about... like my needing to go to work tomorrow." I know I'm bluffing because I'm going to be thinking about this for the rest of the night.

Jade gives me a look but walks past me to go to the fridge. She's about to say something more when my phone's ringtone plays. I guess I forgot to turn it on vibrate before entering Brewed Beginnings.

It takes me a moment to fish the device out of my bag. My eyes land on the phone screen and see Dad's name. My stomach does a weird flip. Why is he calling instead of texting?

"Hey, Dad, gimme a second." I look over at Jade and say, "I'll be right back."

I leave the room without waiting for Jade's response, and once I'm in my bedroom, I close the door behind me. "Okay. What's up?"

"Hey, sweetheart. Did I catch you at a bad time?" Dad's voice is warm, and I can't detect anything strange in it.

"No, no, it's fine," I let out a burst of air from my lungs. "Just got back from... a thing." I sink onto the edge of my bed and cross my legs.

"A thing, huh? Sounds mysterious." There's a teasing vibe to his words. "Also sounds like you don't want to tell your old man about it."

"There's nothing really to tell." That is only sort of true, but I didn't want to do a deep dive into it.

"That's okay. I won't pry. Just wanted to check in on you."

"Everything's good here. How about you?"

There's a pause on the line and I brace for what he's about to say. "Things are going well here too. Work is work and I'm doing a couple of things around the house. You'll probably notice them when you come home."

That doesn't seem too bad. It isn't the first time he's fixed or improved some things while I've been away at school. "Are the projects major things? Is there anything you need help with? I can come home one weekend and help."

"Oh no, no, no." I can feel him waving me off through the phone even before the words come out of his mouth. "I've got everything under control. If I want to do anything drastic, I can ask Henry to come and help out."

I nod along to my father's words. Although Crestwood isn't far from my childhood home, I'd been worried about my dad and how things would be once I moved away. It might be a strange thing for me to think about, but it has been the two of us for so long, I was worried about the change.

Or maybe it is me projecting my own feelings onto my father.

But things have gone well, and Dad still has Henry and others in our community to count on. And for that, I'm grateful.

That reminds me of something. "Dad, I'm putting together an event at Oak Terrace in a few weeks. We're going to have a chess night for some of the citizens there. If you want to come and be there for it..." My voice trails off as I wait for his response.

"Are you kidding me? Of course I want to be there. Just tell me the date and time and I'll be there."

I smile, feeling the warmth of his enthusiasm through the phone. It's a comforting reminder that no matter what else changes, he is a constant in my life. "Thanks, Dad. I'll text you the details later."

"That sounds great, Hailey. But there's something else I wanted to tell you. Related to something we talked about when we went out to dinner."

"What is it? Did you end up getting a dog?" I ask, suddenly nervous about the shift in his tone. A dog to see and play with sounds awesome in my mind.

"Well, I met someone," he says.

Someone? The word bounces around my head with no sign of slowing down. "Oh?" is all I manage to get out. Because what else is there to say?

"Yeah, it was unexpected," he admits with a small chuckle. "At the grocery store of all places. Her name's Angela. We've been talking over the last couple of days and so far, she's lovely."

My mouth drops open as I hop off my bed. It's as if my world has tilted off its axis slightly and nothing is in alignment anymore. But I can't show it.

"Oh wow." The words taste like cardboard on my tongue. Speaking about it is one thing, but now this is becoming real.

I'd done my best to not think about it for the most part after Dad brought it up, but all of those emotions I've tried to hide from myself are back and bubbling underneath the surface.

"I want to be transparent about it, especially because

we already talked about it," Dad continues. "I'm thinking of asking her out to dinner."

I swallow hard, trying to maintain a calm façade over the phone. Thankfully, he can't see what I'm actually doing because he would immediately be able to read me like a book.

I can't explain why I'm panicking about this, but I am. It all seems fast for me, but I'm proud of him for taking this step. I take a deep, shaky breath, trying to steady my voice before responding. "That's great, Dad. I'm really happy for you."

The words sound silly to me, but it's all I can come up with. I pace the length of my bedroom to give my body something to do because I don't know what will happen if I don't.

"Thanks, sweetheart. I know this might feel a little strange for you. It's new for me too. But I want you to know that no matter what happens, you'll always be my number one."

I feel tears forming at the corners of my eyes and I hate it. "I know. It's... it's been the two of us for so long, so this feels strange."

"I know and we don't know where any of this may go anyway."

That's true. It's not as if he's getting married again or something.

Yet. But that isn't something I have to think about right now.

"I'm happy for you, really," I say, trying to keep my voice steady.

"I appreciate you being so supportive. This is all still new; I'm just exploring things with her."

We chat for another minute or two before saying goodbye. As soon as I end the call, the floodgates open. I crawl into bed, burying my face in the pillow as sobs wrack my body, hoping Jade can't hear me.

I cry until the only thing I can do is be a sniffling mess, the pillowcase now damp due to my tears. I can't stop the feelings I'm having even if I know it's selfish. He promises he'll always be there, but so did Mom. I'm scared of losing him, even though I understand he deserves happiness.

Eventually, my tears subside and my breath steadies. I rub my eyes with the back of my hand before sitting up. I don't even know how long I've been crying for at this point.

Wiping away the remaining traces of tears on my cheeks, I take a deep breath and gather myself. I'm not able to fix this alone. I need to talk to someone else about this to work through my emotions.

I sit down at my desk and turn on my laptop. It takes me a little bit before I figure out what I'm looking for and I end up on Crestwood's mental health services web page. My eyes scan over the options and I start filling out the information they require.

I select an appointment slot on their online booking system, hovering over the confirm button. Do I really want to do this? Before I can dissect the answer further, I press the button, and almost instantly, a confirmation notification pops up.

That small action feels monumental, although I'm absolutely scared shitless.

17

LEVI

"Y ou can give me one more rep."

I want to glare at him and cuss him out for suggesting it, but my focus is on bench pressing this weight. New sweat beads form on my forehead and gravity has its way as it trails down my skin. I'm in the zone, feeling every muscle fiber singing with that good kind of burn—you know, the one that screams progress.

However, it doesn't mean that I want to do another rep. I now wish that I had my headphones on to tune him out. Taylor Swift wouldn't force me to do another rep.

I push up the barbell with a grunt, locking my arms before letting it drop back to the rack with a satisfying clank. I'm breathing hard as I try to recover from the effort I just exerted.

Asher claps his hands once. "There it is! That's what I'm talking about!"

I roll my head to the side to look at him. "You're enjoying this too much," I accuse, but there's no real bite to my words.

He picks up my hand towel and tosses it at me. "Hey, you gotta admit, it felt good."

Wiping the perspiration from my face, I sit up and shake my head. "You're right, but it doesn't necessarily mean that I like it."

Asher's laugh is loud in the gym, drawing a few glances our way as he helps me up. Of course, he finds all of this hilarious because he already finished his set.

"C'mon, man. Admitting it is the first step."

I snort as I grab my water bottle and take a long swig, letting the cold liquid soothe my throat. Asher moves on to the next machine, but I stay back for a moment as I try to decide which machine I'm going to use next.

My mind drifts back to yesterday's chess lesson with Hailey. I'd gone in with low expectations, especially after I was late. Heck, I wouldn't have blamed her for leaving, but she'd surprised me.

She didn't hold back from calling me out when necessary, but she also praised me when I made a good play.

"Levi."

I look up at Asher and see he's doing some crunches on the ab machine.

"You're thinking about her, aren't you?" Asher's knowing glance makes me shift uncomfortably.

I try to play dumb. "Thinking about who?"

"Really, dude? You know exactly who I'm talking about."

"Not a clue."

"Hailey, the barista and chess player."

I bite back the sigh. "What? No. I'm just focused on getting through this workout." But he sees right through me.

"Uh-huh. That's why you've got a little smile on your face," he teases. "Your chess session must have gone well."

"It was a chess session," I say nonchalantly.

"Yeah, it must have been something more than that because you're actively avoiding telling me anything about it."

"That doesn't mean anything."

Asher stops moving to stare at me. "We've extensively talked about the women we've slept with and now you don't want to say a word about playing chess?"

Talking about who we've had sex with isn't my finest hour, but for some reason, I don't want to delve too much into what happened between Hailey and me, even to my best friend.

I shrug my shoulders. "It was just chess, nothing to tell."

"Levi, c'mon. Knowing you, you probably talked about more than just what direction a pawn moves in."

I can't help but chuckle. "Well, we did talk, but it wasn't anything that deep."

"Anything that deep, huh?" Asher raises an eyebrow. "Let me guess, you discovered you both like the same kind of drinks?"

I shake my head. "It wasn't like that."

"Then what was it like?"

I pause, considering how to describe it. "It was... good," I say slowly. "Most of it was about chess, but we did get to know each other a little bit better."

Asher's eyes light up. "That sounds like it could have led into pretty deep territory to me."

"It wasn't, trust me." I walk away from him, hoping he'll get the hint and get back to his workout.

He doesn't, instead choosing to follow me around, almost like a lost puppy.

"So, what are you going to do about it?"

I shrug again. "Nothing. There isn't anything to do."

"Who are you? Where's the Levi I know?" Asher asks, his disbelief evident in his voice. "I've never seen you act this way before when it comes to a girl you're interested in."

That's because this whole thing is different and something I've never experienced. Hailey has made it clear that because I'm on the hockey team and have the celebrity status that comes with it, there is an issue for her. It doesn't change the attraction I feel toward her. It also doesn't change my thoughts about her fighting this thing that is growing between us.

"You're not going to quit with this, are you?"

"Nope, so we should talk about it now and then we get to finish our workout for the day."

With a heavy sigh, I look over at Asher and say, "I don't know what to do."

Asher drops the playful tone, his expression becoming serious. "Yeah, I get it. You don't do relationships, but you want to get to know her better, so you feel conflicted."

I nod, acknowledging the truth in his words. "It's more than that too. She doesn't like attention and she would get that if this did turn into something more. That isn't really avoidable."

"So, what's the solution?"

I don't know what the solution is. I feel trapped between my desire to get to know Hailey better and the reality of the situation and her feelings regarding it. I can keep the status quo between us as long as possible, but I'm not going to hold out hope that she'll eventually change her mind about the attention that would come with dating me. However, I don't want to ignore whatever this is either. All of this is happening while I'm trying not to move too fast and screw things up.

"I don't know, and I'm not just saying that because I'm trying to avoid talking about all of this."

"Fair. Okay I'll leave you alone about it. For now."

"Thank you."

As we continue our workout in silence, Asher's words are playing on repeat in my head. What am I going to do? I don't want to ignore the growing connection between Hailey and me, but I also can't ignore the reality of the situation. Even if she likes me, she might never overcome her dislike of the attention that comes along with dating me.

I lift the weights without thinking much about it because my mind isn't into it, but I know it's something I have to do. A part of me wants to give up, to convince myself that I'm doing too much for something that won't work out.

But I'm not a quitter.

Until I know for sure that Hailey wants nothing to do with me, I won't give up. I can't deny the way she makes me feel and I'm not willing to throw it away unless I absolutely have to.

I finish my set, my muscles exhausted, but my mind is still moving at a million miles an hour. As I wipe the sweat from my brow, I glance at Asher, who's looking back at me.

"You'll figure it out," he says. "You always do."

He's right and things will work out the way they're supposed to. Once we finish up our workout, we collect our things and head on out.

Outside the gym, I take a deep breath of the cooler air, a stark contrast to the stuffiness Asher and I left behind. My phone buzzes in my pocket and I take it out half expecting it to be someone trying to spam me with... something. Instead, it's from my father's personal email account.

Swiping the screen with my thumb, I open the email. And I quickly realize I should have ignored it:

"Levi,

I've reviewed the tapes from your last game several times now. While your performance was adequate in terms of scoring, there are things that need to be improved when it comes to defense in both your maneuvers and power play strategies..."

The words blur as I scroll through his message. Words like "improve," "inefficiencies," and "missed opportunities" feel as if they are everywhere. My father's voice repeats in my mind because I can hear him saying every word. It's obvious he thinks I'm supposed to be perfect.

Just like he viewed Caleb.

Not once does he mention the goal I scored or the assists. No mention of the way I rallied the team when we were feeling demoralized. It's a clinical dissection of everything I did that he didn't approve of. There is no hint of pride or satisfaction in my doing a damn good job in helping my team win our game.

I can feel Asher's eyes on me as if he's trying to figure out what is going on. When I finally reach the end of the email, I'm pissed, and I fill Asher in on what just happened.

"This is fucking typical of him. I'm not even surprised. Just disappointed."

"Hey, man, don't let him get inside your head. You can't, or he's going to fuck up your ability to function, let alone play."

"I know," I say with an annoyed groan. "It's more bull-shit I have to deal with when it comes to him and how he views me and Caleb."

Saying his name out loud stirs up a mess of emotions inside me. My throat tightens at the thought of my brother, even after all of these years. The wound that his passing away caused still hasn't healed. I don't know if it ever will.

"There's something that has been on my mind for a while, and I didn't know how to say it, but I think it's something you need to hear right now."

I'd be lying if I said I'm not nervous about what he's going to say. "What is it?"

"Caleb wouldn't have wanted you to live your life like this."

A pin could drop in the car right now and sound like a glass shattering. Deep down, I know he's right.

"I sometimes think about what he'd say if he saw me now," I confess, feeling a rare vulnerability creep into my voice. "Would he be proud?"

"He'd tell you to drop your dad's expectations like a bad habit," Asher replies matter-of-factly. "Caleb played out of passion for the sport, not for approval, even when your father used to hound him."

"Yeah, I can't stand this anymore. But saying that out loud to you versus telling my father is a totally different thing." I don't want to think about this anymore. "But enough about him. I don't want to keep my attention focused on him."

Shaking off the email, I lock my phone and shove it back into my pocket. I'm going to ignore the message for as long as I can. Because though his words may sting, they will not define me.

18

HAILEY

y leg bounces up and down to an imaginary beat in my head. Saying I'm nervous about what is going to happen is an understatement.

I can't believe I've done it. This is probably something I should have done years ago.

I'm sitting in Emily Shaw's office, one of the therapists on Crestwood's campus, debating if I still have enough time to run out of here ahead of my appointment.

My gaze lands on a therapy dog I found out was named Charles, and I wonder if it's worth sitting down there and petting him to calm my nerves. He looks so peaceful laying there with what looks to be soft, golden fur, but I can't manage to make myself walk up to him. It's as if I'm frozen to this seat, unable to move.

I steal a quick glance at the closed door leading to

Emily's office as my anxiety about this whole thing continues to build. All I can do is let out a deep breath and shake my head. It's a silly idea since her assistant has already signed me in, but I won't lie and say the thought hasn't crossed my mind.

I watch as the clock hanging on the wall to my left ticks away, reminding me that every second I'm here is another second closer to me spilling the secrets I've kept from everyone else. Again. Not exactly my idea of a fun Thursday afternoon, but I also know this is what I need to do.

My thoughts are interrupted by a voice calling my name. "Hailey Reed?"

My eyes land on a woman with blonde hair and thin-rimmed glasses standing in a doorway. Dread clouds my mind but I force a smile, which I never do, and my stomach does this weird little flip thing, twisting into knots. My nerves and anxiety are something else.

"Hi," I reply, standing up too quickly. My legs feel like they've been replaced with rubber bands, but I still manage to stay upright. I grab my bookbag and follow her into the office and sit down in a plush navy-blue armchair.

The office emanates a peaceful feeling with the light blue paint I'm sure is done by design. The walls are adorned with diplomas and certificates and a couple pieces of abstract art that aren't meant to be the center-piece of the room. Bookshelves overflow with texts on psychology, human behavior, and a couple of plants.

Emily is dressed in a simple, yet elegant, cream blouse paired with navy slacks that mirror the color of the armchair I sat on. Her blonde hair is pulled back in a way that's both professional and effortlessly chic. She closes the door behind us as I set my bag down.

"Welcome, Hailey," she says with a voice that's softer than I'd imagined. Then again, I'd gone into this without any expectations. "I'm Emily Shaw. It's great to have you here."

"Thanks," I manage to respond, my words feeling clumsy and awkward in comparison to hers. I'm not sure why.

"I know coming to therapy can feel overwhelming, but please know this is a safe space. Everything we discuss here will remain confidential."

I nod slowly. Hearing it from her provides a layer of assurance I didn't have when I walked in here. For that, I'm grateful.

"How has your day been so far?" Emily asks.

"It's been… okay," I reply, trying not to rush the words out because it would give away my nervousness. Then again, I don't think she would judge me for being anxious. "I worked my shift at Brewed Beginnings and then had an environmental science class before coming here."

"Oh? That sounds fascinating. What are you studying at the moment?"

"We're looking into sustainable agriculture methods," I explain, happy to talk about something that's more neutral. "Like the impact of farm runoff on local ecosystems."

"That's incredibly important work. Do you enjoy it?"

"I do, actually. It all can be a lot sometimes. I'm talking about the workload, by the way."

Emily nods. "It can be difficult balancing personal life and responsibilities. How are things at Brewed Beginnings?"

A sigh escapes my lips as I think about my part-time job at the coffee shop. "Brewed Beginnings is... eh. It's like my second home, but I have issues with my manager. My coworkers and customers are usually pretty cool though." I think about how Levi has become one of my regulars now.

"But that's not stressing you outside it being an addition to your schedule?"

I hesitate before answering. "I mean I would prefer to not be doing it, but the extra money helps make ends meet as well as gives me some spending money."

"Understandably. Why don't we talk about what brought you here today."

I take a deep breath, feeling as if I'm about to rip the Band-Aid off, exposing a wound that was barely covered to begin with. "It's... it's my dad," I begin, looking down at my fingers. "He's in the process of starting to date again. It's weird because, well, he hasn't dated since my mom left us."

Emily tilts her head slightly. I notice that her eyes

seem to be kind and attentive, encouraging me to continue without rushing me.

"I somewhat remember how it happened, at least from my perspective anyway," I clear my throat before going on. "My mom walked out on us when I was nine. Just packed up and left without a word to me or my father. Dad mentioned they got into an argument the day before, and apparently, she packed her things while he was at work and I was at school. Dad tried to shield me from it, but he couldn't hide that no matter how hard he tried. I remember I used to wake up in the middle of the night, thinking I'd heard her voice. I'd run around looking for her, only to find no one there."

I shift in my seat, pulling at the hem of my sweater to give my hands something to do. "I also would wake up each morning, and for a fraction of a second... forget. Forget she was gone. Then reality would crash into me all over again. Dad was my rock though. He never let on how hard it hit him. All he did was show compassion and love to get me through that time. And you know what else is interesting about him?"

"What's that, Hailey?"

I pause to take a deep breath as tears began to pool in the corners of my eyes. "He never spoke ill of her, you know? He did everything he could to keep things as normal for me as possible. Even though his life had also been flipped on its head. I'm so grateful for everything he has done, and I want to do a better job at expressing that to him."

"It sounds like your father has been a constant source of support and stability for you," she says gently. "It's clear how much you appreciate and recognize his efforts, even during such challenging times. It's natural to feel a mix of gratitude and concern when family dynamics change, especially given what you've experienced with your mother."

"And now that he's interested in seeing someone, I'm scared," I finally blurt out. "I know I should be happy for him, really. It's been years since Mom left and he deserves happiness. But there's this fear that it might drastically change my relationship with my father. Also, if their relationship progresses and they become serious, what if I let myself trust this woman and... what if she leaves too?"

Emily leans forward slightly, her hands folded neatly on her lap. "It's natural to have these fears, Hailey, considering what has happened to you. But it's also important to remember that we can't predict the future."

"How do I deal with it then? I was full on sobbing when my dad told me there is a woman that he is interested in." My voice is barely above a whisper as a tear falls from my eyes.

"First you need to acknowledge your feelings. But then you must work toward not letting them control your actions or thoughts about others. Your father is his own

person, capable of making decisions for his well-being—
just like you can for yours."

I sniffle and nod once more. What she said makes a lot
of sense, but the fear is still there. Wiping a stray tear
away, I can't help but draw parallels between how I view
my dad's potential new relationship and how I treat the
other relationships in my life.

"I guess..." I start, hesitating as I try to untangle my
emotions, "this fear isn't just about Dad. It's seeping into
other areas of my life. Like with Levi."

Emily tilts her head. "Who is Levi?"

"Levi Jamison is the captain of Crestwood's hockey
team. We met when he came into the coffee shop one day,
and he's sort of been in my life ever since. But I'm keeping
him at arm's length. Probably because I'm afraid to let
anyone in." It feels awkward to admit this out loud, but
here we are.

"It's normal to want to protect yourself from poten-
tially getting hurt."

I tuck a loose strand of hair behind my ear. "Levi
doesn't know about my mom. I haven't told him
because—"

"Because you're afraid of letting him in," Emily
finishes for me.

I nod reluctantly. "Yes, and it's like... every time he
tries to get closer, I find some excuse to push him away."

"Maybe your reluctance to let Levi in is less about him
and more about your need for control. It's another change

and you have a fear of unpredictability in relationships because of what your mother has done."

I have no response because she hit the nail on the head. My childhood trauma has been exposed and everything she said makes so much sense. And this is part of the reason why I came here today.

"I want to change that." And I mean every word.

We talk more, and by the end of the session, my eyes feel heavy from the crying, but the burden on my shoulders feels lighter. As I stand up to leave, I grab my bag and head to the door.

"Thank you for coming in, Hailey," Emily says as I reach for the door handle.

"No, thank you. And I'll definitely be back."

I open the door and walk into the waiting area. I wave goodbye to Emily's receptionist before leaving the building.

As I'm walking back to my apartment, my phone vibrates in my pocket. I pull it out and see a text from Jade.

> Jade: What are you up to tonight?

Oh hell. What is Jade trying to get me into now?

> Me: Nothing. Headed back to the apartment. Why?

As I hit send, another message pops up from her before I can even put my phone back in my pocket again.

Jade: Thought we could hit up Sapphire Tavern, the new bar downtown. I know it's not your exact scene, but I'll buy you a few drinks.

I stare at the screen for a moment longer than necessary. The lure of free drinks is appealing. A night out sounds like something I need after the day I've had.

Me: Alright. I'm in.

19

HAILEY

I stand in front of my bathroom mirror, staring at my reflection with anxiousness and excitement. My fingers hesitantly reach up to the bun that not only keeps my hair off my face but has become a staple in my life. It's a part of my daily uniform to the extent that it feels odd sometimes when I wear my hair down for bed.

It's funny how something as simple as a hairstyle can feel so ingrained in your identity. But tonight, I want to do something different. Maybe it's because of my session with Emily, but I'm feeling a little bit bold.

Slowly, almost ceremoniously, I remove the silk hair tie from my hair. The tension in my head immediately lessens until it's gone. I watch as my hair cascades down my shoulders in soft brown waves, and I barely recognize the person in the mirror. It has been forever since I last let it hang loose and left the house.

The reflection staring back at me now looks more carefree, unlike the controlled version of myself I've presented to the world.

The small change shifts my mindset as I quickly run my brush through it to give it a more polished look. I love the way it looks and wonder why I don't wear it down more.

Because it's a piece of your armor, Hailey.

Shaking off the thoughts that are swirling in my head about the step I am taking, I stroll into my bedroom and walk over to the closet. My whole objective is to do something different, a bit daring. I don't want to think about myself as someone who has abandonment issues and fears that shouldn't still be a thing, but they are.

My fingers brush against a vibrant red dress. I immediately know it's not something that I own and suspect Jade must have snuck it in while I was in the shower. It's a bit daring for me, but also, tonight feels like a night to be daring.

The more I stare at it, the more I realize I actually want to wear it.

As I take the dress off the hanger and slip it on, I can't help but run my fingers down the fabric. The dress clings to my figure, accentuating curves I usually hide under baggy sweaters and hoodies and jeans. Wearing this is going to be an experience in itself because it is predicted to be chilly tonight, but tonight is all about new experiences.

Plus, the longer I look at the dress, the more my confidence about wearing it tonight grows. It's strange how a piece of clothing can change your whole mood, but I'll take what I can get.

"Hailey!" Jade's voice draws my attention to the door. "You ready?"

"Almost. Be there in a sec!" I call back as I zip the dress up and put on a pair of black boots I'd stuffed in the back of my closet when I moved in.

When I step out into the living room of our shared apartment, Jade is dancing to a song coming from her phone, the pink dress she decided to wear tonight shifting with every movement she makes. I watch her for a few seconds with my arms crossed over my chest, and when she finally sees me, her face lights up like it's Christmas morning as she stares at my hair. "Look at the stunner that just walked in here. And your hair is actually down, holy fuck."

"Don't get used to it. I can easily toss it back up in a bun."

"Don't you dare!" Jade exclaims as she takes a step toward me as if she might grab my arms. "If you do, I'm cutting your hands off myself."

I can't help but laugh at Jade. "Alright, I won't put it back up. But only because I know you'd find a way to follow through on that threat."

"You're damn right." Jade grins triumphantly, clearly

pleased to have won this small battle. She gives me an approving once-over. "But seriously, you look fantastic."

"And the same can be said about you. Thanks for leaving your red dress in my closet."

She flashes me a dazzling smile. "You're welcome. Let's finish getting ready."

We both make our way to our bathroom, where Jade starts rummaging through her makeup bag. "You want to wear eyeshadow, right?"

"Sure, that's fine," I say as I watch her remove a compact case with several different colors of eyeshadow included. She carefully applies a brownish shimmery shade to her lids before she looks at me in the mirror.

"I've got this. I'll make sure we both look stunning tonight."

I'm willing to put my look in Jade's hands because I trust her completely. Once she finishes applying most of our makeup, she turns to me holding a red lipstick. "This is going to look perfect with that dress."

I take the lipstick out of her hand, uncap it, and bring the tube to my lips. After I finish putting it on, I can confirm that she's right. This lipstick looks great with this dress and with my skin tone.

"Okay, I think we're all set," Jade says as she takes one final look at herself in the mirror.

"Great. Let me grab my keys, coat, and purse."

"Okay, I'll meet you in the living room."

Both Jade and I leave the bathroom and go our separate ways. I gather the things I need before walking into our living room once more. I say a quick prayer that my coat will keep me mostly warm tonight as Jade joins me and we leave the apartment.

The night air hits us as we step outside, and I shiver in response. Jade tries to talk to me, engaging in small talk, but I'm only half paying attention. My mind is on what tonight will bring and the things I revealed to Emily. It's all a lot to process, but I'm hoping tonight will give me an opportunity to quiet all of the other noise in my head.

We take a campus-owned bus downtown where a bunch of restaurants and shops are located and walk up to a building with Sapphire Tavern written across the front. We push through the doors of the bar, and I'm impressed by what we see.

As we walk into Sapphire Tavern, I start to understand why it is the new trendy spot in Crestwood. The exterior is sleek and modern, and the words of the bar lit up in neon-blue signage are icing on the cake. The interior of the bar is spacious, bathed in a soothing blue glow from the strategically placed lighting. The walls are adorned with contemporary art pieces, giving an even bigger artistic flair to the space.

The central attraction is the long, polished bar counter, topped with sparkling sapphire-colored tiles that shimmer under the overhead lights. Behind the bar, shelves of assorted liquors create a mesmerizing backdrop. This place is stunning, and I can see why it has become the new *it place*.

The seating area is a mix of booths and high-top tables, and near the rear of the venue, there is a dance floor if we want to shake our asses. Once again, normally not my vibe, but if I get enough drinks in me, I can be persuaded to do so.

Jade grabs my hand, pulling me toward the bar. "I promised you a few drinks, so this first round is on me!" she shouts over the noise from the music and the talking.

I smile, letting her lead the way. Once we are there, a bartender immediately comes up to us. "What can I get you? And would you like to start a tab?"

"Two Jack and Cokes and yes, please," Jade calls out to the bartender, who nods and begins mixing our drinks. That drink is my go-to outside of the occasional beer and wine, and I'm not surprised Jade ordered one for herself too.

As we wait, I feel a tap on my shoulder. I turn around, coming face-to-face with Ben, one of my coworkers from Brewed Beginnings.

He grins at me and says, "Hailey, I thought that was you." His eyes shift from being focused on my hair to my face as his smile widens.

I do a double take, still questioning whether I'm truly seeing him outside of work. Then again, he is more than likely more surprised at seeing me outside of Brewed

Beginnings given I rarely go out and party. "Ben! What are you doing here?"

He shrugs, leaning against the bar. "Hanging out with some friends after a long week. You know how it is."

I nod, understanding the sentiment. "Of course. I'm here with my best friend, Jade. Jade, this is Ben, my coworker."

Jade waves at Ben, flashing him a bright smile before handing me my drink. Ben nods, acknowledging her presence.

Ben leans in closer and says, "Can I be honest with you?"

I have no idea where this is going, but curiosity gets the best of me. I need to know what he wants to say. "Sure. What's up?"

"I've noticed you've been a bit more... distracted this week. Is everything okay?"

I take a sip of my Jack and Coke, letting it coat my throat before responding. "Yeah, everything's fine. Just a tough week at work and trying to juggle schoolwork, that's all."

"I know how that can be. I wanted to ask you how you were while we were at work but didn't want to make things awkward."

It is a little bit awkward to be frank, but I don't want Ben to feel that way. "Thanks, Ben. It means a lot to have you looking out for me."

"So what tales can both of you tell me about working at Brewed Beginnings?"

I swear I can't thank Jade enough for being an extrovert because she easily steered what could have been an awkward moment into an opportunity for us to find something else to talk about.

"Marc keeps us all on our toes with his random ideas and demands. Hailey, did you hear what he's thinking of doing next?" Ben asks as he looks at both Jade and me.

I roll my eyes. "Let me guess, another brewing technique?"

"Even better," Ben says with a chuckle. "He's planning on themed days. Like, Mocha Mondays or something."

Jade raises an eyebrow before taking another sip of her drink. "Sounds... interesting."

"Yeah, interesting is one word for it," I reply, dreading this idea with everything in my soul. "He'll probably make Funky Foam Fridays a thing."

Ben laughs. "I wouldn't put it past him. Hey, remember when he tried to introduce that artisan toast thing?"

Ben and I burst into laughter at the memory. "It was a disaster," I admit. "Burned bread isn't exactly gourmet."

Jade chimes in, "But hey, at least it's never boring with him around although, based on what Hailey has told me, he's an asshole."

"You're putting it mildly," I say. I start laughing again at the thought of theme days.

We continue to talk among ourselves when suddenly Jade pulls her phone out of her pocket. The slightly puzzled look on her face has me wondering what she's reading. I lean over and ask her, "Is everything alright?"

It takes a few seconds before she responds. "Um... maybe?"

I share a look with Ben and say, "That's not convincing."

"It's Wilder."

That is the last thing I expected her to say, but at this point, I'm not shocked. "What did he say? Shouldn't he be doing something related to hockey right now?"

"They don't have a game tonight."

Oops. Guess I haven't been paying attention to their schedule even though Levi sent me his. I don't have a reason to.

Regardless, there is still a question I need to find out the answer to. I glance at Ben before I turn back to Jade. "What did he say to put that look on your face?" I ask. Normally I wouldn't be asking this many questions, but the expression on her face is confusing to say the least.

Instead of replying, Jade looks up and moves her body so that she can look around Ben and toward the front door. It is then that she finally puts me out of my misery. "Levi is here. And he's staring right at you."

20

HAILEY

I have no time to prepare myself for the freak out that I'm going through. It honestly never occurred to me that Levi would be here tonight. Hell, I hadn't even thought much about it. Maybe it's because there are so many other places in and around Crestwood he could go to or maybe I assumed he'd have to do something hockey related this evening.

The only thing I've been doing is lying to myself.

I don't want to look at him, instead choosing to focus on Ben in front of me. However, Jade has no issue giving me an update. "He's walking over here and doesn't look happy."

I turn my head slightly to look at her and say, "That's not my problem, is it?" My words sound harsh leaving my lips, but I mean every word. There are a million things

Levi can be unhappy about and it's not my job to police his feelings.

"It's not, but your night is about to get a whole lot more interesting, if I had to guess," Jade replies.

I don't like that she's probably right, but I refuse to acknowledge it. I take another sip of my drink and give the man already in front of me a small smile.

"So, Ben, did you already get something to drink?" There, I can also do my darndest to shift the conversation into a different direction.

"I did. It's at my friend's table."

As Ben answers my question, I'm half paying attention to his response. But I'm on edge from the fact that Levi is walking over here, and it is hard to focus on anything else.

Good thing he comes over and is standing between Jade and Ben.

"Hailey, Jade," he says. "It's good to see you both again."

The moment Levi's gaze locks with mine, I feel like a deer caught in the headlights. I hate that it takes me several seconds to look away because my body is in flight or fight mode, and I can't turn it off.

I clear my throat, trying to stop the butterflies that are dancing in my stomach.

"Levi," I manage to say amid my struggle to maintain an aura of indifference. "What are you doing here?"

Levi chuckles, his eyes never leaving mine. "Here with

some of my teammates. We thought we'd go out and grab a drink."

He gestures toward a group of guys that have now settled in a corner of the bar. I look over at them and recognize a couple of faces before Levi sticks his hand out.

"I'm Levi," he says to Ben, who quickly returns his handshake. Although Levi's words are polite and show-case the golden-boy, hockey-captain image that he has built, there's something lingering under the surface. It's not lost on me that the tone of his voice is different from the one I usually hear him use or that it's directed at the only other guy here.

I try to keep my expression neutral as the two men exchange introductions, but on the inside, my heart is threatening to leave my chest.

Part of me is happy to have Levi here, especially while I continue to explore what I'm feeling as a result of my session with Dr. Shaw. My gut tells me the vibe I'm getting from him is that this is a pissing contest, but I can't tell if I'm overthinking things again.

"Nice to meet you, Levi," Ben answers, his voice cool and collected. His neutral tone eases the tension slightly, but it's still there. "Great game you guys had a few days ago."

Who doesn't know Levi at this point?

"Thanks. I can't complain too much," Levi answers Ben, but his gaze is on me.

We all stand there quietly for a few seconds before

Ben clears his throat. "Listen, I should get back to my friends. I'll see you at work, Hailey?"

I give a quick nod. "Yes, I'll see you there."

I watch as Ben gives a polite nod to Levi and Jade before turning and walking back to his group. And then there were three.

Jade glances between Levi and me, a knowing smile playing on her lips. "Well, this is cozy," she says.

I shoot her a warning look, telepathically telling her not to say anything weird. As much as I love Jade, her playful meddling is the last thing I need right now.

Levi either doesn't notice the subtle exchange or opts to ignore it. His gaze remains fixed on me. "It's good to see you, Hailey," he says. "You look beautiful tonight."

There are butterflies in my stomach again because of the compliment. I smooth my hands over the red dress self-consciously. "Thanks," I reply, aiming for a casual, indifferent tone and failing miserably.

Jade hides her smile behind her glass as she takes a sip. The silence stretches for a beat too long. I rack my brain for something else to say that won't be strange.

"So... how's the season going so far?" I ask Levi.

He relaxes a bit at the mundane question. "It's going well so I can't complain. Just trying to keep the momentum going."

I nod along, hoping he doesn't notice how panicky I feel. I'm painfully aware of his eyes on me, and the only thing keeping my hands from shaking is my holding this drink.

Once again, thank you, Jade. I'm convinced she heard me thanking her because she jumps in to continue the conversation.

"I saw that you guys play WTSU in a few weeks. That'll be a big game."

Levi acknowledges her with a glance. "Yeah, we're focused on preparing for that one. It's an important matchup." He looks back at me. "Maybe you both could come watch? I could leave tickets for you to grab."

I freeze, unprepared for his direct invitation again. Jade's eyes widen in excitement. "We'd love to!" she exclaims.

I shoot her another look. I hate that he's putting me on the spot with this in front of Jade. "Levi, you know how I feel about this."

"Yes, but I was hoping you'd change your mind."

Jade looks between Levi and me, trying to figure out what is going on.

I take a long gulp of my drink, disappointed that I've finished the damn thing. "I appreciate the offer, but I don't think it's a good idea for me to come to the game. As I mentioned before, sports aren't my thing, and my life is complicated enough right now without getting caught up in"—I gesture vaguely—"all of this."

Before Levi can respond, a boisterous voice suddenly interrupts us.

"Hey, guys!"

We all turn to see Wilder barreling toward us, a huge grin on his face. He makes a beeline for Jade, throwing an arm around her shoulders.

"Jade! I've been looking everywhere for you."

Jade laughs, probably because she's used to Wilder's over-the-top personality due to their friendship. "Wilder, hey! Didn't realize this was your type of bar."

He grins. "Had to make an appearance here. Couldn't miss out on Sapphire's famous Thursday specials."

His eyes drift over to Levi and me. "Oh hey, Hailey. Fancy seeing you here." He tosses a wink my way.

I roll my eyes because I swear Wilder and Jade are working together to make something happen between Levi and me. Speaking of, Levi stands up a little straighter, his jaw tightening. I can't deny that I find his reaction interesting and a turn on.

Maybe I have had too much to drink. Nah, that's not possible because I've only had one.

"So!" Jade says brightly, breaking the silence. "Who's up for another round? These drinks won't order themselves."

"I'll come with," Wilder says. "Anyone else want anything?"

If Wilder hadn't offered to go, I would have in order to get some space away from Levi. Instead, we both decline. I need a minute to process everything and with him standing here, I know I'm not going to get it. As they head to the bar, Levi turns to me.

"Sorry about that. I hope I didn't make you uncomfortable with the invitation."

"It's fine. Don't worry about it."

I shift my weight from one foot to the other, trying to find something to say or an excuse to get the hell out of here.

Levi's gaze lingers on me as he reaches out toward me, only hesitating for a second before gently tucking a loose strand of hair behind my ear. His touch sends a shiver down my spine. "Hailey," he begins, his voice low and serious. "Did you wear your hair down for me?"

"Excuse me?" His question completely takes me by surprise. There is no way I heard him right.

"First of all, the last thing I would do is change my appearance for anyone, let alone you. Second of all, are you trying to piss me off? Do you get off on me being mean to you?"

He takes a step toward me and leans into whisper, "That's one of many things about you that gets me off, Rook."

I can't believe he said that. "You've got some fucking nerve," I say back at him. "Move out of my way."

Without waiting for a response or for him to move because I don't trust what he might say to that, I brush past him and head down a hallway straight for the bathroom, my heart beating a mile a minute and cheeks on fire.

When I lock myself in a bathroom stall, I lean my head against the cool wall, trying to breathe. What the hell had just happened?

I'm irritated at Levi for throwing me off balance like that but also irritated with myself for reacting so strongly. Not only did he piss me off, but he also made me want to tear his clothes off, all in one short statement. I let him get under my skin and then I ran to the bathroom of all places.

Smooth, Hailey. Really smooth.

Once I calm myself down, I unlock the bathroom stall and wash my hands. The desire to throw water on my face to cool my heated skin is there, but I'd mess up my makeup if I did so. Instead, I'm left hoping the water on my hands will help settle the chaos in my stomach. It doesn't.

With my hands dried off, I reapply my lipstick and take a look at myself in the mirror. I still look the same, although my cheeks are looking slightly more flushed. After spending a few more seconds attempting to regain my composure, I leave the bathroom.

I step out into the dark-blue-tinted hallway feeling calm, but that is short-lived. I freeze in place when I see Levi standing just a few feet away with his back leaning against the wall. He's watching me like a hawk. Before I can move away, he closes the gap between us and firmly places one hand on my arm, pushing me against the wall. Before I can blink, his other arm is situated above my head, caging me in with his body.

"What do you want?" I ask, not sure if I really want to know the answer.

"I can answer that question in many different ways."

"Why are you standing so fucking close to me?"

"Because I need to fucking kiss you," he says in a way that I can't quite describe. His blue eyes are locked onto mine, as if he's trying to decipher every thought running through my mind. "Tell me that I can kiss you."

I try to come up with a snarky remark to hide my nerves, to hide the way I'm loving being in his arms. But I'm at a loss for words for the first time in what feels like forever. I allow my body to take over instead of my mind and give him a single nod. I'd be lying to myself if I denied I wanted the opportunity presented in front of me. I nod my head quickly and before I can utter a word, his lips are on mine.

As his lips press against mine, all coherent thoughts vanish from my brain. Hell, I swear I forget my own name temporarily. I gasp at the feel of his warm lips, and for a moment, I can't breathe. It's like he's stealing my air, but there's nothing I want more than this. His hand moves from my arm and slides to the back of my head, cradling it gently as he deepens the kiss.

Our connection goes from gently exploring this new feeling to being hungry for one another in a split second.

My hands land on his chest and grip the fabric laying across it. His shirt is nothing but a thin layer standing between us that I'm tempted to rip apart so that my fingertips can touch him, skin to skin.

It's then that I become more aware of where his other hand has gone. It dances along my collarbone before drifting lower to my waist where he pulls our bodies closer to each other. His touch is featherlight, yet it ignites a fire within me I can't ignore.

I melt into him as he removes the space between us. His hand inches upward, and at this point, I don't care if he's bringing the dress with him, exposing my panties along the way. When his hand reaches its final destination, my breast, my back arches into his touch, wishing that this would never end.

It feels so natural being with him like this, yet wrong at the same time. When his thumb runs across my nipple through the fabric of the dress, it's as if I'm being thrown into a pool filled with ice water. This little bubble that we are in bursts, and in my mind, everything crashes down around me. I'm slightly disoriented when we break apart. "No," I shake my head. "This—" I hesitate, my voice thick with emotion. "This can't happen."

Anyone could have walked up and seen what we were doing. They still can for that matter. The fight or flight instinct within me ramps up again, and I need to get out of here.

Although it's somewhat dark in this hallway, I can see

my smeared lipstick all over his face. I can only guess what the state of my face is, but none of it matters.

I wipe at my mouth, my hands shaking, and push past him as I stumble toward the main area of the bar. I don't look back because I don't want to know if Levi is following me.

When I finally reach Jade and Wilder, who are staring at me as if I've grown another head, Jade takes one look at my face and her eyes widen. "Whoa, what happened to you?"

"Nothing. I need to go," I manage to say.

"Hailey? Are you okay?"

"I'm fine," I say, allowing the lie to fall from my lips. "I just want to go home."

Jade looks between me and Wilder before responding. "Okay let's head back home," she insists quickly.

I look over at Wilder momentarily and see Levi over his shoulder, walking toward us, but Wilder's next words force me to focus on him again. "I'll pay for your drinks. Just go."

Without another word, Jade and I leave together. From where we were standing to the front door, I can feel Levi's gaze burning a hole into my back.

But I never look back.

21

LEVI

The harsh beeping of my phone's alarm forces me awake. I groan and fumble to hit the stop button, wishing I had a chance to hit the snooze button instead to get a few more minutes of sleep. Not getting much rest the evening before will do that to you. The chances of me feeling like a zombie today are high.

Pushing the covers off my body, I sit up and run a hand through my hair. The first thing I think of is Hailey and how I royally fucked up last night. How could I have been so stupid? I let my desire to have her in any way I could, get the best of me, and I acted without thinking properly.

Seeing her in that red dress had done something to my brain. More accurately, it had done something to my dick.

I'd wanted to rip that dress off her but knew better than to do it in public.

However, I didn't know enough to keep myself from making out with her in the back hallway of Sapphire Tavern. It was as exhilarating as being out on the ice, and for a brief moment, I pushed all thoughts of potential consequences to the side.

Which is something I shouldn't have done.

I'd wanted to go after her, to talk about what I did and apologize, but Wilder thought it was best that I leave everything alone for the time being.

As much as it hurt, I knew he was right. So I followed his lead, and soon after Jade and Hailey left the bar, I did too.

Regret is all I feel as I realize I ruined her night. From what I know about her, it's rare for her to venture out and do that type of thing. Her life consists of the work she needs to do for her college courses, her job, and chess club.

Fuck.

I hadn't even begun to think about whether she'll want to continue the chess lessons we've been doing together. They are the most fun I've had in a long time and now they might be ruined by my impulsive actions.

But for now, I have to put that on the backburner. My focus is on the day ahead and repairing what little relationship Hailey and I had started to build.

Dragging myself out of bed, I shake off the nagging

thoughts of Hailey, trying to focus on what I need to complete today. My feet hit the rug my mother insisted I needed in my bedroom, and I stand up, stretching my arms high above my head.

I walk to the bathroom, splashing cold water on my face to help myself wake up more before throwing on the clothes I need to wear to practice and grabbing a quick breakfast. This is part of my routine since I started at Crestwood and usually it's an opportunity for me to get into the zone and focus on what I need to do on the ice.

However, the only thing I can think of is Hailey.

That continues as I finish eating, leave my apartment, and head down to the rink. The urge to text her is there, but I need to take my time with this and not jump into it, which is how I got into this situation to begin with.

Once I'm at the rink, I put on my gear and lace up my skates, then step out onto the freshly smoothed ice. I need to keep my mind on this and not on Hailey.

As practice kicks off, Coach Johnson puts us through drills that come one after another. I try to let muscle memory take over, but my focus isn't there and I know it.

A puck slips past me that shouldn't have. A rookie could have easily made the play I just missed.

"Jamison! Eyes on the puck!" Coach Johnson yells, and I feel the sting from his words.

I glance at Asher who shoots me a look across the ice. He waits for us to talk about it until Coach calls for a break. "Dude, what's going on with you today?"

"Wish I knew," I reply with a shrug, trying to deflect his perceptiveness. "Not feeling it, I guess."

Asher gives me a look that says he doesn't believe my shit. "Does it have anything to do with Hailey? Wilder mentioned what happened last night."

It's not shocking that word has gotten to him even though he wasn't there. Wilder has no issue talking, and I didn't ask him not to say anything. I'm also not surprised that Asher is able to put two and two together.

"Yeah, it's Hailey," I confess, taking a swig from my water bottle. "I screwed up last night and I can't think of anything but that. It's messing with me."

"You're not going to be able to stop thinking about the situation or her until you solve it."

He taps his stick against the rubber matting under our feet as I think about what he said.

"I know that too," I finally say.

"You've said before that you need to 'Leave it all on the ice.' Maybe it's time you do that off the ice too. Man, go talk to her after practice. Clear the air."

Wilder strolls up to us, but his trademark smile isn't on his face. "So, are we talking about Hailey?"

"Yeah. Asher's giving me his sage advice." It comes out more sarcastic than I intend, but Asher doesn't take offense. Maybe Hailey is rubbing off on me, and I wish that she was rubbing *on* me.

"Well, let's hear it then," Wilder says as he looks at Asher.

Asher rolls his eyes but repeats himself for Wilder's benefit. "I told Levi here that he needs to go talk to Hailey and take care of this."

"Oh, he's going to need a lot more than talking to deal with Hailey," Wilder adds.

His tone sets me on edge. "Why? Did you hear anything from Jade?"

Wilder shakes his head. "Jade and I are friends, but I know she's not going to betray Hailey by telling me things about her when it comes to this. It's something I respect about her and know she would do the same for me. This is just based on what I saw last night."

He knew exactly what happened the moment he saw me with her lipstick smeared across my face and how she ran out of the bar like a bat out of hell.

The truth in his words hits me square in the chest. I've been trying to figure Hailey out since the day we met. Every time I think I've made progress, she throws up another wall. It's frustrating as hell, but I'm determined to break every single one. There's something there and I need to be patient.

Coach Johnson blows his whistle, announcing it's time for practice to continue.

"Thanks, guys," I say.

"If Jade says anything, I'll let you know. But chances of that are slim," Wilder chimes in before heading back toward the ice.

I put my water bottle down and both Asher and I join

Wilder. I channel all of my restless energy into practice, spending less time thinking about Hailey now that I was able to talk it out with someone. There is still a lot I need to figure out, but the short conversation during our break helped calm the racing thoughts in my head so I can focus on getting the job done at practice.

As the coach blows his whistle for the final time, I feel relieved. Practice is over and I can finally stop pretending like everything is okay. My performance on the ice today was far from my best, but at least I managed to make it through without any major mishaps.

I offer Coach a nod as I come off the ice, and his return grunt is as good as I'm going to get today. It's obvious to everyone how off my game I was today, but no one else mentions it.

Without a word to anyone in the locker room, I hit the showers and change into my street clothes, and for the first time in a few days, my thoughts drift to my father. It's been a few days since his last email landed in my inbox, a laundry list of expectations and thinly veiled disappointment in anything less than perfection.

The weight of my father's aspirations sits heavy on my shoulders, a burden I've carried since we lost Caleb. Hockey isn't just a game. It's a living memorial to my brother who is supposed to be in my place right now.

How have things gotten this fucked up? Or were they always this way?

As I stuff my gear into my duffel, I find myself thinking

how it would be nice to have Caleb to talk with about what's going on with Hailey. I know he would have found the right words that I could use to smooth over last night's mess in a heartbeat. Then my thoughts drift to how different my life would have been in general.

But he's not here and nothing I can do will change that. I zip up my hoodie and sling my bag over my shoulder, shoving the thoughts I'm having to the back of my mind.

As I'm walking out of the locker room, Asher strolls over to me. I didn't know he was still here. "You good?"

I manage a half-smile. "Yeah, I'm going to figure out a way to talk to Hailey. I think it will help a bunch of things fall into place."

"Good plan."

We walk together to my car, and I ask Asher, "Did you drive, or do you want me to take you back to your place?"

"I didn't drive so I'd love a ride back."

"Not an issue." I unlock the car doors and once our hockey gear is in the trunk, we slide into our respective seats.

Before I can start the car, Asher speaks again. "Why don't you reach out to Hailey before we take off?"

That's a great point. It would be easy to do it right now. It gives me the opportunity to lift some of the weight I've been feeling off my shoulders. Plus, at least right now I can somewhat think straight. But I don't want to talk to Hailey about this over the phone or via text.

I need to see her face, read her expressions. So many things can get lost in translation over text or the phone. I pull out my phone, hovering over her name. It's now or never. My thumb hovers over the call button, but then I hesitate. Maybe texting instead to ask if I can see her would be easier for both of us.

I glance at Asher for a second and then say, "Fine, I'll send her a text right now."

> Me: Hey, Hailey. I want to apologize in person for last night. Can we meet up when you're free?

There. It isn't the most eloquent message of all time, but I hope it will do the trick. Now all I have to do is wait to see what her response will be.

22

HAILEY

Days later, I find myself back in Emily's office, staring at her and wondering what the hell my life has become. I need someone to talk to and she is the person that makes the most sense. Talking to Jade would have also been helpful, but that would mean admitting everything that happened at Sapphire Tavern to her. Then again, I suspect she had a good idea about what occurred. While I plan on eventually telling her, I need to get my thoughts straight first. Discussing this with my father is the last thing I want to do at this point, given the new stage he is moving toward in his life. Not to mention, hello awkwardness.

Regardless, my mind is a complete mess and feels as if it's spiraling out of control because I can't make sense of it. But I'm not sure where to begin.

Thankfully, she speaks first. "Welcome back, Hailey. How is everything going?"

"It's going is about all I can say. They're a lot of moving pieces and I'm not sure which piece to focus on first."

"Hmmm... okay. What's the biggest moving piece? Or the thing that is bothering you the most right now? Maybe we can start with that first, if you want?"

I nod my head slowly, trying to gather the courage to admit what has been bothering me the most. "It's Levi. We had an... incident at the bar this weekend, and I'm trying to process how I feel about it."

"What happened?"

I can feel the heat rising to my cheeks as I share the details of my encounter with Levi. Embarrassment grows within me as I recount the events that led to Levi's impulsive kiss and my kissing him back. It's awkward to be admitting this, but I need to tell her in order for her to help me process my feelings.

"And after he kissed you, you left?" Emily prompts, urging me to finish the whole story.

"Yes. Like my ass was on fire." I blow out a huge breath of air. "I needed space from... from whatever this thing between us is turning into."

Emily doesn't flinch at my colorful metaphor. "Space can be healthy, but talking it out with him, since he didn't harm you in any way, might have also been a good idea, don't you think?"

"I know, and part of it was because I was drinking,

although not that much," I admit, tapping my foot to an imaginary beat. "In the past, when my fight or flight response kicks in, I've always done the flight thing, which is what happened that night and probably would have happened quicker if my instincts hadn't short-circuited. I'm not used to someone... someone like him being interested in me."

Emily taps her pen on her chin for a couple of seconds before she says, "Is it Levi himself that's causing these feelings, or could it be what he represents? The possibility of being hurt again?"

I hadn't thought of it that way, but as soon as she says it, something clicks inside me. Levi isn't just any guy. Whatever is happening between us is a test of whether I can take a risk on someone and not be fearful that they'll abandon me like my mother did.

"It's both," I reply after a long pause. "Not to mention, he has some of his own things he needs to work through. Plus, I'm not a huge fan of the amount of attention that he gets for being a star hockey player on campus. Hell, maybe I'm jumping the gun on all of this and I'm overthinking like usual."

Emily nods thoughtfully. "You're right; entering a relationship means intertwining your life with someone else's struggles and dreams. But remember, Hailey, you bring your own strengths into this equation. Your empathy and understanding could be exactly what someone like Levi needs."

"I don't know. There's still the whole limelight issue and my panicking when I ran away from him a few nights ago. He sent me a text message, apologizing to me and asking to meet up so we can talk about it. I haven't responded to him yet."

"And you want to talk to him, right?"

I nod, but for some reason can't say the words out loud.

Emily offers a gentle smile, as if she's read my silence loud and clear. "I'm glad he reached out because there's a conversation that needs to happen between you two. Communication is key in any relationship, friendship or otherwise."

I let out a long sigh, dragging my hands down my face. It takes everything not to pull on my bun. "You're right. I know I need to talk to him. I'm just scared."

"What scares you the most about having an honest conversation with Levi?"

I pause, chewing my bottom lip as I consider her question. "Outside of everything that would come with being involved with him, I guess, on the flip side... I'm scared he'll reject me. Tell me he made a mistake or got caught up in the moment. Or that he'll end up confirming I'm too closed off and difficult for someone like him to date."

"Those are understandable concerns," Emily says gently. "But you won't know how Levi truly feels unless you communicate openly with him. Give him a chance to share his perspective too. He might surprise you."

I nod slowly, knowing she's right but still feeling the vice of anxiety around my chest.

"Hailey, relationships require courage and vulnerability from both people involved," she continues. "I know your mother's abandonment left deep scars, but don't let that close you off to new possibilities. You have so much love and strength within you."

I feel my eyes well up with tears at her words. She's hit upon the root of my deepest fears. I truly feel as if I'm unlovable, which is what I've long believed my mother thought. That's the only reason why she would have left me, isn't it?

"Hey, it's okay," Emily says softly, passing me a tissue from her desk. "I know this is difficult, Hailey. You're trying to heal old wounds and that can be a painful process, but you have already shown so much courage just by coming and talking to me."

I swallow hard and dab at my eyes with the tissue. Emily is right. I have come a long way since my mother left all those years ago. Therapy has helped me continue to process my pain and start building back my sense of self-worth. Levi stirs up intense emotions in me, but it doesn't mean I should run away from it.

"Maybe I'm ready to try having an honest conversation with Levi," I say quietly. "I want to figure out what this is, even if the thought terrifies me."

She smiles. "That's wonderful, Hailey."

Emily and I talk through how I will approach the

conversation with Levi. I want to be open about my fears and I also want to listen to his thoughts about all of this.

By the end of the session, I feel a new sense of hope about my situation. Emily has helped me get clarity on my feelings and given me the confidence to have this discussion with him. As I leave her office and walk back to my apartment after the appointment, I feel lighter, but that could be due to the crying session I had a few minutes prior.

When I get home, Jade is sitting on the couch working on a homework assignment. She looks up when I come in.

"Hey! How was therapy?" she asks.

I sigh and plop down on the couch next to her. "It was good. Rough but good."

Jade closes her laptop and turns to face me. "Do you want to talk about anything?"

Even though I just saw Emily, I want to let Jade in on a part of it too. She's my best friend and knows about my struggles with dealing with my mom even though she wasn't in my life when it happened.

"I'm so afraid of getting hurt again, you know?" I confess. "My mom really did a number on me, and I've mostly avoided entanglements with other people while being here, but this is a different ball game. Or should I say hockey game?"

My little joke makes Jade chuckle as she grabs my hand and squeezes it supportively. "I get that, I really do. But not every person is going to hurt you like she did.

Sometimes you need to take a chance, and it's obvious that Levi has been trying to get your attention if it's something you're truly interested in."

"You think so?"

Jade nods. "I really do. I've seen the way Levi looks at you when we've all been together. That guy is smitten."

"Who says smitten anymore?"

"What's wrong with that? It's just another way to say he has feelings for you, Hailey. Do you want me to say he wants a situationship with you? I'm willing to bet he wants at least that and more. It's been a while since you've gotten laid so it wouldn't be the worst thing..." Her voice trails off as she shrugs.

That makes me laugh. "Fine. I get your point. I should probably text him back."

"I agree. Do it and get it over with."

I take a deep breath and pull out my phone. I stare at the screen for a moment before I finally find Levi's name and open up our message thread.

> Me: Hey, sorry for not getting back to you sooner. I've been doing a lot of thinking and I'd really like the chance to talk in person too. Why don't we keep our usual chess lesson time and talk then?

I stare at the message for a long moment, my finger lingering over the send button. The doubt is still there, but I know this is a step I need to take. Before I can overthink it further, I hit send, turn my phone's sound up, and set the device down.

"There. It's done," I say, looking up at Jade.

She grins and pulls me into a hug. "That's my girl!"

I can't help but smile too as I return the embrace. Despite my nerves, it feels good to put myself out there once more, just in a different way.

I get up from the couch, suddenly feeling restless after sending that text to Levi. My phone sits face down on the coffee table, and I resist the urge to pick it up and check for a response.

Because there shouldn't be one since my ringer is on and it hasn't rung.

"I'm going to make something to eat. Want anything?" I ask Jade. This is a distraction I desperately need, and I know doing homework right now wouldn't provide it.

"Ooh yes, I'll take whatever you're having," she says.

I head to the kitchen and start rummaging through the fridge and cabinets, pulling out ingredients almost at random. My mind is only half focused on the task at hand. I settle on making grilled cheese sandwiches and tomato soup because it's easy and will keep me busy for the time being.

As the scent of toasting bread and simmering soup fills the air, Jade starts a conversation about her latest art project. We engage in small talk as I finish cooking and serve our meal. We're halfway through eating when my phone's text ringtone plays. Jade and I stare at my phone before looking back at each other.

"Are you going to read it?" Jade asks almost frantically.

"Shit, I guess." My voice trails off as I stand from the kitchen counter where we are eating. There's a chance it could be someone else, like my father, texting me. But I doubt it if I'm being honest. I grab my phone from the coffee table, flip it over and read the text.

> Levi: Great, I'm glad it works for you. I'll see you at our usual time for chess. Looking forward to it.

"Well, he's cool with meeting at the same time we usually have our chess lessons. Now I have to mentally prepare for this conversation."

Jade gives me an encouraging smile. "You've got this."

I have to have this because there's no going back now.

23

HAILEY

The next day, I decide to leave my apartment early in order to get to Brewed Beginnings before Levi, giving me time to calm myself down before our conversation. It is a ridiculous thought because the closer I get to the coffee shop, the more nervous I become. The nausea I'm feeling stays at the same level until I hear the chime from the bell above the door of the coffee shop.

But as fate would have it, I manage to get there after Levi anyway. He is already seated at a small table tucked into the corner, looking as handsome as ever. My heart slams in my chest as I approach him because I have no idea how this conversation is going to go.

As if he senses I'm here, Levi's eyes lift to meet mine and he gives me a faint smile. I can't help but notice he's tapping his fingers on the table. It makes me think that he is just as nervous as I am. Without saying anything, I sit down across from him, and we fall into an awkward silence.

I can feel his gaze on me as if he's trying to figure out how to proceed without making things more uncomfortable. Finally, he breaks the silence.

"Hey," he says.

"Hi," I reply, my voice barely audible, especially with all of the noises occurring around us.

We watch each other, I assume we are both trying to read the other person and figure out how not to make this even more uncomfortable.

"Did you want something to drink or eat? I can go grab it for you."

I shake my head quickly. "Thanks, but I'm okay."

Levi clears his throat and I know it's time to rip the Band-Aid off. "Thanks for agreeing to meet me here. After what happened at Sapphire Tavern... I wanted a chance to talk."

"Same. I'll admit, the other night left me feeling..." I trail off, uncertain how to articulate myself.

"Overwhelmed? Uncomfortable?" Levi adds gently.

"Both of those, yes," I agree.

Levi lets out a heavy sigh, running a hand through his hair. "Hailey, I'm really sorry about all of that, but it would be a lie if I said I don't know what came over me."

My eyes dart to the left before focusing back on him. "So you know what came over you?"

"I got caught up in the moment. I'd had a couple of shots before leaving Wilder's place, and then when I walked into the bar and saw you there with Jade and your coworker, I was jealous."

"But there was nothing to be jealous about. Ben is a friend and you and I aren't together."

Levi rubs both hands over his face. "You're right. I know there's nothing official between us and I had no reason to be jealous. But at that moment, seeing you with another guy, I felt... possessive, I guess. I'm not proud of it."

He meets my gaze once again and says, "The truth is, I really like you, Hailey. When we first met, I liked that you gave me shit, to put it mildly, and I thought you were intriguing. As we've spent more time together, I've realized how thoughtful, witty, and caring you are when you start to open up. You challenge me in ways no one else does."

I'm stunned by Levi's honest confession. I hadn't realized he felt that strongly. I take a moment to gather my thoughts before responding.

"Thank you for saying that," I say. "The truth is, I like you too. More than I expected. But this whole situation makes me nervous."

"I get it. The attention that is on me due to hockey can be a lot."

"Part of it is that. I'm a pretty private person and you're basically a celebrity around here. I don't want to end up being gossiped about around school. Heck, us meeting for chess lessons is probably enough to cause people to talk."

"I would never want that either," Levi says earnestly. "Your comfort is important to me. If this, well, whatever this is, is going to work, we need to be on the same page."

"Well, if we want to lay everything out there, there are some other issues that are relevant to this that I think we should talk about."

"Tell me."

I let out a deep sigh. "My mom walked out on me and my dad when I was nine." I wait as the surprise registers on his face. "When she left, it really messed me up, and it still affects me now. I've had a hard time trusting people since."

Levi nods slowly. "That makes sense. I'm sorry she did what she did and caused you trauma that you're still trying to heal from."

Something about the way he says that sets me on edge. "I didn't tell you that so you could pity me."

Levi lets out a sarcastic laugh. "That's the last thing I'm feeling. I think you're stronger than even you know."

And just like that, my irritation fades because I'm touched by Levi's words. For so long, I've felt ashamed of the hurt my mother caused, like it was my fault she left. Hearing Levi acknowledge the wrongness of her actions and recognize my strength makes me feel good.

"I appreciate you saying that. I'm still figuring things out, but the acknowledgment helps." I suck in a deep breath. "That night at Sapphire Tavern made me realize that there is something between us, but we need to take things slowly."

Levi nods understandingly. "Of course. We can move as slow as you want to. I don't want you to feel any pressure. Unlike the kiss I laid on you at the bar."

"I enjoyed the kiss. Probably way more than I should have." I give him a small smile before I continue. "But I don't really want to label this right now. Let's continue getting to know each other and see where it goes."

"I'm good with that," Levi agrees. "Do you still want to do a chess lesson today?"

I think about it for a moment before nodding my head. "Why don't we since we're both here anyway? I'll go grab a set."

Levi's face lights up as I stand up, but he does the same. I raise an eyebrow at him, wondering what he is doing. "I'm going to grab a drink. Do you want something?"

If I'm being honest with myself, I'm happy he asked. I couldn't imagine eating or drinking anything when I first walked in here, but now I could use something. "A chai latte would be great."

"Coming up."

Levi and I go our separate ways and I beat him back to our table. I take my time setting up the chessboard, and by the time Levi comes back, he has two drinks and a small paper bag.

"What did you get to eat?" I ask him, trying to keep things casual.

"Two brownies for us to split."

My eyes widen. "How did you know I like brownies?"

"I saw you eating one when we had our first lesson. Thought we could use a sweet treat after what we talked about."

I like the way he thinks. I smile at Levi's thoughtfulness as I take a sip of the chai latte he brought me. The warmth and sweetness hits the right spot, and I'm the happiest I've been in days.

We settle in across from each other at the small table, the chessboard between us. For a moment, neither of us makes a move, both seemingly lost in our own thoughts.

"I'm glad we talked," Levi says, breaking the silence once more. "I know it wasn't easy."

I nod. "It was needed though. I feel better having been open about how I'm feeling."

"Me too," he agrees. He studies the chess pieces before he speaks again. "I meant what I said about taking things slowly. I care about you, Hailey, and I don't want to mess this up."

"Alright, let's focus on chess now," I say, redirecting our conversation to the familiar territory of strategy and competition.

I take a deep breath and make the first move, moving my queen's pawn forward two spaces. Levi responds by also shifting his queen's pawn, mirroring my action. As the game progresses, I walk him through various strategies, emphasizing the importance of developing pieces in the early game. He listens attentively, nodding as I explain each concept.

Despite being new to the game, he quickly demonstrates a knack for anticipating my moves. When I capture one of his pawns with my knight, he responds by putting my king in check with his queen. I'm impressed by how quickly he's picking up on things.

"You're a fast learner," I remark as I block his check.

"I have a good teacher," he replies without a second thought.

I bite my lip and shake my head, choosing to focus on our game. I counterattack, putting his king in checkmate. "Checkmate in fifteen moves. Not bad at all," I say.

Levi grins. "Ready for another round so I can try to beat my new record?"

"If that's what you want to do," I say before sticking a piece of brownie in my mouth.

He laughs, a genuine and carefree sound. "If there's one thing you should know about me, I'm not one to give up easily."

I absolutely believe that. With him not being turned off by my snarkiness or my pushing him away, he must have the patience of a saint.

Levi moves first this time, pushing his king's pawn into the center of the board. We fall into a rhythm that feels natural and any nerves I had when I first arrived are long gone.

As we play, I realize that despite my reservations about getting involved with someone like Levi because of his popularity, I'm beginning to appreciate the person he is beyond the image. His humor when he feigns shock at my aggressive moves, his gentle way of teasing when I take too long to decide on a move, all of it is calming to me. It's beginning to feel more and more normal.

"You know," Levi says after I've taken one of his knights, "I was reading up on chess after our last lesson. Did you know they call it the game of kings?"

I snort lightly. "Yeah, because historically, it was played by nobility or because of the king chess piece. What are you trying to say? That you're king material?"

"Well," he draws out the word with a playful smirk. "Considering my last name is Jamison and James means supplanter, which could loosely be interpreted as one who takes over, a king isn't too far-fetched."

I laugh harder than I probably should have at his logic. I don't remember the last time I laughed this hard, and the grin on Levi's face only grows. "I'll remember not to underestimate King Levi when it comes to chess then."

"Don't underestimate me when it comes to anything. I know what I want, and I go after what I want full stop."

His words send a shiver down my spine, and I can't help but think about what it might be like when we finally give in to the tension that is coursing between the two of us.

The game continues and this time it stretches longer as Levi becomes more cautious with his moves. When we finally conclude our second game, he manages to extend his record to twenty-five moves. But what's interesting to me is that after our conversation and subsequent chess lesson, the energy around us is more friendly and, at least in my opinion, our connection has grown stronger.

"It's getting late," Levi comments as we pack up the chess set. "Thanks for sticking around for a couple of games."

"It was fun," I admit truthfully. Part of me didn't want to leave, and that's when another thought came to my mind. "When are you going to be able to help me with the chess event at Oak Terrace?"

Levi pauses his movements for a moment as he processes the question. "Yeah, we need to do that. How about we meet up at either your place or mine in the next couple of weeks?"

I pull out my phone and start looking through my calendar. "When do you have an evening free? I'm working several early shifts this week. Why don't we meet at your place?" The last thing I need is for Jade to see Levi walking around our apartment.

"What about two Thursdays from now?"

"I can come over after chess club."

"That would be perfect. Why don't I also fix dinner for us if you think you'll be hungry."

I tilt my head and stare directly into his eyes. "This is beginning to sound more like a date."

"And what if it is? Do you have a problem with that?"

I smile for what feels like the millionth time since I came here. "Not a one."

24

HAILEY

I need to stop staring at my phone. It's doing nothing but getting me into trouble. I can't take my eyes off it for longer than a few minutes because of Levi. We've been texting back and forth since we talked about what happened at Sapphire Tavern a couple of weeks ago, and tonight is the night I'm going over to his place to talk about what I envision for the event at Oak Terrace.

Well, first I have to make it through chess club. I press one of the buttons on the side of my phone and see another text from him.

> Levi: Wait until you see what I've got planned for tonight.

> Me: Oh? Should I be worried or excited?

> Levi: Definitely excited. I might have a surprise or two up my sleeve.

Me: As long as it doesn't involve spiders or doing anything too crazy, I'm all in. Any hints?

Levi: Not a chance. Surprises are no fun if you know what they are.

Me: Fair enough. I'll just have to prepare myself for anything then.

Levi: Exactly. Just make sure you bring your appetite.

Me: This is definitely sounding like a date. Are you ordering food?

Levi: Something like that. You'll see soon enough. Just know I'm looking forward to tonight.

Me: Me too, Levi. Can't wait to find out what you're up to.

Levi: See you soon?

Me: See you soon.

I close out the application and notice that time is up for chess club. I quickly give off some last-minute tips and help everyone pack up the chessboards and pieces before I make my move to head out. The chime of the bell on top of Brewed Beginnings front door draws my attention as I open it before I look back at the people I am leaving behind.

"I'll see everyone next week. Hope you have a good

rest of your evening," I say with a small wave as I walk out of the coffee shop for the second time today.

I notice Jeff's skeptical look as I turn away and I bet he's wondering why I'm in such a good mood. What he doesn't know is I've been ready to walk out of here since the moment I arrived. Time has been ticking by at the pace of a snail, and I've never been happier to leave chess club since I joined.

Stepping out into the crisp air of the evening, I pull my coat tighter against my body to help me stay warm. I curse myself for not deciding to drive over to Levi's as I watch my breath materialize in front of me. My reasoning is that Levi's apartment is so close to Brewed Beginnings that walking there now almost feels like a death sentence. I know once we are done with whatever Levi has planned, I'm going to call an Uber to come pick me up because there is no way I'm walking home in this chill.

As I make my way to his apartment, my stomach flip-flops a little from excitement. I have no idea what is going to happen outside of Levi brushing me off slightly when I mentioned ordering take out.

My hand trembles slightly as I reach out to open the main door of the building that Levi gave me the address to. Already the outside of this place is much nicer than mine, but it's also not surprising. He doesn't live on Crestwood's campus while I do, and that's not to say that Crestwood's grounds aren't kept nice and well maintained.

I feel a flutter of nerves as I walk into the building and

approach the front desk. My apartment on campus is nice, but this place is out of my league. The lobby is large and open with modern décor and bright lighting. Clearing my throat, the woman sitting at the front desk looks up at me with a warm smile.

"Hi, I'm here to see Levi Jamison. My name is Hailey Reed." My voice gives away that I'm nervous as hell.

The attendant offers a polite nod before picking up the phone and clicking a few buttons. "Mr. Jamison, your guest, Ms. Reed, is here," she announces.

After a brief pause, the attendant nods again before saying goodbye and hanging up the phone. She stands up and gestures toward the elevator and says, "If you'll follow me, please."

As we walk, I'm trying to calm my nerves. They have nothing to do with where I currently am but everything to do with the man I'm about to see.

The elevator ride up to his floor is smooth and quick. The attendant leads me down a hallway where we stop at number 413. As she turns to leave, she offers me a reassuring smile. "Have a nice evening, Ms. Reed." And just like that, she's gone, leaving me alone in the quiet hallway.

Before I can knock on the door, it swings open. I'm greeted by Levi who is standing there in a white t-shirt, dark jeans, and bare feet.

"Welcome to Chez Jamison," he says as he steps aside to let me in.

The apartment is warm, and scents of garlic and something else greet my nose as soon as I walk over the threshold. He's set his dining room table for two and I stare at the candles flickering softly, creating a romantic mood. I'm thoroughly impressed. There's no other word for it.

"I hope you're hungry," he says as he closes the door behind me and leads me further into his apartment.

"Starving," I admit. "I forgot to eat lunch today and only had a protein bar while I was at the library studying."

I shrug off my coat and drape it over the back of a chair and turn to Levi. "What are you making?" I ask.

"Butternut squash risotto."

I do a double take. I don't know what I was expecting him to say, but that wasn't it. "I've never had that before but I'm excited to try it."

"Great. It's done. I'm keeping it warm."

I follow Levi into the kitchen and ask, "Where did you learn how to cook?"

"Well, my roommate freshman year taught me a thing or two before he ended up transferring out of here to go to culinary school," he says as he takes the lid off the pot.

For a moment I watch as he stirs the risotto, and the smell is amazing. I feel my stomach growl and am thankful that Levi doesn't show any indication that he hears anything. I lean against the counter as he takes out two bowls and plates up our dinner. This all feels very domestic, for lack of a better description, and I'm not running for the hills... at least not yet.

We leave the kitchen and walk into the dining area, and Levi pulls out a chair for me. I thank him as he takes his seat opposite mine. "So, this is pretty fancy for us chatting about a chess event," I start, picking up my fork and diving into the risotto.

Levi chuckles. "You mentioned this was starting to sound like a date, remember?"

"Right. How could I forget?" I take a bite of the risotto, and it's like an explosion of autumn on my taste buds. "This is incredible, Levi."

His smile widens as he watches me enjoying his cooking. "Thanks. Glad you like it," he replies before taking a bite himself.

As we eat, our conversation drifts from classes to the latest hockey game. Levi recounts a play-by-play of the winning goal, and while he has to take some time to explain some of the concepts to me, he looks to be enjoying it.

Levi grabs his napkin and wipes his mouth before he says, "Hey, there's something I need to tell you."

"I don't like the sound of this," I reply, wondering what this can be about.

"I knew how to play chess before I asked you about it."

I slam my hand down on the table, making it shake. The look in Levi's eye tells me he's worried I'm upset, but that isn't the case at all. "I knew it! You were picking up on concepts super-fast. Not that it isn't possible for someone to do that, but the chances of it happening are rare."

Levi laughs so hard that I think it's from relief that I'm not pissed at him. He reaches into his pocket and pulls out a tattered photograph, unfolding and placing it carefully on the table between us. It's a picture of two young boys, one unmistakably Levi, with his brown hair and bright blue eyes, and the other, slightly taller with a similar build. They're sitting at an old wooden chess table with a man standing near them.

"That's my brother, Caleb," he says softly, tapping the image of the other boy. "And our grandfather was there. Our grandfather was great at chess and taught us quite a bit before hockey took over our lives. Caleb and I used to play quite a bit and now it's something we won't ever be able to do again."

I draw in a sharp breath because his tone tells me he's been hurt. "What do you mean?"

"Caleb died a few years ago in a car accident." I set my fork down and reach over to grab his hand. "I'm sorry," I say. Although the words seem inadequate, I hope that they are helpful.

Levi shrugs, but I can tell it's an attempt to brush off the sympathy. "Thanks. His accident... It changed everything. He was supposed to be the hockey star, you know? Had all this talent on ice. At least, more than I ever had."

"But you're amazing out there," I say, even though I haven't been able to see it for myself. If he's the captain of the team, he must be talented and it's something he needs to hear.

He shakes his head almost dismissively. "I worked twice as hard after he died; not for me, but because his dream was left unfinished, and I needed to complete it. Dad always pushed him the most, but with him gone..." Levi trails off and there's a haunted look in his eyes that makes my chest tighten.

"It became all about you," I finish for him.

"Yeah." Levi exhales heavily and stares down at the crinkled photograph again. "I guess I didn't want to disappoint him any further."

"So, is playing hockey and now us playing chess together... Is that your way of staying connected to Caleb?"

He nods slowly but waits to respond. "Yeah, something like that. I knew hockey was, but I didn't consider starting up chess again might also be. It's a way to connect to both of you."

"I get it," I murmur after a moment. My mother may have left by choice, but abandonment and loss are connected in their own twisted way.

Levi looks up at me then. "You do?"

"Yeah. While I don't understand what you're going through exactly because I haven't lived through it, we've both struggled with huge losses from those that were close to us."

"I suppose we have," he says. "It's weird, isn't it? How life just... goes on, even when yours feels like it's stopped."

I can't agree more. "That's probably the truest thing you've said all night."

Levi pushes the photo aside. "So, your mom," he starts, but then stops as if he's thinking about how to word this. "You don't have to talk about it if you don't want to."

But I want to. Maybe it's the way he's opened up to me or how comfortable this makeshift date feels, but I find myself wanting to share more of me with him. "She left when I was still a kid," I begin. "Just packed up one day when I was at school and Dad was at work. Dad tried to explain it to me in a million different ways, but I still don't understand."

"Hailey," he whispers my name like it's a secret he's never told anyone before.

I move my hand that was holding his and grab my wineglass. I take a sip before I speak again. "I'm fine, really. I've had a long time to get used to it." But as I say it, there's a question forming silently in my mind: Am I really fine?

"We're quite the pair, aren't we?" he says with a light chuckle that doesn't quite hide his sadness.

"We are," I agree. I snort and shake my head. "Look at us, we're like two characters in some indie movie."

"Yeah, but make it a sports romance," he replies, matching my tone. "We have hockey, complex family drama, and a situationship of sorts that started out with you hating me to now just tolerating me."

"I can't stand you," I say jokingly. "I don't know if I should be flattered or worried that we're ticking all the boxes of a cliché though."

He leans back in his chair, folding his arms. "Oh really? So you do like me or something?"

"I thought we established this already. I wouldn't be here if I didn't. So what happens next in our cliché sports romance?"

Levi grins widely. "Well, if I had to guess... the star hockey player who's hiding his pain behind his talent does something unexpected."

"Oh?" I prompt him to continue.

"He takes a risk," Levi says softly.

"And what risk would that be?"

It takes what feels like forever for him to respond. "Asking if I can kiss you right now."

The words hang in the air between us, an unspoken challenge. I feel a familiar flutter in my stomach like the one I got just before he kissed me at Sapphire Tavern.

"Are you always this forward?" I ask.

"I told you I go after what I want, full stop. But only when it feels right, and with you, it does, Rook."

I push my chair back to stand up and walk over to him. He looks up at me before joining me and pulling me toward him as his hands rest on my waist.

"We don't have to—" he starts but stops when he sees me open my mouth.

"We do if you want to. Because I do."

He towers over me slightly but bends down to meet me at eye level. His gaze softens just before our lips meet, and once they do, all bets are off. Our kiss deepens as everything fades away.

Right now, this is exactly where I'm meant to be.

25

LEVI

"God, I've been wanting to do that all evening," I confess before my lips land back on hers. Hailey's hands end up in my hair, pulling me closer to her. I went into this wondering where the night would lead, hoping we might be on the same page about where we wanted tonight to go. If she wants things to continue in the direction they seem to be going in, then great. If she wants to stop, that's also fine.

I break our kiss and I never thought I would see the day when Hailey Reed began to whine, but I lose the fight with the chuckle that I've been struggling against. "I want to confirm that you're okay with this, Rook."

She bites her lip and nods shyly. "Yes, I'm okay with this."

I smile because that's all I need to hear. Her consent

and being comfortable is my priority, but there's something I need as well. "Take your hair down."

"Why don't you do it?" she asks with a smirk.

"You don't have to tell me twice." I reach up and gently
tug at the silk band holding her hair in its messy bun. As
it falls loose around her shoulders, I brush my fingers
through the soft waves before my eyes land back on hers.
"Much better," I whisper before leaning in again.

I start to nibble my way down her neck, and she
moans in response. I smell the same vanilla and citrusy
aroma that I did the first time when she was interacting
with me at Brewed Beginnings. It's intoxicating, and I
know it's something I could smell for the rest of my life
and never grow tired of.

I shift back slightly so I can help her remove the
purple chess club sweater she wore over here tonight.
Being able to see a touch of her stomach as she lifts up her
arms is making my cock harder than it has ever been
before.

What the hell kind of spell did she have over me?

I run my hands down her back and trace the delicate
fabric of her bra. My light touches cause goosebumps to
appear on her flesh, a hint that gives away what I'm doing
to her body.

"Fuck, Levi," she moans, pulling me closer to her.

"You don't know how much I love the sound of that."

"Why don't you show me?" Her question sounds innocent, but there's some bite in her words that comes across like she's daring me.

There is no way I can deny her request. The challenge in her voice only encourages me to prove how fucking hot this could be between us.

How good we could be together.

I need to explore this. I hold back a growl of approval as I unclasp her bra and find myself staring at her tits. "You're so fucking beautiful, Hailey," I whisper against her skin. Her nipples are hard nubs under my gaze, and I can't wait to get my mouth on them.

But first, there is somewhere else we need to go.

I bend down and toss Hailey over my shoulder. The second thing I didn't expect her to do tonight was laugh and squeal. Her laugh takes me by surprise. Not only is it rare to hear, but it sounds like a melody I could listen to on repeat for the rest of my life.

"Levi! Put me down."

"Your wish is my command." I place her down on the bed and I refuse to lie and say I don't enjoy watching her breasts jiggle as a result.

"There's something I need to tell you."

I pause at the foot of the bed and stare at Hailey before some words fall out of my mouth. "Are you a virgin?"

Hailey does a double take. "What? No. I was going to say I've never gotten off with a partner before."

My eyes narrow because I'm not sure I heard her properly. "None of the people you've slept with have given you an orgasm?"

All she does is nod.

"That's a fucking sin and it's never happening again."

I waste no time climbing onto the bed after her and my lips land on her jawline. I make sure to leave a trail of kisses along it. Even when she shivers beneath me as a result, I know that my job has only just begun.

"Do you want me to stop?" I ask, but it's nothing more than me mumbling against her skin as I kiss my way down her collarbone.

"No, this is what I want," she says, the words rushing out before a moan leaves her lips because I've reached her breasts. I lick around her nipple before sucking it into my mouth, feeling her gasp against my lips. Her taste is addictive, and it drives me crazy how responsive she is under my touch.

I make sure that I don't leave her other nipple without attention for too long and use my fingers to play with it, bringing it to a stiff peak rather quickly. I bite down gently on the nipple I've been sucking on. She arches her back as if to get closer to my mouth, which only encourages me to suck and nibble harder.

Watching the look of pure bliss on her face makes my dick grow harder, but I fight to do anything else but serve her. She deserves all of this and more, and I'm willing to give it all to her.

My hand wanders down her stomach and past her waist, until I reach her cotton panties.

"If I would have known we were going to do this, I might have found something sexier," she says as my eyes meet hers.

"You think I give a damn about what underwear you're wearing? The only thing that matters is that they're going to end up on my bedroom floor."

I make my way up to my knees and just stare at her as she lays across my bed. I guess I've been staring at her for too long because she moves up onto her elbows and looks down at me.

"What are you doing?"

"Staring at your perfect body. Will you let me touch and taste your pussy? Please?"

The only answer I receive is in the form of a moan, letting me know I've said the words she wants to hear, so I continue.

"Does it turn you on, me begging on my knees to taste you?"

"Yes, it does, and yes you may."

I slide my fingers under the edge of her panties, teasing her skin with more light touches. I know where she wants me to go as her body squirms in anticipation. I can't help but smirk at her impatience just before my fingers finally make their way to the place she wants me most.

"Fuck, you're so wet already." I pause for a moment to look into her eyes. "And we've only just begun."

I part her other lips with my fingers as I lean in to lick my way up one of her thighs. She tastes sweet, salty, and all mine. I want more.

Her underwear is another barrier that is keeping me from getting to all of her, so I take them off as quickly as possible. I'm left staring at her naked body, wondering how I got this lucky. "You're so beautiful."

I take a moment, letting my eyes roam over her body, drinking in the sight of her. A low groan escapes my lips as I lower my head, trailing kisses down her abdomen, each one causing her to shiver under me. I make sure to take my time, savoring every inch of her before I reach my destination.

Although I want to put my mouth on her, my fingers want to have their fun first. I run them up and down her slit twice before slipping my middle finger into her.

Her lips part as she moans and the sound that leaves her lips is like music to my ears. As we stare at each other, the connection we forge while I'm fingerfucking her is electric. And that's before her body starts moving in perfect sync with my hand.

I'm determined to make her come on my hand first. It's a travesty that she hasn't had this experience before, but I can't say I feel guilty about her first time having this be with me.

I add another finger to her pussy and once I brush

against her G-spot, she almost loses it. She's growing closer to the edge, and I can't wait to see her fall over it.

I shift my body while not losing too much of the pace I'm keeping. My mouth makes its way to her pussy, and I inhale deeply, taking in the intoxicating scent that surrounds me. I give her several small licks, teasers for what is about to come until I make it my mission to devour her.

"You taste so damn good," is all I can manage to say before I continue licking and sucking. My utmost priority is not to ignore her clit because I have no doubt in my mind that it will drive her wild.

"Oh fuck!" she screams, and I look up at her. "Don't stop."

I smile against her skin and debate whether to tease her about having manners but decide against it. Instead, I increase the pace I've set because all I want to do is watch this beautiful woman come undone just for me.

Her hips buck against my face as her hands find their way into my hair. The last thing I'm about to do is complain because I've thought about this very moment for weeks.

As I listen to her breathing speed up, I know she's close to coming apart. I take a second to move away from her pussy and say, "Come for me, baby." Then it's as if I've never left because I'm right back on her.

There's a short moment of silence before she

explodes, and I make sure not to miss a drop of everything she's willing to give me.

"That's my good girl," I say. Her pussy continues to clench around my fingers as she comes down from the high. I pull them out of her and hold them up to her lips. She hesitates for a moment before she licks them clean.

That is the second hottest thing I've ever seen. The first was watching Hailey as I gave her an orgasm, and I am determined to make sure that it wouldn't be the last.

It takes Hailey a moment to catch her breath, but she sits up, leaning on her elbows and says, "I want to return the favor."

"Not this time, Rook," I let out a shaky breath. "If I feel your lips on me, this is going to be game over before we even begin."

"Well come on then, Jamison," she says.

I can't help but smirk at her using my last name. "What do you want?"

"I want you to use your cock to fuck me until I can't walk tomorrow."

If it wasn't obvious that Hailey wasn't shy about demanding what she wanted before, then those words would have removed all doubt.

"That can be arranged."

"Do you have a condom?" she asks as she watches me take off my shirt, her gaze burning a trail across my body.

I unbutton my jeans and unzip my fly. "I do and I'm

clean. Crawl up toward the headboard and lay back down."

She stares at me before she says, "I am too," and to my surprise, she does what I say.

I stand there for a couple of seconds, watching as her ass and pussy are on full display for me as she moves before I pull off my jeans, followed by my boxer briefs. I can't help but smirk as she stares at my cock in amazement without making a sound. If I've stunned her into silence, I'll take it as a win. I follow her onto the bed and lean over to dig into my bedside drawer to grab the thing I just promised her I had.

I roll the condom on as Hailey opens her legs, giving me plenty of room to work with. But she has gone back to resting on her elbows.

"Lay back," I tell her again and she does so without hesitation. "Fuck, I've created a masterpiece. If only you could see how pretty your pussy looks right now."

A small blush appears on her cheeks at my words, which is kind of funny to me given what we've just done. Regardless, I feel grateful she's chosen me to experience this with.

I position myself between her legs and without a second thought, I enter her. She gasps and I manage to stop myself from moving too quickly, for fear that I might be harming her.

"Am I hurting you?" I ask, wanting to make sure she's comfortable.

"N-no. This feels amazing. Better yet it is amazing."

I take that as my sign to sink into her, inch by inch. Every move I make causes new sensations to form in my body and I only crave more of her.

More of this.

More of us.

"Still feeling good?" I ask her and all she does is nod.

Not wasting any more time, I pull back before sinking into her body once more. "Fuck." How is this real?

Her pussy has me and my cock in a chokehold. When I imagined this happening, I never expected it to be like this.

The walls of her pussy clench around me off and on, making it difficult to keep a rhythm. Yet I manage because my goal is to make sure she finds bliss again. Hailey's eyes are half closed and the only thing she is focused on is the pleasure I'm giving her. It takes everything in me not to tell her that I love the look on her face.

When I change the pace I've been keeping to one that matches the way her body moves against mine, she lets out a loud moan, telling me I've made the right move. All of this is addicting, and there is no way I'll get enough of the way she feels underneath me.

I stare at the way our bodies move in harmony. I thought she was beautiful from the moment I saw her for the first time, but those words run through my mind on repeat like a mantra.

I lean down and capture her lips for a brief kiss that

doesn't disrupt our movements. "You're mine, Rook." I'm slightly concerned about what her response will be to it, but I needed to say the words.

Her mouth forms into a perfect O-shape before answering, "I am."

While there are still some things we need to work out, hearing her say those two little words rocks my entire world and spurs me to move faster.

A grin forms on my face when I watch her eyes roll back into her head. This is because of what I am doing to her, and I refuse to do anything half-assed.

I place my hands on her waist, allowing me to pull her down harder on my cock. Her small gasps and moans fill the room, and I can't stop.

"Fuck, Hailey."

"I'm going to come," she rushes out in between trying to catch any semblance of her breath.

"Do it for me, baby. Come now."

That's all it takes for her to come apart once more, and fuck, it's the hottest thing I've ever seen. The way her body reacts to the pleasure is everything and more. I feel myself about to lose control, and when it happens, I swear I'm seeing stars.

My roar of approval is the only warning I give before I shoot my load inside the condom. My shaft twitches as we both ride out the aftershocks of what we've just done.

"That was..." she starts, barely able to form the words.

"That was incredible," I finish for her.

I pull out of her slowly, savoring the feeling of her body against mine one last time. Carefully, I dispose of the condom and walk into my bathroom where I prepare a warm washcloth. Once I clean her up, I lay down and gather Hailey in my arms. Having her resting her head on my chest and being able to touch her like this does something to me. It's not about sex. It feels healing in a way, but I'm not sure what she's healing me from, and I don't dare question it.

"I still can't stand you," she says, and I can hear her breathlessness.

"Huh. Yet your body can."

The silence that follows is interrupted by Hailey sitting up and slapping my chest before plopping back down.

I chuckle because of what she just did. "Any time you want to do that, day or night. Doesn't even matter if I'm dead asleep."

"Duly noted."

"I meant what I said, Hailey," I tell her once we've both caught our breath. "You're mine."

She looks up at me with those beautiful hazel eyes of hers and smiles. "I know," she says simply. "And you're mine."

I chuckle and press a kiss to her forehead. "Damn right."

26

HAILEY

The next morning, I can feel myself slowly drifting back to consciousness, but I'm not sure I want to. Right now, the thought of getting up and diving into whatever the day is going to bring feels like too much.

It's still dark outside or that's what the lack of sunlight behind my eyelids is telling me. As I shift my body slightly, I feel an ache from muscles I didn't know I had. And I can't help but notice the hard warm body that I'm currently curled up against.

The immediate question is where the hell am I?

It takes me a second to remember the night before.

Levi and I having dinner at his place, which sounded suspiciously like a date.

The evening ending in his bedroom.

Me being so exhausted from sex that I'm positive I passed out almost immediately.

I had sex with Levi Jamison, and it was magical.

That thought makes me open my eyes and I'm greeted by what I thought I would be: almost complete darkness. The peace that surrounds me is lovely, but I know it can't last forever.

The sliver of light coming in through the window casts a dull glow around the room. I let my eyes adjust to the dimness, taking in the sight of Levi's peaceful face. His features are softened by sleep, and I find myself tracing my fingers lightly over his chest. The realization that I'm in his bed, wrapped up in his arms, makes me question everything.

His chest rises and falls slowly as my fingers draw imaginary designs over his pecs. The sheets are cool against my bare skin and tangled around our legs as if we'd been rolling around in them all night. Which is exactly what we did until we both passed out.

My hand starts to move lower and lower before my fingers are playing with the edge of the sheet where it rests on his waist. He's none the wiser, remaining asleep under my caresses.

I move my hand lower until it brushes over his cock and I can't help but smile. An idea pops into my mind as soon as I decide that I want more. After all, he did tell me if I needed more sex at any time, I could go as far as to wake him up. There's no time like the present.

My hand slips under the sheet and finds his dick already hard and ready for me. I pull the covers over my head and slowly wiggle my body, releasing myself from the hold he has me under. I pause for a second, happy that both of us decided clothes weren't necessary because it only makes my job that much easier.

I open my mouth and lick the tip before I wait to see if he acknowledges the sensation. When he doesn't, I repeat the move before sucking on the tip gently. It only takes a few seconds before a groan escapes his lips as he stirs in his sleep. His hand comes down to my hair and pulls but not enough to hurt me. I shiver when he moans my name as if it's the only word he knows. His hips jerk up on instinct, showing me that he's seeking more.

And I'm willing to give it to him.

I move my lips, allowing me to take him deeper in my mouth. He tastes salty and so damn good. Knowing I'm the reason why he's losing his mind only further encourages me.

"Fuck," he whispers, and it takes everything in me not to laugh. So he does know another word.

I bob my head up and down, taking him in deeper each time. One of my hands holds his cock while my other plays with his balls. His hips start to buck against me, grinding him into my face. I feel his grip tighten on my hair, pulling me closer to him. He moans, and I swear it bounces off the walls. I take him down my throat and then back up slowly.

"Rook," he pauses, and he takes in a shit ton of air. "You're going to have to stop right now or—"

His words die on his lips as I start moving faster. Adrenaline is driving me, and I won't be happy until he comes. I look up at him and find him staring at me, watching my every move. Well, at least for a moment before he closes his eyes tightly and throws his head back on the pillow.

His hand further tangles itself in my hair and I can feel his fist just behind my ear. He looks down at me, but even in the dim light, I can see he's struggling to focus on anything.

"I'm not going to last." His words come out at three times speed. "I'm going to come into your mouth."

I moan around his cock, letting him know I'm fine with that plan. The next sound that leaves his mouth, I can't quite describe. It sounds like a mixture of him trying to speak a groan, and it happens just before his cock jerks in my mouth. He comes on my tongue and down my throat in a hot wave. I swallow every last bit of it, and when I'm done, I wipe my mouth.

"Good morning," I say with a grin.

"Fuck. Good morning to you too." There's not a trace of sleep left in his body after the show I just put on. "What was that all about?"

"You told me to wake you up whenever I wanted sex. I woke up this morning wanting to give you a blow job. Is that okay?"

"Absolutely," he says as he pulls me back down on his chest. We both end up chuckling before he rolls me over so he's now on top and places a searing kiss on my lips. When our kiss breaks apart, he pulls me back into his chest. "That was mind-blowing."

"Literally or figuratively?"

"Both."

I chuckle at his response, and I have to agree with him. Even though I was on the giving end in this instance, seeing him come apart like that is something I won't ever forget.

"What are you up to this weekend?"

His questions make me stop laughing as I think about what he said. "Jade and I are going to visit Oak Terrace tomorrow. We plan on seeing her grandmother, and I'm going to talk to the activities director to make sure we have everything set for the chess event. Why?"

"I was going to invite you to my hockey game again, despite knowing that chances are high you're going to say no."

I feel somewhat guilty that he already assumed what my answer is going to be. It's not as if he's wrong, but the comment still stings.

Before I can think of something to say, he speaks again. "Don't you have to work a morning shift today?"

Those words make every nerve in my body stand at attention. My time spent here with Levi has thrown off my schedule completely although the fading darkness outside should have clued me in on what time it was.

I groan from the pain of it all. "I do. How did you know?"

Levi throws a smirk my way before he responds. "I saw you for the first time on a Friday. Figured it was your usual shift."

The fact that he kept track of it is sweet. "What time is it?"

He manages to find his phone and says, "Almost five-fifteen."

"Shit," I say as I scramble out of bed, looking for my clothes.

Levi doesn't move an inch. Instead, he chuckles from the bed, watching my frantic search.

"I'll get you there on time," he assures me as he turns on the lamp closest to where he's lying. "How about you shower here while I fix you a quick breakfast, and then I'll drive you back to your place so you can change? Then, if you want me to, I can drive you into work."

I stop moving as if I'm frozen in place. There's no way he said that, right?

"You'd do that? For me?" My voice cracks, and I hate how vulnerable it sounds. I'm so used to doing everything myself that I hadn't even thought to ask him for help.

He props himself up on one elbow, his eyes meeting mine and they don't waver. "Yeah, Hailey," he says softly with a small smile. "I would."

"I thought we were keeping things casual? No labels, right?"

He rolls his eyes at me, and I can read the annoyance loud and clear. "I can help you without being your boyfriend, Rook."

He makes a good point. I've just never expected kindness from most people without strings attached.

"Fine. Thank you so much."

Levi's grin returns to his face. "Now get your pretty ass in the shower so we can head out in a bit."

I don't need to be told twice. I dash into the bathroom, and it takes me a moment to figure out how to turn on the hot water. I tie my hair into a messy bun and pray it stays where it is. Once again, being fully naked is a plus because it makes it that much easier to step into the shower.

As water cascades down my back, I take a moment to relax some of my achy muscles before I get to work on quickly washing up. Soon I'm scrubbing away sleep and any traces of what happened last night. While showering, I think about everything that has transpired over the last twenty-four hours and what might come next. But no matter how hard I try, I can't seem to find any answers.

I step out onto the bathroom mat and wrap the towel around my body. The mirror is fogged up, but I can still see the redness in my cheeks. I'm not sure if it's because of the shower or because I've felt heated from the moment I stepped into Levi's home.

By the time I emerge from the bathroom, Levi is nowhere to be found, but there are a pair of black sweatpants, t-shirt, and a hoodie next to my clothes that were neatly folded on the bed. Assuming they are for me to wear, I quickly put the clothes on, making sure to roll the waist down so the pants will somewhat fit me. When I walk out into the kitchen area, Levi has breakfast laid out on the counter. As I'm staring at the fried egg and avocado toast with a cup of water, I'm impressed. My stomach growls as I walk over.

"You cook breakfast too?" I ask with raised eyebrows as I slide onto a barstool.

He gives me an exaggerated bow from where he's leaning against the counter. "I am a man of many talents," he says with a smirk.

I roll my eyes and we both eat quickly because time is of the essence. Once we're finished, I quickly pack my backpack with most of the clothes I wore yesterday. Levi grabs his keys and together we walk out of his apartment and to his SUV. He disengages the locks and opens the passenger door for me.

As I settle into the leather seat, Levi starts the engine and pulls out onto the road.

"FYI, I probably should have said something earlier, but I sometimes get nauseous when I'm in a car and I'm not driving."

"Okay, I'll take it easy then and won't pretend I'm driving a Formula 1 car."

The joke pulls a laugh from me and the rest of the ride back to my place is quiet, but it's a comfortable silence. As I glance down at the clock, I'm slightly worried I'll be late because it all depends on how quickly I can change my clothes and unpack and repack my bag.

When we pull up outside my apartment building, the sky is turning a soft shade of blue-pink as the sun is beginning to rise. Levi turns off the ignition and looks over at me.

"I'll wait here," he says as if reading my thoughts about asking him to come up. Having him come up will further complicate things in my mind given what he's doing for me, so having this space is the right call. I could tell him that I can drive myself to work, but I don't really want to because I have class about an hour after my shift and parking near the campus building I need to go to is a pain in the ass.

Instead, I nod before exiting the car. Once I'm inside my apartment, I move as fast as possible to finish the tasks I need to do while doing my best to not wake up Jade. I change my clothes, redo my bun, brush my teeth, and double-check that my name tag is in my bag.

As I head back downstairs and outside, the cool morning air finally feels wonderful against my face because I know that I should be able to get to work on time now. I don't realize how fast I'm walking back to Levi's SUV until I'm sitting in the passenger seat with my seat belt on and I'm kind of out of breath.

"Made it," I say as Levi starts the SUV.

"Excellent. Let's head out," he says as he pulls away from the curb.

"I'm not looking forward to today. Having to deal with Marc."

"Marc..." Levi's voice trails off as if she's trying to piece together who I'm talking about. "Isn't he the guy that interrupted us the day we met?"

I nod. "Yes, that's him. He's my manager and is a pain in the ass. He makes my life a living hell at the coffee shop."

Levi doesn't say a word for a moment, then he says, "Something should be done about him."

"What do you mean?" I can't help but question.

"Don't worry about it, Rook."

"Why do you call me that anyway?"

"Because Queen didn't flow as well."

I roll my eyes. "Tell me the real reason."

"It's one of the most powerful pieces on the board and that's how I view you and your strength."

I have no words and thankfully we're only a block away from Brewed Beginnings. We get there in record time, thanks to it being super early in the morning. He pulls up close to the entrance and throws the SUV into park.

"Thanks for the ride—and for breakfast," I say as I unbuckle my seat belt. The words sound lame coming from my lips, but I'm not sure what else to say after his nickname explanation.

Levi turns to me and says, "Anytime."

If this was a romance novel, this would be the moment where we lean into each other slowly and kiss over the console. But this isn't a romance novel.

Instead, I pull back and grab my backpack. "See you later then," I say with a small wave as I step out of the SUV.

"Yeah, later," he says as I close the door behind me. I can feel his eyes on me as I walk toward Brewed Beginnings. I shove any thoughts of Levi into the furthest corner of my mind because if I don't, there's not a chance in hell I'll be productive for the remainder of the day.

27

HAILEY

I roll my eyes for what has to be the fiftieth time in the last twenty minutes.

Okay, maybe I'm exaggerating a little, but it doesn't negate the fact that every second that ticks by is one second closer to us being late for the meeting I need to attend.

Jade, who is usually on time, is running late because she overslept after hanging out with some of her other friends too late last night. I'd suspected something like this might happen, so I even built in a small buffer by telling her we needed to leave ten minutes earlier than we actually did, but we are still cutting it close.

I let out a heavy sigh and drum my fingers on the steering wheel. I'm debating sending another text message telling her to hurry up or just giving up on getting there on time.

I grab my phone out of the cupholder and stare at it, willing Jade to at least text me and give me an update. No dice.

But there's something else I can do while I wait.

My thumbs hover over the screen of my phone. Biting my lip, I find the text message thread between my dad and me and start typing.

> Me: Hey, Dad, how was the date last night?

Without Emily's help, there's no way I would have been able to send that text message without having stared at it for ten years to make sure I actually wanted to send the message. To my surprise, Dad texts me back almost immediately.

> Dad: It went great! She's amazing and we had a great time. Thanks for asking.

> Me: Of course. I want to know about your life, and I want you to be happy. This is a win-win.

> Dad: I definitely am. It feels good to be getting out there again, and she's really easy to talk to. We're planning on going out again next weekend.

> Me: That's awesome, Dad.

Just as I'm about to ask him about what he did on his

date, I get a notification for another message—a text from Jade this time.

> Jade: On my way! SORRY!!!

> Me: It's okay. Hurry up though because we're late.

> Jade: Gimme 2 mins.

I shake my head as I go back to texting my dad.

> Me: What did you do on the date?

> Dad: We went to this little Italian place close to her house and then we strolled around the park for a bit to talk and get to know each other better. I liked it a lot and she said she did too.

Before I can type another word, I see something out of the corner of my eye, so I look up. Jade is a few yards away and she's power walking toward my car with a sheepish grin on her face. My irritation melts away because she's finally here.

With the click of a button, I unlock the doors and she slides into the passenger seat.

"I have to start setting, like, ten alarms," she says with a sigh as she buckles up. "I need to tell Gran we're going to be a little late."

"Okay and alarms would have been nice for today," I respond as I start my car.

I pull out of the parking spot as Jade flips down the sun visor. She quickly swipes lip balm across her lips before turning back to me.

"Okay, spill. Something else is going on here. It's not just because I was running behind," Jade says as I feel her stare on me.

"Nah, it's not you... well, not only you," I admit. "I texted my dad about his date."

Her eyes light up with excitement. "And? How did it go?"

"Sounds like it went well," I reply, sparing a glance at her before turning my attention back to the road. "He said they both enjoyed themselves. I'm happy for him."

Jade claps her hands excitedly, her curly hair bouncing with the movement. "Oh my gosh, that's amazing! And you're taking this well."

I can't help but laugh at Jade's enthusiasm, releasing some of the tension that had been trapped in my body. "Yeah, I know. I'm proud of him, and I'm proud of myself."

"As you should be. Plus, you have plenty of things to focus on when it comes to your own dating life."

I purse my lips together to keep from blurting something out. "I have no idea what you're talking about."

"Now we both know that's a lie. You didn't come home the night before last."

I can feel the heat rising in my cheeks and I hate that I can't control it. We hadn't had an opportunity to talk about Thursday night because we hadn't seen each other on Friday. There was no doubt in my mind that Jade would know I wasn't home that night, but I hadn't been expecting us to talk about it now. I grip the steering wheel a little tighter, suddenly interested in a nonexistent spot on the windshield.

"Unsurprisingly, I was at Levi's," I confess without looking her way.

Her response isn't immediate, and the pause stretches long enough that it has me stealing a glance at her. Jade's got this knowing smile playing on her lips, and I brace myself for what is going to fly out of her mouth.

"I knew it!" she exclaims, punching the air. "So? Details, Hailey! I need details! Was it romantic? Was he a gentleman? Did you..." Her voice trails off as she wiggles her eyebrows, making it easy for me to pick up on what she is referring to.

"It was... nice," I begin, picking my words carefully. Nice is an understatement; it was more than nice. "He made dinner. We talked... a lot."

"Talked, huh?" Jade winks at me, and I can tell she's not buying my PG-13 rated version of events.

"Okay, fine." I chuckle a bit as I shake my head. "We might have done more than just talk. It was amazing, Jade. Everything was if you get my drift."

Jade grabs my arm. "I'm hearing it loud and clear, trust me. This is HUGE, Hailey!"

I glance down as she holds on to my arm before looking back at the road. "J, I'm trying to drive."

"Oh yeah," she says as she lets me loose. "I'm sorry."

I keep my eyes on the road but can't stop the small grin that forms on my face. "Yeah, it was definitely not what I expected. But I don't want to make a big deal out of it. Both of us agreed to not put any labels on this."

I can feel the look she's giving me without having to turn toward her. "No labels, huh? You say that now. Maybe if you continue repeating it, you'll make yourself believe it too."

Jade's comment hits its mark, and I don't like that she, knowingly or unknowingly, called me out. I have been repeating the no labels line in my head since Levi and I agreed to it. The agreement is meant to protect me, but it did little to fix the confusion I have about all of this.

I clear my throat to not only make it easier to speak but also to remove the thoughts from my mind. Or so I hope. "Look, I want to enjoy whatever this is without over-thinking it."

"Hailey Reed, not overthinking? Now, that's a headline."

I can't fight the laughter that escapes me. It's true—overthinking is my Olympic sport, and I've won many gold medals in that event.

"But seriously, I need this to be simple. Life's complicated enough and I have too much to do."

"I get it. You want something that's not going to throw your world upside down."

Funny enough, he has already done that, but I don't

say it out loud. We continue to chat for the rest of our trip and soon I'm parking in a spot near the entrance of the main building on Oak Terrace's campus.

Jade hops out of the car first and I find myself trailing behind her. Part of it's my nervousness, but it's also obvious Jade wants to see her grandmother.

The automatic doors sweep open with a soft whoosh as we enter the lobby. Immediately I'm greeted by the sight of residents living their lives, some walking slowly with canes, others zipping through in motorized wheelchairs.

Jade waves at an older man who is positioned strategically by the window, sunlight casting a gentle glow around his silver hair. "There's Mr. Kowalski! Gran and he sometimes play bingo together."

I smile at her enthusiasm. Jade has this talent for making everyone feel welcome and like they are her best friend. Since I don't have that ability, I find myself in awe and sometimes slightly annoyed because that means people then come over and talk to me.

We make our way to the activities director's office after a few more hellos and introductions, courtesy of Jade. Stepping into the office, we find Mrs. Linda Rafferty, her round glasses perched on the end of her nose as she scrutinizes the documents in front of her.

"Mrs. Rafferty?" Jade says as she knocks on the already open door, her voice filled with the same warmth she extends to everyone.

The older woman lifts her gaze, and a soft smile finds its place on her face. "Jade! And this must be Hailey. Thank you so much for coming out here today."

I step forward to take the lead, my fingers lightly gripping the strap of my bag. "Thanks for having us. We're here to go over the final arrangements for the chess event this Saturday."

Mrs. Rafferty nods, pushing her glasses up the bridge of her nose as she gestures for us to sit across from her. "Of course. We're all very excited about the event. The residents have been playing and practicing with one another and it's a beautiful sight to see."

I can't help but smile because the thought makes me so happy. It's one of those moments that makes me realize how worth it all of this is.

I pull out my notebook, flipping past scribbled notes about environmental policy levels until I find my checklist for the event. "So, we'll need to confirm the setup for the tables and chairs in the main hall..."

Mrs. Rafferty interjects, "All taken care of. Your diagrams were very detailed—I will make sure maintenance sets everything up the way you've asked."

"Excellent," I reply. This is going better than I thought. "We'll bring some more chess sets from campus because we'll need more. Also, we'll have more chess club members coming from campus who can help with teaching and playing with those who might not have an opponent."

As Mrs. Rafferty and I continue to run through logistics, from accessibility accommodations to outlining emergency procedures, the nerves fall away and my passion and love for chess as well as this event returns. My impostor syndrome has been laid to rest for the time being, giving me the ability to think and act more freely.

Finally, with everything addressed down to the last detail, Mrs. Rafferty leans back in her chair with a satisfied sigh. "Well, it looks like we're prepared for an afternoon of chess! You've done an excellent job coordinating this, Hailey."

"Thank you," I say sincerely. The proverbial ball for this event is rolling and so far, so good. And I was damn proud of it.

Jade clasps her hands together excitedly before standing up. "This is going to be so great! I can't wait."

As we leave Mrs. Rafferty's office and head toward the wing where Jade's grandmother resides, our conversation drifts to how well the meeting went and what we need to do next to make sure things go off without an issue.

We come to a stop outside room 215 and Jade gives a quick knock before turning the doorknob and pushing the door open. "Gran? We're here!" she calls out.

Seated by the window is Mrs. Hazel Samuels, and as we step inside, a smile spreads across her face when she sees Jade.

"There's my girl!" she exclaims, holding out her arms.

Jade immediately goes to her grandmother and gives

her a gentle hug. Mrs. Samuels pats Jade's cheek affection-
ately before her gaze settles on me.

"And you must be Hailey. I've heard so much about
you from this chatterbox granddaughter of mine."

I can't help but laugh. "It's nice to meet you, Mrs.
Samuels. I hope Jade hasn't been spreading too many
stories about me."

"Oh nonsense, she only has wonderful things to say,"
Mrs. Samuels says with a wink. The neatly arranged cards
on the table in front of her make me think she was playing
a game of solitaire before we arrived. She pushes the table
aside to stand and greet us properly.

Mrs. Samuels points to the stylish bar cart on the
other side of the room that has lemonade, water, and
cookies on it, "I've set up a little treat for us. Don't be shy,
pour yourselves a drink and grab a snack."

Jade jumps into action, assisting her grandmother
with the refreshments. Taking a glass of lemonade, I
thank Mrs. Samuels. I'm touched by her thoughtfulness as
I settle down onto her couch.

Once we eat the snacks that we wanted, Jade speaks.
"Hailey's the one that is organizing a big chess event here,
Gran," she says. "You mentioned that you couldn't wait to
participate."

Mrs. Samuels' eyes light up. "That's right. I'm so
excited about it!" She settles back into the armchair across
from us, smoothing the navy slacks she has on. "Tell me

about this event, dear. I'd love to hear more and only know the basics."

I explain the details, how we plan to have residents play against chess club members from the university as well as each other. "It's meant to be a fun social activity; a chance to engage with the students too," I say.

"A wonderful idea. You can certainly count me in. I played with your grandfather when he was still here, Jade." The pause gives Mrs. Samuels a moment to share a sad smile with her granddaughter. "With my chess skills, I'll show those students a thing or two!"

We all laugh, and I have no doubt that she can teach me some new tips and tricks.

"I am certain you'll be a challenging opponent," I say. "I'm looking forward to seeing your skills in action."

"Just you wait, young lady. I may be old, but my mind is still sharp as a tack," Mrs. Samuels assures me.

The conversation flows naturally as Mrs. Samuels asks more about my goals and interests, and Jade gets to fill her grandmother in on the latest things that are going on with her life. I find myself opening up more than I expected, sharing things I normally keep private.

As we get ready to go, Mrs. Samuels' positive words have given me a much-needed boost of confidence for the chess tournament and my ability to make everything run smoothly. Mrs. Samuels walks us to the door, where she gives both of us hugs, and soon we are walking back down to my car.

Jade and I are quietly talking when my ringtone goes off. I pull my phone out of my bag to see a new text from Levi.

> Levi: Hey, still up for coming over to play chess tomorrow?

"Everything okay?" Jade asks, noticing the change in my expression.

"Yeah, it's a text from Levi about getting together to play chess tomorrow. I'm just surprised he's texting me now because I think he's preparing for a hockey game," I say nonchalantly.

Jade grins. "Wait, that isn't the usual day you have your lessons. Is this a date?"

I roll my eyes but can't help the butterflies in my stomach at the thought. "It's not a date. We're just hanging out."

"Mm-hmm, sure," Jade says in a singsong voice. "As I said earlier, it's as if you need to keep repeating yourself in order for you to believe it."

I roll my eyes again. "I told you, it's not a date."

"Call it what you want. As long as you go over there."

"Fine. I'll go. You don't have to tell me twice." She didn't have to tell me at all because there was no way I was missing this.

Jade grins. "Excellent and remember to give me all the juicy details after."

I laugh as we reach my car. There's no way I'm doing that. "You're the worst."

"I've been called worse, so I don't care," Jade says as she gets in the passenger seat.

I shake my head, unable to keep a small smile off my face as I start the car. Before I pull away, I send Levi a reply.

> Me: Chess at your place sounds good. See you tomorrow evening and good luck today.

I read it over one final time before gathering the courage to press send. The weight of my decision hangs heavy in my mind as I tap the phone screen. I don't know where any of this is going to lead, but I guess I'm trying something new. That is the point of all of this, right?

28

HAILEY

The next evening when the elevator doors slide open, I step into the sleek metal box and take a deep breath. Moments ago I'd arrived at Levi's apartment, and I'm not prepared for anything that might happen tonight. I suck in another deep breath even though I'm not exerting a large amount of energy. I can only assume it's the excitement getting to me, though I would never admit it out loud. If it's anything like what happened the last time I was here, I'm one hundred percent down.

It's only a chess game, Hailey. Calm the fuck down.

Easier said than done.

The ride up to Levi's apartment feels like it takes forever, even though it's only a few floors. At least this time I didn't have to be escorted up because Levi now has me on a list of approved guests.

I don't want to spend time dissecting that right now.

When I arrive at his front door, I ring the doorbell, and I swear on everything, the sound of the bell bounces off every corner of my mind. Suddenly the door swings open and I find Levi standing in the doorway, looking perfect in a Crestwood University hoodie and gray sweatpants. Once again, he still manages to look put together, and I can't help but wonder if he wore those pants for my benefit.

"Good evening, Hailey." He greets me with a grin and motions for me to come inside.

My stomach flips at the sight of him. I try to act casual as I follow him to the living room, but my nerves are getting the best of me.

"Would you like something to drink? Eat?" Levi asks. Although he's standing behind me, grabbing my coat, I can still hear the smile in his voice.

"Just water, thanks," I reply, hoping he can't detect the slight tremor in my voice.

In a flash, he lays my coat across a chair and returns with two glasses of ice water from his kitchen. He places them on opposite sides of the coffee table. They are now in front of where each of us would sit down to play our match.

"Ready for me to kick your ass in chess?" he asks.

I roll my eyes. "In your dreams, Jamison."

"That's not the thing that I tend to dream about..." his voice trails off. "But before we begin, how about we make this more interesting?" he says as he's about to move one of his pawns.

I raise an eyebrow. "What do you have in mind?"

"Strip chess. For every piece I lose, I have to remove an article of clothing and vice versa."

"Were you thinking about this before I got here or is this something that just popped into your head?"

"I've been thinking about getting you naked again since before you left my bed days ago," he admits without hesitation.

I swallow hard in an attempt to coat my suddenly dry throat, but I fail. *Fuck.* "What do I get if I win?"

He shrugs as if what is happening between us isn't rocking his entire life. "I'll give you a surprise."

"What is it?" I don't care for how eager I sound, but it's too late to take it back and try again.

This time he smirks again. "Wouldn't be a surprise if I told you what it is, now would it?"

I do my best not to roll my eyes at his cockiness as I experience a sense of déjà vu from the last time I was here. "What do you get if you win?"

Leaning forward, resting his elbows on his knees, Levi locks eyes with me. "Another one of those fantastic blow jobs you woke me up with."

The memory of that morning floods my mind and sends a shiver down my spine. Doing that to him again is enough to make me debate losing so that we can take it there. I hesitate for a second, but the desire to wipe the smug look off his face overrides everything else.

I stick my hand out for him to shake. "You have yourself a deal."

Levi's eyes widen before he catches himself. Is he surprised I decided to participate? I'm not sure, but he grabs my hand and turns it palm side down before he brings it up to his lips. He slowly kisses each of my knuckles and I can't help but be hyper-fixated on what it's doing to me.

But now it's time for us to play this out on the chessboard.

Levi opens with a pawn to e4, a familiar move that has started countless games before. However with this being strip chess, it feels as if we are charting unknown territory.

I mimic his opening and push my pawn to e5. And so our game begins.

The room is silent except for the clinking of the pieces as they hit the board. It's hard to be focused on what is happening in front of me because the fact that I more than likely will be losing at least a piece of clothing is at the forefront of my mind.

After about ten minutes, I lose my first pawn, and I can feel the heat growing on my cheeks. I decide to pull off the black sweater I'd thrown on last minute, happy that I had the foresight to do so before leaving my apartment. What I hadn't done was wear a long sleeve shirt under said sweater. Goosebumps appear on my skin because of the slight chill in the air.

When I snatch his bishop, Levi almost gleefully unzips his hoodie, and he, too, is left in a t-shirt. For some reason, I am expecting him to be shirtless. Or maybe that is wishful thinking.

When it's my turn to lose my bishop. Levi's smirk grows. "You owe me a piece of clothing," he says.

I stand up and unbutton my jeans, shimmying them down my legs. I catch him staring as I fold them and place them on the chair. Now clad only in my t-shirt and underwear, I feel exposed under his gaze.

Yet I'm loving it.

When I capture Levi's knight, he pulls his shirt over his head in one smooth motion. I take in the defined muscles of his chest and abs, allowing myself to admire him. He notices and chuckles. "See something you like?"

I shake my head to hide my embarrassment at being caught staring. "Your cockiness is off the charts tonight. What gives? You're usually worried about the things you say to me."

"How do you know that?"

"It is obvious."

Levi shrugs. "Well, to answer your question, I'm confident because I know that I win no matter what the outcome of this game is."

"That's sweet in a twisted way."

"I thought so too."

The game continues and pieces fall steadily from the board. My pulse quickens as clothing flies off, and soon Levi is down to only his gray sweatpants and his boxers.

When I capture his rook, fittingly enough, he stands, sliding his sweatpants down his muscular legs. I try not to stare so he doesn't call me out again. I shift in my seat, clenching my thighs together in a silly attempt to relieve the desire building within me.

Levi notices my discomfort and a knowing grin tugs at his lips. "Getting distracted, Rook?" His voice is husky, and he knows exactly what he's doing to me when he uses that voice.

I clear my throat and force myself to meet his heated gaze. "You wish, Jamison. I'm still in this game." And I am because I fully believe that I'm going to win.

Levi makes his next move swiftly, capturing my remaining bishop. I hesitate for only a moment before pulling my shirt up over my head. His eyes rake over my nearly naked body hungrily, but I keep my expression neutral. I will not let his need for me become a distraction.

The game progresses tensely as we both seek to gain the upper hand. I manage to take Levi's remaining knight with my rook. Levi stands, his fingers sliding beneath the waistband of his boxers. I hold my breath, waiting for him to expose himself fully to me. At the last moment, he pauses, cocking an eyebrow at me, but he doesn't say a word.

If he is naked, but the game isn't over, did I still win? "Am I the winner since that's your last piece of clothing?" I'm proud of myself for making a cohesive sentence all the while staring at his V-line.

"Not so fast. The game's not over until you take my king."

He slides his boxers down inch by inch, maintaining eye contact with me the whole time. I forcefully shifted my eyes up to his face when he started removing his boxers. Now I'm trying to keep my eyes on his face, but they inevitably wander down his muscular frame. He steps out of the boxers and kicks them aside, completely naked before me.

"Your move," he says, sitting back down across from me. I tear my eyes away and study the board, forcing myself to focus again. I have to be strategic if I want to win this.

After contemplating my next move, I advance my remaining knight and put his king in check. "Check," I say, meeting Levi's gaze again.

He moves his king out of check, but I quickly counter and check him again with my other rook. But he escapes again. We continue in this pattern with me checking his king while he barely escapes.

After a few more turns, I finally yell, "Checkmate!" when there's nowhere for his king to go. Holy shit, I won. This is the most excited I've been about winning a chess match in a while.

Levi nods as he studies the board. "Well played."

I had faith in myself that I would win, but Levi had given me a run for my money. My heart pounds against my ribs as I meet Levi's heated gaze.

"So..." I say, suddenly feeling shy under the intensity of his stare. "What happens now?"

Levi stands up from his chair and walks toward me. "I guess I owe you the surprise now, huh?"

I like the sound of that. But adrenaline is coursing through me and I'm feeling playful. Who am I and what has happened to Hailey? Before I overthink something else, I stand up too and take a step back just before Levi would have reached me. And then I take another.

Neither one of us utters a word before I turn around and run into his bedroom with him hot on my heels.

I stop abruptly near his bed, spinning around in time to see Levi entering the room. His eyes darken with desire as he closes the distance between us. Before I can respond, his lips crash against mine. It's a hungry, passionate kiss that causes me to melt against him. My hands have a mind of their own as they slide up and down his chest. He groans into my mouth when I lightly rake my nails over his abs.

Levi's hands grip my hips as he deepens the kiss, pulling me closer to him. It's my turn to moan as his tongue dances with mine. I can feel his dick pressing against me and the only thing standing between us is the very thin barrier of the lace underwear I decided to wear tonight.

He breaks the kiss, both of us breathing heavily. "Eager, are we?" he says, leaving a trail of hot kisses along my jaw and down my neck.

I nod, not trusting my voice to work at this juncture. His hands slide up to caress my breasts through my bra and I arch into his touch. He is already driving me wild, and we are only just getting started.

"I should give my girl the surprise she's earned," he whispers in my ear before guiding me down onto the bed. I watch him as he kneels between my legs, hands stroking up and down my inner thighs with light touches.

"Close your eyes and if there's anything you don't like, tell me immediately, okay?"

I hesitate for a second as Levi enters a more dominant role in the bedroom. I'm used to being the one that tells people what to do and how I want things done. This is a change that I'm willing to experience. "Okay," I repeat, but my tone is more breathy than his is. With one last glance, I close my eyes and wait for further instructions.

I can sense when Levi leaves his position between my legs. There's some shuffling around in the room, but I can't pinpoint exactly what he's doing or what my surprise can be.

He must have found whatever it is he was looking for because I feel a small kiss on each of my inner thighs before I sense that he's between my legs once more. His hands massage my thighs before one of his hands reaches my panties. His fingers dance along the fabric and I can feel myself growing wetter. It is then that I feel something smooth and hard pressing at my entrance. My eyes pop open when the device starts vibrating against my clit.

"My surprise for you," he says over the low buzzing, making me squirm against the vibrator.

"Do you like it?" he asks as he watches my reaction closely. I manage a nod, already overwhelmed by the new sensations coursing through my body.

It's then that I notice the small white remote in his hand, and when he presses a button, the speed increases. I gasp loudly and throw my head back. There is no way that this is real life.

"Fuck, Hailey," Levi says, and it only adds fuel to the fire that's burning inside of me. He rests one of his hands on my abdomen, rubbing soft circles that only intensify the sensation. "I want you to play with your nipples for me."

It takes me a second to register what he asked me. But when I do, my hands immediately begin alternating between lightly pinching and soothing my nipples. My climax is closing in, letting itself be known.

"Levi," I moan out his name. He adjusts the vibrator slightly, allowing the device to hit the right spot. I feel like I could come at any second. He puts more weight down on the hand that's resting on my stomach so that he holds me down without keeping me prisoner.

When he uses the remote again, I can't hold back anymore.

I cry out as my climax crashes down on me, leaving me panting and shaking. It's like nothing I've experienced before but in a good way. He keeps the toy pressed to me, waiting until I've ridden the full wave of my orgasm. When my breathing tries to level out, Levi reaches for the remote and switches it off.

He kisses a path up my body until he reaches my earlobe where he whispers, "Good girl."

I'm once again aware of how hard his cock is. I want it in me and now. "Fuck me."

Levi stares down at me for a moment before he says, "With pleasure."

He reaches into his nightstand and tosses a condom my way while I watch. Part of me wants to put the condom on him myself, but I'm still gathering my bearings after that mind-blowing orgasm.

Once he rolls the condom on himself, he positions himself between my legs, but before he can enter me, I hold up my hand. "I want to ride you."

"Are you sure?"

"One hundred percent."

He nods and says, "Ride me then."

We adjust our positioning and within seconds, I find myself lowering my body onto his cock. My eyes close as I enjoy the feeling of him sliding into me, inch by inch. As I begin to move up and down, his hands end up on my waist, and I'm listening to the sighs we're making as we become one.

I'm still questioning whether this is my reality or not. What I do know is that this is what I needed.This is where I belonged, right here with him.

If it weren't for what we are doing right now, the thought would have hit me like a ton of bricks.

I begin to move faster, my hair flying in every direction. He moves his hands from around my waist and before I know it, the vibrator is once again on my clit and soon the humming of it greets us both.

"That feels good," I mutter but I'm not sure if I've actually said the words out loud.

"You feel good," he whispers back before closing his eyes with a groan.

Our moans and grunts fill the room as we both approach our climaxes. The weight of what this means is heavy between us, but I can't focus on it without losing my concentration. All that matters is us right now and this is how it should be.

I feel the now familiar sensation growing and I know it's going to be over soon. "I'm close," I warn him as I start rocking my hips faster, pushing myself down on his dick.

He smiles up at me and says, "So am I."

The rhythm that we've set intensifies to the point where Levi throws the remote and places his hand back on my waist. Our breaths become ragged as our movements grow more desperate for a release.

I come first due to the vibrator, and I'm left in a mess with me calling his name. When Levi joins me, he grunts out a curse and follows me over the edge. I push him away a little but end up resting my forehead on his chest to catch my breath. His cock slips out of me, and I can't help but chuckle.

Levi's fingers tenderly brush strands of my slightly damp hair away from my face. I lift my head from his chest and gaze into his eyes, not sure what I'm searching for in them.

Levi's breathing slows down to match mine as his hand remains on my cheek. A soft chuckle escapes his lips, breaking the silence. "You okay?" he asks.

"Yes. I don't know what my expectations were, but this exceeded them."

His smile widens, his thumb tracing circles on my cheek. "Good," he whispers, leaning in to press a soft kiss against my forehead. We lay like that for a few moments before Levi gathers some strength to get up and clean both of us.

When he crawls back into bed, I see the vibrator, and I immediately recognize the shape. "Is that a white pawn? The vibrator is in the shape of a chess piece?"

Levi chuckles as he pulls me close to him. "Yes. I thought it would be cute and funny. Plus, it did the job, right?"

I can't help but laugh out loud even though I'm exhausted. "That it did. That. It. Did."

29

LEVI

"Jamison! Get your head in the damn game!" Coach yells from the sidelines.

I hear him loud and clear, but I can't bring myself to look over and see the disappointment on his face.

I try to focus on my job tonight, but tonight my mind and heart aren't in it. The biggest reason is because I'd caught a glimpse of my father in the stands, arms crossed, frown on his face. Of course he has no issue with coming to this game as well, even though we are playing a college that is about an hour away from Crestwood.

Looks like my attempts to ignore him have come to a head, and I imagine that when he finds me after the game, his version of hell will break loose.

The puck feels as heavy as a brick as I struggle to

control it. My passes are sloppy, my shots way off target. As captain, I'm supposed to be leading this team, but tonight I'm letting everyone down.

The final buzzer sounds and I slowly skate over to the bench with my head hanging low. We lost and it is, in part, because of me.

Coach shakes his head as I sit down, exhausted and defeated. "I expected more from you tonight, Jamison. Get it together."

His words sting, even though I know he's right. I should have played better. I should have been a better leader for this team.

It has been almost a week since I've seen Hailey, and the distance is getting to me. The reasoning behind us not seeing each other is because of our busy schedules this week, but I can't help but wonder if there might be more to this on her end. I hope I'm wrong, but this isn't an excuse for how shitty I played today.

Once I head into the locker room and hit the showers, I allow the hot water to run over my aching muscles. However, it does nothing to soothe the stress and pain that are overpowering any other emotion I could possibly have right now.

And this is all before I've spoken a single word to my father.

Everyone can sense that something is off with me today, and it's not just because of my performance in the game. They're all avoiding me, including Asher, who usually puts up with most of my shit on a regular basis. Some days I can push through and put on a good face. But others, like tonight, it all feels like too much. I'm not the perfect son or student or captain my father wants me to be. And I'm disappointing everyone—my team, my coaches, my family.

I take my time getting my things together, dreading the confrontation I know is coming. I can picture my dad waiting outside, pacing, and ready to pick apart every mistake I made on the ice tonight. He won't hold back because he doesn't care who hears him tear into me.

When I finally emerge, Frank Jamison is there as expected. He barely waits for me to take a step toward him before he snaps at me. "What the hell was that out there? Do you want to explain to me how the captain of one of the best college teams in the nation managed to cost his team the game?"

I stare at the ground, unable to meet his eyes. "I'm sorry," I mumble. "I was off my game tonight."

"Off your game?" he snorts. "You're damn right you were off your game! That was a piss-poor performance. What's wrong with you? You've been playing like shit."

His words feel like a slap in the face as his criticism slices me in the heart. It hurts even more so because hockey is so much a part of my identity and my father's approval means everything, even though his love feels conditional.

"Things have been... rough lately," I admit.

"Rough?" He shakes his head, dismissing my response. "Do you think anyone gives a damn about your problems off the ice? Get your head straight and leave whatever is happening to you off the ice. I didn't raise a quitter."

I flinch at his words. The truth is, I don't know how to get my head straight these days. Between my father's expectations, my trying to figure out things with Hailey, and the pressure I put on myself, I feel stretched thin, like I might flip out at any moment. But I know better than to talk back or make excuses.

I clench my jaw and stare at the ground, telling myself I shouldn't respond. Arguing will only make things worse.

"Are you even listening to me?" my dad asks. More like demands, if I'm being honest.

"Yes sir," I mutter, avoiding his gaze. "I hear you and it won't happen again."

"See that it doesn't." He waits a beat before he turns and walks away, not even bothering to say goodbye.

Of course he doesn't. It would be too much like doing the right thing and having compassion for the only child he has left.

I readjust my duffel before shoving my hands into my pockets and leaving the arena.

I start the walk back to the bus, replaying the game in my head. Each missed shot, each fuckup—it's all there in excruciating detail. All I want to do is get back to my apartment so I can be alone to lick my wounds. The only thing I can think of that can possibly help me feel better is Hailey, but I also don't want her to see me in this state.

Lost in thought, I barely notice when Asher catches up to me halfway to the bus.

"Hey," he says as he falls into step beside me. "You gonna talk about it or are we gonna pretend everything's fine?"

I give a halfhearted shrug but don't say anything.

Asher's silence is needed. He doesn't push like others might; he waits because he knows eventually, I'll crack.

Finally, I let out a long sigh. "Tonight was a shit show," I confess without looking at him.

"But it happens. We'll kick ass and win our next game."

I glance at him out of the side of my eye. "I know you're trying to be cheerful to help me feel better, but you feel as shitty as I do after that game."

"But as Coach likes to tell us, one game doesn't define us."

I shake my head, understanding what he is doing but also not believing him. "Easy for you to say. You didn't play the worst game of your career and didn't have your father waiting for you after the game so that he could tell you how much of a disappointment you are."

"I know this is easier said than done, but fuck what your father thinks of you. You know we've all had those games where we can't seem to do anything right. Doesn't change the fact that you're a damn good captain."

I let out a dry laugh. "Thanks, Ash." I run a hand through my hair, feeling the frustration about this week's events clinging to me like a second skin. "It feels like I'm carrying around this... I dunno, this expectation that I should always be at the top of everything for who knows how long, and some days it all tumbles down."

"That's because you usually are, man. But you're human, and it's okay to have off days. Besides," he adds with a lopsided grin, "there's more to life than hockey, although it's hard for us to remember that at times."

We arrive at the bus, and I turn to look at him. "What, like classes? Had a hell of a week with them as is. I'm also trying to not fuck up things with a girl who deserves someone with less baggage."

"Since you brought her up, how are things going with Hailey?"

"It's... complicated and I know that is shocking," I say sarcastically.

"What isn't complicated at this point?" Asher asks as we slowly walk onto the bus.

"Touché." I finally give in to a small smile. "She's amazing, man. Different from anyone I've ever met."

"That's a good thing?"

"Definitely. She challenges me, makes me want to be better." The admission feels heavy on my tongue, but it's the truth. "However, she doesn't want to have anything more than... whatever is going on between us."

Asher throws himself into a seat near the window before he says, "How does that make you feel?"

My head involuntarily jerks back before I side down into the aisle seat next to him. "What are you, my therapist?"

"Your deflection isn't going to work here."

I sigh. "It sucks because I really like her. But I get it, you know? She doesn't want to be mixed up in going public with me and is dealing with her own shit."

"Even if it's not something you want."

"Yes," I reply, though every part of me screams otherwise. "I'll take her anyway I can get her."

"But how long will you be happy with just having a piece of her?"

Asher's question hangs in the air because I'm not sure how to respond.

Deep down, I'm afraid to admit the truth—even to myself. The possibility that I'll never be satisfied with a small part of Hailey bothers me, but the alternative—pushing for more and possibly driving her away—is a risk I don't want to take. I'm determined to follow her wishes.

"I don't have the answer," I finally say.

"Fair. You know what? Why don't you come over to our place and blow off some steam tonight?"

The invitation is enticing to say the least. The thought of spending time with good friends and forgetting about my troubles for a while is a welcome relief.

"Sounds good. Let me know when you want me to show up."

"Deal. Let me shoot Knox and Blaise a text to clarify a couple of things, but it should be fine."

I nod, grateful for the distraction. We ride the rest of the way back to campus in a comfortable silence. As the bus pulls into the parking lot, I feel my phone buzz in my pocket. Without looking, I know it's likely my father, probably with something to add to the criticism he spewed at me earlier. I have no problem ignoring him.

When we get off the bus, Asher pulls me aside and says, "I'll see you later tonight, right? The guys said maybe you can come over in forty-five minutes."

"Sounds good. See you in a few."

We part ways, and I head toward my SUV. Once I throw my bag into the back seat and I get situated in the driver's seat, I drive back to my apartment on what feels like autopilot. It's not until I park and drag myself up to my place that I'm tired. But that's not stopping me from going to Asher, Knox, and Blaise's place.

I dump my stuff on the couch and fall into it in an attempt to release the tension from my body. I close my eyes for a moment and that turns into thirty minutes. Luckily, I wake up before I need to leave because I refuse to stay here all night.

Asher's right. A change of scenery and some time with the guys outside of hockey will do me some good.

I change my clothes, deciding to dress in a well-worn

pair of jeans and a warm Crestwood hoodie. After, I double-check to make sure I've grabbed the essentials— my wallet, phone, and keys. After closing my front door, I lock up my apartment as I gather my second wind, deter- mined to put this hellish day and week behind me.

30

HAILEY

My apartment is silent except for the low voices coming from the latest reality television show that is more so watching me than I'm watching it. It is Saturday night and I'm enjoying my time alone.

Jade tried to convince me to go out, but I had a date with a book I've been meaning to finish. I'm curled up on our couch, wrapped in the knitted blanket Jade's grandmother made for her. Since Jade has no issue with me using it, I have no problem laying underneath it.

The cup of hot chocolate I made before I sat down is tempting me and, in a flash, I'm bringing the drink up to my lips. I take a sip and as the warmth spreads through me, I can't help but think that this is the perfect evening.

That is, until I start thinking about Levi. Despite my best efforts to ignore the impact he is having on my life, my thoughts have drifted toward him more often than I would like.

I know he has a hockey game tonight, but I promised myself I wouldn't check how the game is going. After all, I wouldn't understand what was going on outside of what the final score for both teams would be. Yet the urge to check is still strong. Maybe I'll read for a bit and then go pull up the game to see what's going on.

I adjust the hold I have on the mug so I'm holding it with both hands, and I take another sip of my drink. When I'm done, I place it back on the coffee table and turn my attention to the book in my lap.

I don't know how long I've been reading for, but the piercing sound of my phone ringing brings me back to reality. My phone is in the other room, and I'm too lazy to get up and check it. Chances are the call is spam anyway.

But when the ringing stops and quickly starts back up again, I toss the idea out the window. Someone is obviously trying to get in touch with me and I'm not sure why.

My heart jumps into my throat because the first thing that comes to mind is that it's about my dad and there is some sort of emergency.

I scramble to my feet, allowing the blanket to slip from my shoulders as I rush to where my phone is charging in my bedroom. The screen lights up with Levi's name as I reach for it, confusing me. Why would Levi be calling me now? Isn't he still at the game?

"Hello?" My voice betrays that I'm breathless from having sprinted into my bedroom.

"Hailey, it's Asher." The words come out in a rush as if he doesn't have much time to complete this task. What the hell is he doing calling me from Levi's phone?

My heart slams harder against my ribcage. "What's wrong? Is Levi okay?"

"He's... It's hard to explain over the phone," Asher says after a moment. "He needs you."

"I think you've got this all wrong. If he's hurt, you need to call nine-one-one," my voice trails off because I'm not processing any of this.

"He's not hurting in the way you think, but I—and him too, to a certain extent—know that he needs you."

The urgency in his voice acts like a shot of adrenaline to my brain. I forget all about the warmth of my apartment, my comfort in being alone, my book and hot chocolate.

"Where are you?" I ask as I'm grabbing my house and car keys and wallet from my desk. I'll have time to examine why I'm even leaving the house to do this later.

"At my place. I'll text the address to you. Please get here as soon as you can. Please."

I end the call without another word and jam my feet into a pair of old sneakers, and as I do, I receive a text message from Levi's phone. With Asher's address in hand. I walk into the living area and pick up the coat that I'd thrown over a chair. My eyes land on the book I'd been reading, now almost forgotten on the couch. I'll get back to it later.

I leave my apartment and my fingers tighten around my keys as I make my way down the stairs. It isn't because of a safety issue, but more because it gives me something to do with my hands.

The night air hits my exposed skin as I step outside. It's colder than when I'd returned home earlier, and for a moment, I question whether I should've grabbed a thicker coat. But I don't have time to go back now. Plus, I'm going to be driving over there so I'll be in a warm car soon enough.

When I reach my vehicle, I slip into the driver's seat and start the engine, taking a few deep breaths to try to calm myself down before I drive off. It doesn't help much, but I appreciate that I tried to tame my racing heart. I pull out of my parking spot and the drive to Asher's is a blur. My focus is on what could have happened that caused Levi to need me desperately.

What I might find could change the way Levi and I see each other forever. This is supposed to be an exclusive situationship but whatever this is, hadn't been included in the unwritten rules.

When I finally park down the street from Asher's place, I realize he lives in the typical home that owners rent out to college students. I barely give the houses nearby a second glance as I leave my car and quickly walk up to the house number Asher sent to me. I ring the door-bell and it's answered by Asher himself.

"Thanks for coming," he mumbles, closing the door behind me.

I nod stiffly, trying to avoid the awkwardness I feel about this whole situation. "Where's Levi?"

He leads me through a cluttered hallway lined with sports gear and equipment. We make our way into a small but cozy living room, where Levi is slumped over on a well-worn couch.

Levi looks up as we enter, his blue eyes hazy but they immediately lock onto mine. His hair is disheveled, his hoodie looks wrinkled and is hanging off one shoulder. I'm not sure what to think about the sight in front of me outside of him looking worse than he did when I saw him for the first time at Brewed Beginnings.

"Hey," he says, his voice hoarse as if it takes a lot of effort to speak.

I quickly cross to him, crouching down to get a better look at him. "What happened?" I demand softly, reaching out to gently adjust his sweater.

"He had a bit too much to drink after the game," Asher explains from somewhere behind me. "Wanted to blow off some steam."

I turn to glance at Asher questioningly, searching for something unsaid in his wary gaze. But before I can press for more details, Levi's hand finds mine. His touch brings a sense of comfort and I hope my being here does the same for him.

"Do you want me to take you back to your place?" I ask quietly.

Levi nods, but he hesitates slightly, making me wonder if he can actually make it to my car and not suffer too much on the ride home.

"Are you going to be sick?"

Levi shakes his head and I stare at him for a moment to see if he'll prove himself to be a liar about this. When he doesn't, I turn to Asher and ask, "Can you help me get him to my car?"

Asher walks over to us and together he and I help Levi to his feet. His body leans heavily against mine, although he tries to support more of his own weight.

As he moves his body closer to mine, I worry he might lose his balance and fall. If that happens, Asher and I will have a bigger problem on our hands.

Instead, he tells me, "Thank you."

Thankfully, everything is okay. Although we have to take our time, soon we have Levi in the passenger's seat of my car, and I turn to Asher after I've closed the door behind him.

"Why didn't you let him sleep it off here?"

Asher shrugs. "He asked specifically for you and kept making demands to go and find you. I've been drinking too and didn't want to have to chase him down, and the other guys all left and headed to the bar."

That makes some sense, but I've also now chalked this up to this being the result of everyone involved outside of me drinking too much. "I'll get him home safely."

"He's lucky to have you, you know," he says quietly. "Not many people would have come to his rescue."

"I know," I find myself saying without thinking about it.

With a small nod, Asher walks away, returning to his house and leaving me alone to care for Levi.

Once I walk around the car, get into the driver's seat, and start the engine, I glance at Levi. His eyes are half closed, but he manages to give me a weak smile. I take it as a reassurance that everything is going to be fine, and we'll make it to our destination unscathed.

The drive to Levi's apartment is quick and mostly silent outside of the soft music I have playing in the background. I park as close as I can to his apartment building and help him out of the car. We make it up to his apartment without incident, and I lead him inside. Once there, I guide him over to the sofa and help him sit down gently. He looks up at me and I'm shaken by what I see in his eyes.

Vulnerability.

The typical golden boy façade is gone, replaced by something that is much more raw. Whatever has driven him to this moment has hurt him deeply, and to say I'm concerned is an understatement.

"I'll get you some water and an aspirin to take. Are you

hungry? I can throw something together if you have some ingredients in the fridge?"

What the hell am I doing? I barely know the layout of his apartment and now I'm having to navigate it as if I'm here daily and not just here when we fuck.

Levi winces before he responds. "Sure, that'd be great."

I head for the kitchen, switching on lights as I go. I rummage through his cabinets and fridge, finding ingredients that can help me throw together a simple omelet with some toast. Before I start cooking, I fill a glass with water and grab some aspirin from the bathroom. Once I've handed those things to Levi, I get back to fixing him a quick meal that will help him deal with the alcohol flowing through his system.

When I've finished cooking, I walk back into the living room with the food and find him sitting up on the couch looking down at his hands. Him being able to do that gives me hope that he is starting to sober up.

I place the plate of food on the coffee table in front of him, along with a fork. He looks at it for a long moment before picking up the utensil and starting to eat. I watch him for what feels like eternity before sitting down next to him.

"You want to talk about it?" I offer gently. I'm not sure what else to say.

He shakes his head. "Not tonight," he says.

"Okay," I reply, knowing that pushing him isn't the way to deal with this. Plus, given the state of whatever this is that is going on between us, we probably shouldn't be having this type of conversation anyway.

We sit in silence, the only sounds in the room coming from the occasional clink of the fork against the plate as he scarfs the food down. To be honest, I prefer it because it gives me an opportunity to start thinking about how I feel about all of this.

"Thanks for doing this," Levi's words break through the silence. His voice is stronger now. He doesn't look at me as he speaks, instead concentrating on a small piece of egg he's chasing around his plate with his fork.

"It's no big deal," I reply softly, though it feels like I'm lying to both of us.

He finally looks up at me and I swear my heart stops beating. "No, Hailey, it is a big deal. You didn't have to come."

I brush off his gratitude with a shrug. "Well, someone had to make sure you got home safe."

I decide not to mention that he could have easily stayed with Asher. What's done is done, and now we're at his place. Speaking of, since he's doing better, it's time for me to head back to my home.

"I should go," I say as I stretch my arms in front of me, mentally preparing for the drive back to my place.

"You don't have to," he counters softly, almost too quietly for me to hear.

I pause, slightly confused. "Wait, what?"

Levi puts the fork down and turns to me. He runs the

back of his hand along my jaw, and I shiver against his touch almost immediately. "Please stay."

Our eyes lock, his intense gaze cutting straight through me. It's a stark contrast to the nervous energy he gave off when we first met and the dominant nature he'd showcase in the bedroom. Every fiber of my being tells me to push him away, to uphold the carefully crafted walls I've built. But when I have Levi staring at me as if I'm his lifeline in a chaotic world, I can't say no.

"Okay," I concede. "I'll stay."

31

HAILEY

The next morning, I wake up slowly and peacefully. There isn't a blaring alarm from my phone or someone banging on the front door. It's just me naturally waking up after a full night's rest.

It's strange, yet I love it.

I open my eyes and I notice I'm not alone. Given where I am, it doesn't make sense that I would be.

I turn my head until my eyes land on Levi, who is still sleeping beside me. His chest rises and falls in a steady rhythm, and it seems as if the demons he's fighting when he's awake allow him to rest when he's asleep. My fingers are itching to play with his messy hair, but I refrain, not wanting to disturb him.

I watch him silently, taking in the strong lines of his jaw and the faint stubble. Deciding that I can't spend my time just staring at him while I wait for him to wake up, I slip out of his bed and manage to not wake him up.

I make my way into his kitchen to grab a cup of coffee. I can't help but look through what he has in the way of coffee, and I'm mildly impressed. He has a selection that would make most coffee shops envious, beans from all over the world neatly lined up in mason jars with handwritten labels. I must have missed this last night when I was distracted by his drunken state. I pick out a blend that promises notes of caramel and chocolate because I know it's going to be good.

When did he get this? Not that it matters.

I settle onto a barstool at his kitchen island, the mug warming my hands. I've barely taken my first sip when I hear footsteps against the hardwood floor. Levi comes into view, and I can't help but stare at him. He's definitely still half asleep but looks much better than he did last night.

"Morning," he says, the huskiness in his voice sending an unexpected shiver down my spine. "Not going to lie, I'm surprised you're still here."

"Good morning, and there was no way I was leaving you before I confirmed how you were doing this morning," I reply with a small smile. "I hope you don't mind, I made myself some coffee. I didn't know you had this fancy set up."

He smirks and pulls a mug down from a cabinet. "I didn't until recently."

"Oh really?"

Levi's smirk grows into a full-fledged grin as he pushes the hair from his forehead. "Wanted to impress a certain coffee barista I know as well as make her feel more comfortable at my apartment. Figured coffee might be the way to her heart," he admits, pouring himself a cup and taking a seat next to me.

I can't stop the smile that spreads across my face. "Well, you were right," I admit, taking another sip of my coffee. "This does make me feel more at home."

There's a comfortable silence between us as we both enjoy the peacefulness of the morning. I'm struck by how cozy this all feels, and although I want to tell him this, I fight the urge to break the silence.

"So," he starts, breaking the silence as he turns to me, "about last night..."

I put down my mug, preparing to listen to whatever he is willing to say. "What about it?"

"I just wanted to say thanks. Not only for coming to Asher's but for sticking around afterward. You didn't have to, and I know that." He runs a hand through his hair, pausing as if he's searching for the right words. "Having you there, it meant a lot to me. After having to deal with my father putting me down again, it felt good to have someone there that I felt was there for me and only me."

"Your father is what led to you spiraling last night?"

Levi nods. "I had a bad game, and he was determined to make my evening worse, so I decided to get drunk enough that I didn't have to think."

I stare at him, hoping that he's telling a joke that isn't funny. He's going to say that he's just kidding right?

Wrong. He doesn't say anything to take it back.

"You don't know how much I want to storm over to your parents' house and speak my mind."

"That won't help much."

"You never know if you don't try it. Sometimes I like to watch things burn before asking questions," I say, and I mean every word.

Levi gives me a dry chuckle. "I can see how that would work to your advantage."

"Regardless, as I said last night, it's no big deal," I say, but it's more so me being nervous about where this conversation could be going that has me trying to put another wall up.

This time he leans over to touch me, allowing his hand to hold onto mine. I've quickly learned this is a comfort thing for him. "And as I said, you say it's no big deal, but it is. You didn't have to come last night when I was in the midst of... whatever that was, but you did."

He's right, I didn't have to go to him, but I did. And I'm finally willing to admit that.

"Okay, it was a big deal, mostly because I left the warmth and comfort of my apartment to go to you." I wait a beat to see his reaction and when he shakes his head and smiles, I continue, "But seriously, it's a big deal because not only did you want me in your time of need, but I also wanted to be there for you."

"That means more than you'll ever know. Because I needed you last night. More than I've ever needed anyone else." His hand squeezes mine gently.

I don't pull away or mask my feelings with sarcasm. Instead, I let the connection we share remain because it makes me feel whole. I think it's helping him too.

"Just so you know, all of this is frightening to me. This is supposed to remain a casual thing, Levi."

"I know, but that doesn't mean things can't change if we want them to."

Once again, he's right, and while I'm not too keen on the thought of change, maybe it wouldn't hurt to try. I hesitate before I finally gather enough courage to say the words on the tip of my tongue. "Is this something we want to do?"

The tables have shifted slightly. I feel more vulnerable by asking the question because I'm afraid of his answer.

"So, I talked to Asher yesterday... before everything happened at his place."

I nod and wait for him to continue.

"And he asked me if I would be okay with things between us remaining as they are."

"And? What did you say?"

"I told him I would because if that's the only way I could get you, then that would be enough. But that was a lie."

I swear I can hear my blood pounding in my ears.

There's no doubt in my mind he's going to say that he wants more than just a casual relationship with me.

He takes a deep breath before continuing. "I'm saying that I care about you, Hailey. A lot more than I ever planned to. And I don't want to keep pretending that this is just a casual thing between us. At least on my end."

I'm stunned into silence as I process Levi's words. Is this really happening to me? The sincerity I see in his eyes tells me it is as he waits to hear what I have to say in return.

Part of me wants to pull back, to retreat behind the walls I've built around my heart after having a front-row seat to my mother abandoning her family. But I don't want to run and hide anymore. I owe it to myself to explore this and if it leads to my getting hurt in the process, at least I can say I tried.

"I agree that what's going on between us isn't casual anymore."

Levi raises an eyebrow at me. "Does that mean you're agreeing with me, and you want to see where this goes? On a more serious basis?"

"Yeah. I mean, I can't promise it'll be easy. My issues with trust and commitment won't just disappear overnight." I pause, chewing my lip. "But I want to try. With you."

Levi reaches out, brushing a strand of hair behind my ear. "That's all I'm asking for. We'll take it one step at a time. But I need to do this first."

He lets go of my hand and pulls the stool over so that my legs are now between his. He leans forward and lays a searing kiss on my lips, leaving me breathless.

As we break apart, he rests his forehead against mine.

"I've wanted to do that all morning," he says.

"But you've only just woken up," I reply.

"And I've been wanting to do it since I cracked my eyes open."

I can't help but laugh at him. "Well, I'm glad you finally did. And I'm glad we finally did this," I say, gesturing between the two of us.

"Me too. You know what the next step in taking this one step at a time is?"

"What's that?" I ask as I'm wondering where this is going.

"Ordering breakfast to be delivered. Let me grab my phone," he says as he reaches for the device that either he or I must have put on the kitchen counter when we got back last night.

"So is this what boyfriends do?"

Levi pauses, his hand hovering over his phone on the counter. A slow smile spreads across his face.

"Boyfriend, huh?" He licks his lips. "I like the sound of that."

Heat rises in my cheeks. I meant it casually, testing the word out, but it hits me that I just took a running leap over the ledge into relationship territory.

Levi grins but doesn't try to save me from myself. In

fact, he continues staring at his phone, searching for some place we can order from.

"I mean, we don't have to put a label on it yet if you don't want to," I backtrack quickly, wondering if I took a step too far. Hell, I only threw it out there to see how I liked the sound of it and didn't think before I said it.

"You know," he pauses as he looks up for his phone, "every time I think I've got you figured out, you surprise me in the best possible way."

Levi steps closer, puts his phone down in front of me, but gently cradles my face in his hands. "It's okay. I'm all in on this, Hailey. One hundred percent. And yeah, boyfriend does sound nice."

My heart flutters hearing him say it outright like that. I try to play it cool, shrugging my shoulders.

"Oh, alright then. Boyfriend it is."

Levi laughs, drawing me in for another long kiss. When we finally break apart, he keeps his arms wrapped loosely around my waist.

"As your new boyfriend, it's my duty to make sure you're fed. Pick what you want and I'm going to run to the bathroom real quick."

"Sounds good to me," I say as I grab his phone and he leaves the room. As I'm scanning the menu, Levi receives a text message from a group chat called Ice Kings and it doesn't stop going off. Part of me knows I shouldn't do it, but I click the notification anyway.

Group Chat: Ice Kings

Wilder: Morning, guys! Cap, you alive after last night?

Knox: Dude, let him breathe. Probably still sleeping.

Wilder: True, but you know, just checking in.

Blaise: Are you though?

Asher: Actually, Levi's fine. Made sure he got home okay.

Wilder: Oh? And how do you know that?

Asher: Because I was there. Hailey was too.

Knox: Hailey? Barista Hailey?

Wilder: Wait, back up. Hailey was at your place?

Asher: Yep. She helped Levi get home because I wasn't in any condition to.

Blaise: ...

Wilder: Well shit.

Knox: Let's not make a big deal out of it.

Asher: Exactly. It's Levi's business, not ours.

Blaise: Agreed.

Wilder: Alright, alright. Just hope he's doing good. The state he was in before we left was...

Asher: He's fine. Trust me.

"Did you figure out what you wanted to eat?"

I jump two feet in the air at the question and place my hand on my heart. "Make a little noise, why don't you?"

"Sorry about scaring you," he says as he sits back down in the barstool he'd abandoned.

"And I'm sorry that I checked your text messages. One of your group chats was going off and making it hard to concentrate on ordering food."

"Which group chat?"

"One labeled Ice Kings."

Levi shrugs. "Typical."

Since I'm clearly on a winning streak, I continue. "Your teammates know I'm here."

"Is that a concern for you?"

"I'm not sure if I'm being honest."

Levi places his hand on my knee before he says, "Their opinions don't mean a thing to me. Only you do. Now let's finish ordering food."

His nonchalant attitude about the whole thing put me at ease and that is all I can ask for at this moment.

And some food.

Definitely some food.

32

HAILEY

I never thought I would look forward to going to my therapist's office, but I do. It could be because I love our conversations, or it could be because Charlie is here, and I love hanging with him while I wait for Emily to call me back.

"Hey, buddy," I say as I place my bag into a chair to my left before I drop to my knees.

His soft fur slides through my fingers as I move my hand, giving him plenty of pets. He bumps his nose against my hand in a friendly hello. Just being here with him dials down the chaos in my head. He adjusts his head so that it's resting on his head on my knee like he knows I need this.

"Hailey?"

Emily's voice pulls me from my moment with Charlie. I give him one last pat before standing up and turning to face her. I grab my bag and follow her into the office, leaving Charlie behind.

The moment I sit down across from her, I do feel more calm, and what a pleasant feeling that is.

Emily gives me a bright smile as she settles in the chair across from me. "How's everything going? Are things going well with your dad? You look super happy."

"I feel happy, so I guess it's shining through. I'll start with my dad. Things are getting better there. He's actively dating and he's happy, which is what I wanted most of all."

"And has it changed your relationship with him in any way?"

"It has," I admit, folding my hands in my lap. "At first, as you know, I was really worried about how his dating would affect us. But seeing him happy has helped me see things differently. Our relationship has actually gotten stronger. We're more open with each other now."

"That's a significant shift, it sounds like you're coming to terms with change, both in your father's life and your own. Does this influence your feelings when it comes to Levi?"

"I think so because we are officially dating now," I announce.

Emily's eyebrows raise slightly with surprise, but her smile doesn't shift. "That's wonderful news. How are you feeling about this new development?"

I tuck a strand of hair behind my ear and let out a deep breath. "Excited, but still nervous because this is all so new. We're keeping things low key for now, which works for me. The thought of his... celebrity for lack of a better word, still makes me concerned."

"It's perfectly normal to be apprehensive about what you don't know since none of us can predict the future. But it seems like you're handling things well by setting boundaries that make you comfortable."

"Yeah, I guess you could say that. I've also been debating going to one of his hockey games."

"That's a big step given what you've mentioned before. Is this because of the change in your relationship status?"

I play with the hem of my sweater as I consider how I want to answer the question. Finally, the words come to me although they aren't as elegant as I would like. "It's a bit of that, and I want to be there for him. His mother hardly attends his games anymore and his father is an asshole to him. He doesn't have someone who roots for him in the crowd that he knows personally, and I want to be that person."

"That's thoughtful of you and it sounds like you're willing to step outside your comfort zone for Levi. Make sure you're also taking care of your own needs in the process."

I nod, because isn't that what I've been trying to find all along? Balance. The tightrope between following my routines and trying something new. This is definitely veering into the territory of throwing myself into the deep end though.

"I think it's important for me to try. Levi has his own struggles, especially with the loss of his brother and the pressure he's under as a result. His dad is... it's a lot. And I might not understand everything about hockey or the fans, but I get what it's like to feel alone surrounded by people."

Those words hit me harder than I thought they would and the fact that they came out of my mouth says a lot. I hate that I understand the feeling of being alone, to be abandoned by the person who is supposed to love you the most.

I can see the gears turning in her mind as she processes what I've said. "What I'm about to say might sound strange but hear me out. Sharing someone else's burdens doesn't mean you have to carry them. Remember, it's about offering support, not fixing everything."

I take in a slow breath and let it out. Fixing things has always been my go-to. It is a coping mechanism, making me feel as if I have control in a life that was filled by chaos after my mother left. But she's right; I can't patch up Levi's past any more than I can change my own.

"I think I'm going to talk Jade about going, and if I finally decide to do it, keep it a surprise from Levi. No matter the outcome of his game, I hope that my presence there will make his day brighter." Having a tentative plan helps with my anxiety about all of this.

"That's a great idea. During our next session, you can tell me what you decided, and if you did go, how it went."

"Thank you," I say as I stand. "I'll definitely have a lot to talk about next time."

As I step out of Emily's office and walk toward my apartment, the only thing on my mind is Levi and this hockey game. There is little doubt in my mind that Jade is going to encourage me to go, but she'll have my back no matter what I decide to do.

By the time I reach my door, I'm pretty sure I know my decision about the hockey game, but I'm ready to chat with Jade. I unlock the door and the first words out of my mouth are, "Jade? Are you home?"

"Yeah! I'm in my room. Give me a second."

I take off my outer gear, hang it up, and drop my bag near my bedroom door. While I'm doing this, I hear some shuffling before Jade emerges from her room. Her curly black hair is pulled up in a ponytail and she's wearing an oversized black sweatshirt and dark gray leggings.

"What's up?" she asks, plopping down on the couch.

I take a seat next to her. "So, I had therapy today and talked to my therapist about going to one of Levi's hockey games. Maybe surprise him?"

Jade's eyes grow wide. "Whoa, really? That would be a huge step for you."

"Yeah, it's kind of scary for me to think about being there, but I want to support him. He works so hard, and his family... is pretty shit at cheering him on. Well... at least his father is."

"Aw, that's really sweet of you," Jade says. "I'm sure he would love it if you went. I'll go with you too! It'll be fun."

I smile, thankful that she also wants to come. Not that I thought she wouldn't. "That would be amazing. But I'd need to figure out a way to keep a low profile. I don't want the spotlight on me whatsoever, and there's already been some chatter about us being a thing."

Jade taps her chin thoughtfully. "Hmm, good point. Let me think about what we could do..."

We sit there in silence as I join her in trying to figure out a way we can be more incognito. It's hilarious that we are spending this much time thinking about it while we probably have more important things to do, but it is what it is.

Out of the corner of my eye, I see Jade jerk as if someone has scared her, and then she turns to me. Her movements cause me to give her my full and undivided attention, and I notice that her eyes widen before she jumps up and sprints out of the room.

"What the..." I mumble to myself before I yell out, "Jade? What happened? What are you doing?"

"Give me a second. I'll be right back."

This is the most déjà vu thing I've experienced in a while, but I don't say a word. Instead, I wait for her to come back, and when she does, she has her phone in hand.

"What's up and am I going to need a drink for this?"

That forces a laugh from Jade. "No? I don't think so at least."

I try to tame my involuntary reaction to it, but goose-bumps appear on the back of my neck. "I don't like the sound of this."

"I promise it will be fine," Jade says as she waves me off, but her eyes don't veer from her phone.

"So you're not going to tell me what this is all about?"

Jade looks up from her phone and I can see the excitement in her eyes. That has me concerned even after she starts speaking. "Okay, so I think I figured out a way we can go to the game and not draw any attention."

Her phone buzzes in her hand before she turns her phone screen to face me. I realize she's showing me a text message conversation between her and Wilder.

> Jade: Hey, can I ask you a favor?

> Wilder: Depends... and you might owe me depending on what it is.

> Jade: If Hailey and I wanted to attend a game without drawing attention to her, how could we do this? Also this is a surprise for Levi so DON'T tell him.

> **Wilder:** What if you and Hailey wear jerseys (pick someone besides Levi) and wear baseball caps? That way you'll blend in with the crowd more. I can give you one of mine and I'll grab someone else's along with tickets to the game. Levi won't suspect anything. And don't worry, I'll keep all of this quiet.:)

> **Jade:** OMG Wilder you're a genius!! I knew we could count on you. Thank you!!

> **Wilder:** You're welcome and you owe me.

My eyes widen. "That's actually brilliant. As rude as this sounds, I'm surprised he came up with it."

Jade beams at me. "Right? He really came through."

"What are you going to owe him for this?"

She shrugs. "He always says things like that and never mentions it again. I'm not worried about it."

I tilt my head because I find this weird. "As long as you're fine with it, I guess."

Jade places her phone screen side down on the coffee table before looking back at me. "So what do you think? Want to do it?"

I don't say a word about the obvious change in subject. Instead, I can't help but laugh at how dramatic this all is, but hey, it just might work. I take a deep breath, feeling the nerves and excitement swirling within me. "Let's do it. But I still might need a drink in order to pull this off."

33

HAILEY

I've lost count of the number of deep breaths I've taken within the last ten minutes, but they've been warranted. I'm about to walk into the Crestwood Arena for the first time ever.

Every inhale is an attempt to prevent my heart from slamming into my chest, but it does little to help. As I leave the cold air and walk inside the warmer venue, the butterflies in my stomach only increase. Why does it feel as if the chances of me making it out of this without suffering from a panic attack are slim to none?

To stop myself from dwelling on it too much, I tuck a piece of my hair behind my ear, feeling slightly self-conscious because I had to wear my hair down due to the baseball cap on my head.

Jade grips my arm and I can feel every bit of her

excitement although she's trying to keep it under wraps. "Are you doing okay?"

"I'm surviving." Thankfully, no one is paying attention to me, which is the exact thing I wanted.

"Okay, let's find our seats."

As we navigate through the sea of red and white jerseys and other merchandise, I can't help but feel like an impostor with Asher's last name stretched across my back. It's like wearing a disguise, and part of me wonders if it's overly dramatic for me to do this. But I'll take the sliver of confidence it is giving me.

Jade finds our seats near the ice, courtesy of Wilder, giving us an up-close view of the action. The sound of hockey sticks clinking and pucks slamming against the boards fills the arena as the Crestwood Red Wolves wrap up their warm-up before taking on the West Haven Stallions. It doesn't take me long to find Levi, and once I do, I can't take my eyes off him.

While I know nothing about hockey, the best way I can describe Levi is that he looks to be a force of nature on ice. There is a power in the way he moves, and I'm able to notice it even before a second of the official game is played.

Then, almost like he can sense that someone is staring at him, Levi's gaze flicks up to the stands and locks onto mine. I soon learn that my heart rate isn't at its maximum speed because it picks up speed again. He breaks into his signature smirk until his eyes catch on to Asher's number written across my jersey instead of his. I swear I see a flash of something like annoyance cross his features before he turns back to the game. I'm left wondering if he really recognized me or if it is wishful thinking on my part.

The blare of the starting buzzer snatches away the quiet moment. The crowd erupts as both teams take their positions on the ice. Jade leans over, her words barely audible over the cheers. "I think he saw you! And did you see that look?"

"Yeah, I saw it," I mutter, trying to maintain any sense of decorum because I'm completely flustered. The look he gave me afterward is one that he's given me several times before. It haunts my dreams because it means he's about to fuck me into another dimension. If I continue to focus on that look, there's no way I'm going to be able to pay attention to this game without thinking about running onto the ice and letting him have me anyway he wants.

What has he turned me into?

With a shaky breath, I brush the thought away as the game begins.

If I thought the arena was alive before the match officially started, it's absolutely on fire now, that being ironic since we are at an ice rink. I take in the action on the ice and am impressed by the agility of the players. My attention, however, is repeatedly drawn to Levi as he maneuvers past defenders with ease. His skill as a player blows me away and helps paint an even bigger picture of the man I've come to know.

The period breaks are a chance for everyone to breathe, including me. I never realized how intense hockey could be, nor did I expect to be so invested. Jade's animated commentary fills in gaps in my knowledge, and I'm grateful for her enthusiasm and for her being here.

As the final period approaches, I'm more tense than I've been in forever. We are deadlocked with the Stallions, and I don't know which way this is going to go. To say I'm nervous is an understatement.

Despite my initial reluctance to even attend, my voice joins everyone else's in the arena shouting encouragement and chanting, "Let's go Red Wolves!"

When the final buzzer sounds, it's a narrow win for Crestwood, and the arena explodes into cheers. Levi's face is flushed but the happiness and excitement is obvious as he raises his stick to the fans. My heart does somersaults as pride swells so fiercely within me. He's done it. The team has done it.

When we grab our things and start weaving through the crowd, Jade nudges me with her shoulder. "Come on, let's go congratulate them!"

"Is that something we can do?"

Jade gives me a big grin. "Of course!"

We make our way down toward the locker rooms where family and friends are already gathered. It takes a bit, but soon, Levi emerges, his hair damp and his eyes scanning the crowd until they settle on me. A mixture of emotions plays across his face that I can't quite figure out.

Ignoring the sea of people around him, he makes a beeline toward where I'm standing with Jade. I swallow hard and I'm even more nervous about what he might say than when I walked into the arena.

"Hey," Levi says when he reaches me. I can hear the exhaustion in his voice. "Jade, do you mind if I talk to Hailey alone for a moment? Wilder is looking for you and he was behind me last I saw."

"I'll go find him. Congrats on the win," Jade says.

"Thanks," Levi responds before turning his attention back to me.

"Hey, yourself," I reply once Jade is out of earshot, trying to ignore how his damp hair makes him look even more attractive. How is this even possible? I clear my throat and say, "You were great out there."

He flashes me a grin that could stop my heart if it wanted to. "Thanks, Rook." His eyes flicker down to the jersey I'm wearing, and his smile lessens. He leans toward me and says, "I don't want to see you wearing his number again."

Normally, someone saying that to me would have pissed me off. How dare he tell me what to do? But the look in his eyes and the tone of his voice, meant only for me, makes me want him more. "I was trying to be incognito. You know people are looking at us, probably talking trash about us."

"You're doing pretty well with the attention we're getting right now. To me, it makes sense for us to make this more public. I want people to know you're mine. Cause seeing you in anything but my jersey is making me see red and not in a good way."

I almost make a joke about him seeing red and the jerseys also being the same color, but now isn't the time. Because everything about this shows me how serious Levi is about all of this.

"Fine. Make sure that I have the proper attire to wear to your games then."

The grin returns to his face. "Yes, ma'am, but you're going to pay for all of this later. You have no idea how much it meant to see you here tonight."

I'm stunned by his confession, but I'm happy he shared it with me. However, what did he mean by me paying for this later? "I didn't want to miss it. Being here for you is the only thing that mattered to me," I tell him honestly.

Before I can ask him about his other comment, a look of relief washes over his face and he pulls me into a hug. I hate that the hug is brief, but it needs to be given where we are. As he steps back, he keeps one hand on my arm like he isn't quite ready to let go completely.

Our moment with one another in this crowded space is short-lived though. Levi looks away from me and I watch as his posture stiffens immediately. Based on where we are and his reaction, I can guess who is behind me without turning around.

"Good game tonight," a voice says behind me,

prompting me to pivot and come face-to-face with a man who is unmistakably an older version of Levi. His features are sharper, more defined than his son's. His hair, once likely the same rich brown as Levi's, has faded to silver at the temples and is slicked back. They both have similar blue eyes but his have an icy undertone that Levi's warmer gaze lacks. His height and broad shoulders remind me of Levi's athletic build, yet I would best describe him as having a stick up his ass versus his son's relaxed posture. That is, until his father showed up.

"Thanks, Dad," Levi replies. I watch as Levi's jaw clenches tightly and it's taking everything in my power not to drag him away from whatever this is about to become. It isn't lost on me that his father didn't try to introduce himself to me and neither did Levi.

"You've still got work to do on your defensive positioning in the neutral zone. And your breakouts were sloppy at times," Mr. Jamison states.

Levi takes a slow breath before responding. "I appreciate the feedback. My defensive play is something I'm focusing on improving."

His father gives a curt nod. "See that you do. Can't have the captain slacking off."

I resist the urge to jump to Levi's defense. This is his battle to fight, and I need to remember that. After all, like Emily said, I don't need to fix his problems, but I can be there to offer support.

"I know you want what's best for me and the team. But

I need you to trust that I'm putting in the work. I'll keep improving, but I can't let your criticism shake my confidence either. I know my capabilities. What you don't realize is that I'm not Caleb and I'm never going to be him."

I hold my breath as Levi stands up to his father. I can only imagine how difficult this is for him. Mr. Jamison's eyes narrow slightly at Levi's words, and he crosses his arms over his chest.

"You're right, you're not your brother," Mr. Jamison says after a tense pause. "But that doesn't mean I'm going to lower my expectations of you. You have potential, and I want to see you reach it."

Levi shakes his head. "I know you do. But you need to back off."

"All I'm asking you to be is the best version of yourself. And sometimes, that means pushing you harder than you might like."

Levi shakes his head. "But at what cost? I'm out there on the ice, giving it my all, not for me, but for an idea of what you think I should be. It's exhausting and I feel like I'm always falling short."

There's a shift in Mr. Jamison's stance. "I'll think about what you've said."

I get the feeling this isn't enough for Levi, but based on what Levi has told me, this might be the first step forward they've ever had.

"Okay." Levi doesn't elaborate further, choosing to

hold back even though I can see that there is more he wants to say.

Mr. Jamison leans forward and puts his hand on Levi's shoulder for a moment before his eyes land on me. He gives me a swift nod before turning on his heel and walking away. We're left watching him leave until Levi lets out the deepest exhale, forcing my attention toward him.

"Let's get out of here," Levi says as he finds my hand and grabs it.

"That's fine... but what about Jade? She and I arrived together."

"Text her and let her know I'm going to take you home. She's with Wilder anyway so she's fine. You need to pay up, Rook."

34

LEVI

There has been no doubt in my mind that it would all come down to this.

I squeeze Hailey's hand before letting it go and having it join my other hand on the steering wheel. As I drive down the mostly deserted road, the lights of the arena have long faded from my rearview mirror, but the confrontation with my father is still in the front of my mind.

Enough was enough for a while and it was about time I'd stood up to him. What I hadn't expected to happen was that Hailey would be there when I did.

"I'm sorry you had to see that," I murmur, breaking the silence between us. It isn't something I wanted her to witness. Part of me wants to look over at her, but it would be hard to read the expression on her face given how dark it is.

"It's okay," she whispers back. "I'm so proud of you for standing up for yourself and not letting him continue to walk all over you."

"Thanks. It was a long time coming and I'm happy that I finally did it."

The silence that falls in the car after I speak gives me time to dig into my thoughts. Reflecting on the events, I'm struck by the irony of it all. I've always stayed in the roles that I was supposed to—the impeccable athlete, the loyal son and brother, the devoted captain. Yet, in the heat of the moment, I tossed all of those things to the side to showcase what I needed to say, without fear of retribution.

I tap along to a beat in my head, quickly figuring out that it's another Taylor Swift song that I can't get out of my head. My thoughts drift away from my father because I've spent enough time on him.

Instead, they latch onto Hailey, which is where I rather they be. To say seeing her at the game was a surprise is an understatement. I know coming tonight was a lot for her, and while she's proud of me, I'm the same for her.

Even if she is wearing Asher's jersey.

I still need to get my payback for that. Maybe the time for it is sooner rather than later. I press my foot down on the gas as I pass the exit that would lead us back to Hailey's apartment.

"Where are we going?" Her question lets me know that she is paying attention. Good.

"Hmmm?" I pretend like I didn't hear what she said.

It's the kind of sound that's more of a vibration in my throat than an actual word.

"Where are we going?" she repeats, but a little more seriously this time.

"Just thought we could use a little detour," I say, as if it's the most natural thing in the world to switch things up without explanation. I look at her for a split second before turning my attention back to the road.

"Levi Jamison, are you kidnapping me?"

The way she says my name is all drawn out, but I can hear the laughter in her voice.

I chuckle, keeping my gaze on the dark stretch of road ahead. "Only in the most romantic sense of the term. Is that something that appears in one of your romance novels?"

"Possibly," she says in a teasing tone. "Have you been reading my books?"

"Not yet, but I'm not opposed to it."

"Seriously?" she asks as if she doesn't believe me.

"Yeah, because it'll allow me to learn more about you, what you like and need."

Her laughter forces me to take another glance at her. She's thrown her head back against the headrest and her right hand has landed on her heart.

A thought appears in my mind, something I've been thinking of for a while but need to get out now. "You know something? Winning hockey games makes me happy, but seeing you laugh like that blows everything else out of the water. Your smile is my victory, Rook."

She's silent for a moment, and when she finally speaks, her voice is softer than I expect. "You can't just say things like that, Levi."

"But I did and there's nothing you can do to take it back," I say, as I take a left and turn down a road that is covered with trees on both sides. The road eventually opens up to a clearing with a view of Crestwood in the distance. I pull over but leave the engine on to keep the heat low in the car before turning to Hailey.

"What is this place?" Hailey asks as she watches the scene before her.

"A quiet spot that I discovered when I missed a turn one day. I come back here sometimes when I want to think, and I want to share the place with you."

I unbuckle my seat belt and shift to face her more directly, taking in the expression on her face. The moon-light casts a soft glow on her face and that damn jersey. I'm determined to get it off her as soon as possible.

"You have five seconds to take that jersey off." My eyes study Asher's number before my gaze lands on hers once more.

"Wait a minute. I—"

"One." She's not going to be happy with me cutting her off, but we'll deal with it later.

"You can't be serious."

"I'm very serious. Two."

Hailey folds her arms over her chest. "I'm not doing a damn thing."

"Three."

"You can stop counting, Levi."

"Four."

"Make me," she says with a smirk as she changes tactics.

The look on her face tells me she's proud of herself, thinking that she's winning because she refuses to obey my order. That's okay though. If she wants to act like a brat, I'll treat her like one.

"Five."

The smirk on her face dims for a second, showing that she's suddenly not sure whether she's made the right choice or not. But she can't turn back time and now needs to deal with the consequences.

I don't waste any time unbuckling her seat belt and reaching for the hem of her jersey. She shrieks and tries to stop me, but I'm faster, yanking the offending article of clothing over her head and discarding it on the floor of the front seat.

She's left in the hoodie that she's worn underneath it and the rest of the clothes she wore to the game. They will all be gone soon enough too.

"Get in the back seat."

"What if I—"

"Now isn't the time to argue with me, Rook. Unless you don't want me to fuck you until you can't stand anymore."

Hailey's eyes widen before she realizes that they are, and I'm left holding back a laugh because of the new expression on her face. I wonder if she's going to fight me on this too.

I'm shocked to watch her freak out briefly before almost throwing herself into the back seat, which I'm impressed she manages to do without stepping out of the car. I, on the other hand, know the chances of me making it to the back seat in the same matter are slim to none so I opt to use my doors.

I slide in beside her and once the overhead light is off, we're surrounded by darkness besides the lights that are coming from Crestwood. The only thing that matters is her.

I move a piece of hair out of her face, allowing myself to stare at her beauty that is illuminated by the soft lights from a world that seems so far away now. Her eyes showcase a mixture of softness and fire, something that makes Hailey uniquely her. I lean closer, letting my lips brush against her, giving her a taste of what is about to come.

"Stop playing with me, Jamison."

I grin at her use of my last name. "Why, when it's so fun to do so?"

"Because I want to experience this payback that you speak of. Making me pay for wearing Asher's jersey." Lust is evident in her eyes and now I'm more than determined to make her eyes roll into the back of her head before this evening ends.

"Remember you asked for this." With that, our lips meet in haste as if we're trying to make up for lost time. Her hands roam over my chest, gripping the hoodie that I'd thrown on after the game while my hands land on her waist and pull her closer.

Hailey pulls away for air as she gasps for breath. "Someone might see us."

"We're alone, Rook. And if someone tried to so much as glance at you at this point in our relationship, I'll knock them the fuck out."

My mouth trails from her lips down to her neck, enjoying the little gasps and moans that flee her lips because of what I'm doing. My sole purpose right now is to make sure that I keep her on the edge of her seat and make her come.

The sounds she's making urge me forward and all I want to do is hear her get louder and louder. "Lose the jeans."

"You can at least say please. Manners are important."

"The only manners I care about is you screaming 'please' while you beg me to fuck you. Lose the jeans, Rook."

She gives me a look that screams defiance and desire at the same time. She's not one to back down easily, but tonight, I can tell she's into playing this game as much as I am. With a playful huff, she undoes her belt and jeans in slow motion, drawing out the moment. Her jeans slip down inch by agonizing inch, but I don't say a word. Soon, the buckle of her belt clinks faintly as it hits the floorboard, and her pants and shoes are off her body.

Since she's determined to test my patience, this time I use my hands to move to her sweater and it takes me a second to find the hem and start pushing it up. Hailey is more than willing to help me because she lifts her arms without hesitation, and soon I'm throwing the piece of clothing somewhere else in the car. What I don't realize until a few seconds later is that I took off the t-shirt she had on underneath as well, saving both of us even more time.

I grab her around the waist, and she squeals as I gently lift her and place her on my lap. Her breasts are now inches from me; the white lace bra cups aren't doing a thing to hide the fact that her nipples are already hard and begging for my attention. I hook my fingers on the straps, pulling them down with ease and exposing her perfect breasts.

She is mine. All mine.

I brush my lips along her collarbone before putting one of her hardened nipples into my mouth. She moans out my name, gripping the headrest, letting me know this is exactly where she wants to be for the time being. I can do this all night, but Hailey's rocking her hips against my jeans, begging for more contact between us.

I take the hint and one of my hands finds its way to her

hip, guiding her movements. It's definitely a mistake because this is only increasing the likelihood that I'm going to bust my load in my sweatpants.

"Levi, please," she says when I switch nipples, making sure I give it the same amount of attention.

I stop sucking on her breast to say, "Ah there are those good manners."

She starts to laugh, but it quickly turns into a gasp when her nipple ends up back in my mouth. Point one to me for making her speechless.

My hand drifts down until it touches her panties. I can feel her wetness through the fabric, and she grinds into my hand. I debate whether I want to tease her through her underwear, but I'm too impatient. I want her on my cock as much as she wants to be on it, and the teasing would only prolong the inevitable.

I push her panties to the side and slide a finger between her slick folds, drawing a long moan from deep in her throat. Hailey arches her back, thrusting her tits into my face. I can't resist and flick one of her nipples with my tongue.

As I continue to explore her with my fingers, a sudden realization hits me. The heat of the moment almost made me forget about safety precautions. I pull back reluctantly because I'm not as prepared as I thought I was. "Fuck. I'm going to need to get a condom out of my bag."

"Don't worry about it. I'm clean and have the shot."

"I'm clean as well. Got checked about a week before we met. Are you sure about this?"

She responds by pulling my face to hers for a searing kiss that says more than words ever could. When we surface for air, she whispers against my lips, "I've never been more certain of anything."

It's all the convincing I need. My hands reach the front of my sweatpants, and once Hailey lifts up, I push them and my boxer briefs down just enough to free myself.

I can't take my eyes off her as she positions herself above me. I hold my breath as I guide myself to her pussy, and once I'm in position, Hailey sinks down onto me slowly. She begins to move, and I can tell she's trying to pace herself, but her body is betraying her. Her hips start moving involuntarily, and I get the feeling that she's about to try to take all of me at once.

"Fuck," I groan out, my hands instinctively gripping her hips to steady her and to control the pace. Being inside her without a condom is a completely different feeling, something I know I'll be addicted to. "You're so damn tight."

All she can do is moan as she continues to move, finding a rhythm that forces both of us to lose our breath. I watch her, first her tits as she bounces up and down on my dick, before my stare makes its way up to hers. Her eyes are locked on mine, and there's a wildness in them that makes me want to toss her on this seat and fuck her harder.

Instead, I decide she's in control and this is her show. But I can't stop myself from meeting her halfway, thrusting up into her from below. The chokehold her pussy has on me is driving to the brink, but I'm trying to hold back in order for this to last for both of us.

"Faster," she whispers hoarsely, and I comply without hesitation.

Our movements become more frantic, desperate even. The sound of skin slapping against skin grows louder, but I can barely hear it over the sound of our panting and moans.

Her hands find my shoulders, giving her something to hold on while she's riding me. I'm drunk on the feeling of having her on top of me. With every move, she matches my intensity like she does in life. This is why we fit together so well, and I'm determined to do whatever it takes to make this work.

Her breaths are short now, like she can't catch her breath. "Levi," she throws out, "I'm close."

Hearing her say that is my undoing. I tighten the grip I have on her waist with a newfound determination for us both to reach our orgasms, but she needs to get hers first. Her nails dig into my shoulders, and I welcome the sting they leave behind.

"Come for me, baby. Come for me," I say, demanding that she gives me the orgasm she more than deserves.

As if my words start the revolution, her whole body shakes as she comes undone above me.

Her climax triggers mine, and I follow right after her, a low groan tearing from my throat as pleasure washes over me in waves. We cling to each other, our bodies still joined as aftershocks ripple through us both.

For a long moment afterward, we're too spent to move. Hailey's head rests against my chest while her breathing slowly returns to normal. My fingers trace lazy circles on her back, skin slick with a thin sheen of sweat from the activities we partook in. The heat in the car is almost suffocating now, but neither of us makes a move to change anything.

There's some cleaning that will need to be done and clothes that will need to be put back on, but for now, the only thing I care about is having her in my arms. It's at this moment I realize how hard I've fallen for her.

There's no doubt in my mind that I love her, but I can't tell her right now because she's going to think it's because we've just had sex. So I keep the words to myself, promising to tell her sometime soon even though the thought of her not feeling the same is terrifying.

But not ever telling her feels a whole lot worse.

35

HAILEY

The next week, I watch as the last customer for the evening finally leaves; the jingle of the bell over the door signaling the end of my shift.

I made it through this unscathed.

I let out a long sigh, feeling the stress from the day lessen somewhat as I start to close up Brewed Beginnings.

The quietness of the café at this time of night is soothing, a world away from what I experience in the morning. During my regular shift, the quiet in the mornings is just the calm before the storm, whereas now, this is almost zen-like. Well it would be if I wasn't working. The only reason I'm here is because another coworker took off due to exams and I could use the extra shift. Thankfully, Jenna and a couple more people are also working this shift too.

I wipe down the front counter with a rag that's seen

better days, moving on autopilot as I think about the chess event that I'm putting on at Oak Terrace this weekend. I can't believe the time has finally come, but to say I'm nervous is an understatement.

"Hey, Hailey, can you mop the floors as well?" Marc calls out from the back, breaking my concentration temporarily.

"Sure thing," I reply without looking up, not in the mood for one of his trademark snarky exchanges. I go back to work, choosing to zone out instead of having to think about Marc for one more second. I wonder if Levi's busy right now. I'll call him on the way back to my apartment.

"Hailey? Are you listening?" Marc stands near me now, his arms crossed as if he's been waiting for me to look at him for a while.

"Of course," I lie, glancing up to meet his gaze.

"I'm transferring," he says abruptly, "to a new Brewed Beginnings location that will be opening soon."

"Transferring?" The word repeats in my head and I'm not sure how to feel. No more dealing with Marc's attitude on the daily? That could be a win. But who would replace him? I can't decide if I should be worried or throw a mini celebration right here, right now.

"I'm helping the new location launch because of the success of this location." He shrugs, as if it's no big deal. "Anyway, I thought you should know. I've already told everyone else."

"Right," I say, keeping my face neutral. What does this mean for me? For everyone currently working at Brewed Beginnings?

"Try not to look too happy about it," Marc adds. "I'll still be around temporarily until the transition is complete and we have another manager in place here."

A memory from when Levi dropped me off at work one morning pops into my mind. When I was bitching about Marc, he said something along the lines of, "Something should be done about him." Is this something Levi has a hand in? I can't let Marc know that I suspect something, so I focus on his initial news.

"How could I?" I shoot back, the sarcasm rolling off my tongue. But inside, my mind is spinning. Marc is an ass, sure, but he's the devil I know. Who knows what kind of fresh hell a new manager might bring?

"Good luck, I guess," I offer halfheartedly as he grabs his jacket and heads for the door. What the hell do you say to the person who has tried to make your life a living hell since you arrived now that they're leaving?

"Thanks. Have a good night... I guess?" And with that, he's gone.

As the door closes behind Marc, silence once again falls over Brewed Beginnings. That is until I hear Jenna's voice coming from the seating area, where she's clearing the last few tables.

"Was that Marc leaving for the night? I can't believe he's leaving for good!" Jenna calls out.

"Yeah, he's gone," I say back.

Jenna laughs as she peeks out from the kitchen. "Do you think jumping for joy would be too much?"

That makes me chuckle. "It might be. After all, he isn't gone yet. I don't trust him not to pull a fast one on us."

I toss the rag under the counter and walk to the back to grab the mop and bucket. As I begin to sweep it across the floor, I hesitate when the bell above the door chimes again. I glance up, expecting to see Marc returning or a customer ignoring the fact that we're closed. Instead, I'm shocked to find Levi standing there, looking completely disheveled.

"What's wrong?" I ask immediately, propping the mop against a wall before making my way toward him.

However he doesn't say a word. He meets me halfway and pulls me into his chest, holding onto me as if I'm his only lifeline. I decide that this is what he needs at this moment, so I don't try to get him to speak to me immediately. If this hug helps soothe him, then so be it.

We stand there for what feels like an eternity but is probably only a couple of minutes. I can hear someone's soft footsteps coming closer to us, but they stop short, and I hear them walk away again.

Finally, Levi's grip on me lessens just enough for me to pull back and look up at him. His blue eyes showcase a storm that is brewing, and I realize he's been holding back tears. I let out a shaky breath and brace for what he's about to tell me.

"It's my dad," he finally says, his voice hoarse. "He had a heart attack."

"Is he okay? What can I do?" My questions tumble out one over the other. I'm not sure I'm even making sense.

"I—I don't know yet. He's at St. Mary's. Mom couldn't tell me much over the phone outside of him being alive." He runs a hand through his hair and it's obvious that he's been pulling on the strands.

Without a second thought, I start walking toward the back and my eyes land on Jenna. "I'm coming with you," I decide.

"But you need to close up..." Levi starts to protest, but it's half-assed.

He needs me and I want to be there for him.

"Zac and I can take care of everything else," Jenna says.

"Thank you so much and I'll make it up to you both." I don't know if I've ever been more grateful.

Jenna waves me off. "Don't worry about it, Hailey. Just go."

I grab my bag and coat before hurrying back to Levi. We don't say a word as we leave Brewed Beginnings, but his hand finds mine and grips it tightly until we reach his SUV.

"Do you need me to drive?" I ask, hoping to take something off his plate.

"No, I got it," he says in a clipped tone, but I don't take it personally.

The drive to St. Mary's is a blur. For a guy who's usually so in control on the ice, seeing him this vulnerable has me freaking out, but I'm trying to remain strong for him. As we pull into the hospital parking lot, my heart lands in my throat as I stare at the big building we're about to walk into. We quickly get out of the car, and he grabs my hand as we walk through the sliding glass doors that welcome us into a completely different world.

I'm looking around, trying to take in my surroundings when I hear Levi mumble, "Mom."

I turn to see where he's looking and follow his gaze to where I find a woman dressed in a cream-colored Chanel suit with pearls around her neck. She looks more like she's about to attend a meeting or a dinner party than sit in a hospital waiting room. Mrs. Jamison's eyes are red-rimmed, betraying the calm façade she's trying to maintain.

Levi squeezes my hand for a split second before we walk over to her. "Mom, this is Hailey."

She gives me a small watery smile before she pulls her son in for a hug. Although I can't hear anything, based on how her shoulders are shaking, I can see that she's crying. I awkwardly hang back, not wanting to interrupt the moment between mother and son because it isn't my place. They deserve it.

After a minute, Mrs. Jamison releases Levi, uses a tissue to wipe her tears from her eyes and turns to me, extending a perfectly manicured hand. "My name is Ella Jamison. Thank you for being here," she says, her voice as controlled as her appearance.

"There's no other place I could be right now," I say as I shake her hand.

She nods but turns her focus back to Levi. "They said we should hear something soon."

Levi passes a hand over his face and lets out a deep sigh. Instinctively, my hand finds his and holds onto him. It's a small gesture of support, and I hope it reminds him that he's not alone in all of this.

We all sit down and wait for who knows how long, but when a nurse approaches us, we jump up.

"Are you here for Mr. Jamison?" she asks, her voice gentle yet professional.

"Yes, we are," Mrs. Jamison replies.

"I need you to come with me."

Levi joins his mother and stands up, but I remain behind. Levi looks over at me and raises an eyebrow.

"You guys go, and I'll stay. I'm not a part of the family, and you're going to be talking about medical information that I shouldn't be involved in. I'll support you from here."

Levi hesitates before nodding, though I can see he's questioning my decision. "If you're sure."

I give him an encouraging smile. "Of course. Go. I'll be here when you get back."

With one more lingering look, Levi follows the nurse

and his mother through a set of white doors. Sinking back into the hard plastic chair, I pull out my phone to tell Jade what is going on and to give myself something to do.

After all, I suspect this is going to be a long night.

36

LEVI

The hospital room is quiet except for the steady beep of the machines that are in front of me. I stand by the bed, looking down at my father, whose face is softer as he gets the rest his body so desperately needs. It's strange seeing him like this—vulnerable and human for lack of a better word. It's a complete one-eighty to how I've envisioned him my entire life.

It's been a couple of days since I got the call from my mother about my father's heart attack and although I've spent countless hours here, the shock hasn't completely worn off yet. Between trying to be here for my mother and still doing my best to keep up with school and hockey, I'm swamped. Thankfully today is Saturday, and we don't have a game or practice so my focus is on being present at my father's hospital bed.

Dad is going to be okay even if all of the machines that

he's hooked up to say differently. He's only napping now and with some changes in lifestyle once he leaves here, he'll be able to live a normal life. I have to remind myself this isn't the same thing that I had to live through when Caleb was connected to every machine known to mankind before he died.

I check my phone to look at the time. Nine in the morning. I send Mom downstairs to get some food and to get some fresh air because she's been by his bedside since they let us come in the room with him. Hailey is probably preparing for the chess event at Oak Terrace right now. I decide that right now is the perfect time to send her a quick text.

> Me: Good luck at Oak Terrace today. I wish I could be there with you.

> Hailey: Thanks, I wish you could be too. We'll speak after?

> Me: Absolutely.

As I'm putting my phone away, Dad stirs. He blinks open his tired eyes, and they finally focus on me.

"Levi." His voice is barely a whisper, but I hear him loud and clear.

"Right here, Dad," I respond as I pull up a chair to his bed and sit down.

His eyes scan the room, then meet mine again. "Where's your mother?"

"She went downstairs to get something to eat and to take a small break."

"Ah," he says as his gaze narrows. "You're missing your game," he says, his voice sounding somewhat strained.

I shake my head. "No game today. The only place I need to be is right here."

He thinks about that for a moment and his gaze drifts to the window where the sun has painted the room in a soft, warm light. "You should be out there, practicing... training..."

"It's okay, Dad. Hockey's important, but you're my priority right now."

"Even after everything I've done?"

I can hear the regret in his words, and I'm taken aback by the stance he's taking. The role reversal leaves me stunned as I try to find the right thing to say.

"We all make mistakes, and you need to focus on getting better." I reach out and place my hand over his. The last thing I need right now is for him to get stressed out depending on how he's trying to steer this conversation.

For a moment, he's silent, just staring at our hands. Then he gives a small nod. "You're a good son, Levi. Better than I've deserved."

"Don't talk like that." The words slip out before I can stop them. "You've always pushed me because you wanted the best for me. It's... been hard to see that sometimes, I guess."

"That's no damn excuse. What you said after the game the other night is right. I shouldn't have been trying to force you to live up to the legacy Caleb left behind."

I swallow the lump in my throat. This is the most open conversation I've had with my father in a long time, if not ever.

"I need you to trust me to find what's best for me," I confess, holding his gaze. "And maybe I can still make you proud by doing that."

He squeezes my hand weakly. "I am proud, Levi. I always have been, even if I haven't always shown it."

I'm not sure how to respond. All of this is new territory for me. I've spent years trying to gain his approval through hockey, pushing myself to the limit to be the best. But now, here in this hospital room, all of that is unimportant.

"I appreciate you saying that," I finally reply. "I know having me succeed in hockey has always been important to you."

He nods slowly. "It's time for me to let go of those expectations. You need to chart your own course. Hell, if you wanted to quit hockey today, I'd be sad, but I would support you."

I feel a weight lift off my shoulders hearing him say those words, but this conversation is far from over.

"Dad, I've never blamed you for how you pushed me after Caleb... you know..." My voice trails off. Even now, it's hard for me to say my brother's name out loud at times. "But I need you to understand how much that hurts. For years, I've felt as if I'd never measure up to him."

My dad's eyes glisten with tears. "Losing Caleb nearly destroyed me. I was so blinded by grief and anger that I lost sight of what really mattered—you. My remaining son."

He inhales a shaky breath, his chest rising and falling in uneven rhythm. I squeeze his hand tighter, hoping this conversation isn't doing more damage to his heart.

"After the accident, I was desperate to hold onto anything that connected me to Caleb, and hockey was a big part of that. So I pushed you relentlessly, trying to relive his glory days through you. It wasn't fair to you, and I'm sorry, Levi. Truly sorry."

"I wanted to make you proud," I say quietly. "All the extra practices, the diets, the training... I did it all to try and live up to an impossible standard. And it was never enough for you."

My dad shakes his head, his eyes full of regret. "You have nothing to prove, son. Your brother was one kind of man, and you're another. There's enough space in this world for both even if one is gone."

When I don't respond right away, he continues. "I know I've got a lot to make up for and this has been a wakeup call once again alerting us to how precious life is," he says quietly. "But I'll do better from here on out."

I let out a deep breath in order to control my emotions. "I'd like that. For us to start again."

He gives my hand a weak squeeze. "Me too, son."

A nurse comes in to check on him, and I stand up to give her space. She asks my dad some questions and records his vitals, informing us that the doctor will be in soon.

As she leaves, my phone vibrates in my pocket. I pull it out and see a text from Hailey.

> Hailey: Okay. Can't wait to talk to you later.

She's been my rock through all of this. I wish I could be there with her, but I don't want to leave my dad's side.

"Who's that?" my dad asks, noticing me looking at my phone.

"It's Hailey," I say. "She's teaching chess to some of the residents at Oak Terrace today."

"She seems like a special girl."

I can't help but smile a little thinking about her. "She is. I don't know what I'd do without her right now."

"Are you supposed to be there with her today?"

I nod. "I am."

"But you stayed back because of me?" When I confirm his assumption, he speaks again. "You should go to her. I'll be alright," he urges.

"Are you sure?" I ask hesitantly. I don't want him to think I'm abandoning him.

"Positive. Go ahead and do something for yourself. Your mom should be back soon anyway."

I weigh my options, torn between staying with my dad and spending time with Hailey. It's been nonstop chaos since his heart attack, and a break sounds fantastic. Plus, I can help her.

"Alright. If you're sure you'll be okay. I really don't mind staying."

"I'm sure," he insists. "Go spend some time with your girl. Tell her I said hello, and I look forward to meeting her properly when I'm out of here."

"Will do," I promise. I grab my coat and take one last glance back at my dad. He gives me an encouraging smile. With that, I head out into the hallway as I'm pulling my coat on. I wave to one of the nurses that I recognize because he's been caring for my dad and take the elevator down to the ground floor. I need to find my mother and let her know that I'm heading out.

I find my mom sitting at a small table in the corner of the hospital cafeteria, a cup of coffee in her hands, her gaze distant.

"Hey, Mom," I say.

She looks up, and a small, weary smile touches her lips. "How is he?" she asks, setting her coffee down.

"He's resting now. Looks a lot better than when we first got here," I reassure her. "I, uh, I'm going to head out for a bit. I want to go help Hailey with her big event and Dad said he was okay with me doing it."

Mom's smile widens at the mention of Hailey's name.

"Hailey... I'm glad she makes you happy. It's wonderful seeing that for a change."

"Yeah, she's... she's something else," I admit. "Call me if anything changes, okay?"

"Of course, dear. You go see Hailey. We'll be fine here."

"Okay, I'll see you later." I promise.

She stands up and gives me a huge hug that is reminiscent of some of the ones she used to give me when I was a kid. When we break apart, a small kiss from her lands on my cheek and she takes the opportunity to push a piece of hair out of my face.

With a final wave to my mom, I turn and leave the cafeteria. I leave the hospital behind, and as I'm walking through the parking lot, I reach for my phone before I pause.

Surprising her is so much more fun than showing up announced. The idea brings a grin to my face as I spot my SUV. After her supporting me throughout all of this, I'm glad that I can return the favor. But first, I have a couple of stops to make and hope that I can do the things I need to do and get to her apartment before she leaves.

37

HAILEY

W hy did I think this was a good idea?

Volunteering to organize a chess tournament at Oak Terrace seemed like a good idea at the time. But now I'm having other thoughts. The day of the event has arrived, and my nerves are completely shot. I've checked and re-checked everything at least fifteen times this morning to make sure that I have all of the things I need for today. All I have to do is wait for Jade and bring everything out to my car.

And finish the speech I need to make at this event.

Fuck.

I look up and watch as Jade leaves her room with a big smile on her face. She claps once and then says, "Let's get this show on the road."

"I really hope this goes well," I say as I do one final check of the small prizes I bought for today.

"Are you kidding? The folks at Oak Terrace are going to love this," Jade assures me as she grabs one of the bags I packed. "Getting to play chess, socialize, and win some fun prizes? It's going to make their day."

She's right. I've put a lot of thought and effort into making this event fun and engaging for the seniors. Everything will go fine.

As Jade walks to the door, there's a knock that causes both of us to jump. Jade opens it, freezes, and then looks over her shoulder at me. "I think this is for you."

She steps out the way and opens the door and there I find Levi with a small bag from Brewed Beginnings.

"Need a hand?" His lips form a smile.

I drop all of the things in my hands and run toward him. Jade moves out of the way again as I launch myself at Levi. "What are you doing here?" My words fall out as if I stumbled down some stairs.

"Thought you could use some muscle." He flexes playfully and I laugh, relieving some of the stress I'm feeling.

"How's your dad doing?" I'm still confused about how he's here right now.

"My dad's doing better, thanks for asking. In fact, he's the one who encouraged me to come. But enough about that. Today is about you and bringing some joy to the residents at Oak Terrace. I'm happy to help in any way I can."

It takes everything in me not to cry at his words. His willingness to jump in and assist me with no questions asked, makes tears well up in my eyes.

"Hey, no crying. We have to get going, right?" Levi wipes the tears that have fallen.

"Well in that case, these bags need loading into my car. Jade grabbed one already—" I gesture to where she stands grinning, holding up a tote bag.

"On it," Levi says. He easily hefts two large bags up onto his shoulders. "Actually, wouldn't it make sense for us to take my vehicle? I have more room and you both don't have to worry about driving."

I share a look with Jade and when she gives me a small nod, I say, "Yes that sounds like a great plan."

As we make our way downstairs, I catch him up on all the plans for the event. His eyes light up as I describe the small trophies I found for the winners.

"This is incredible. You've put a lot of thought into this. Then again, I'm not surprised by that at all."

I feel my cheeks warm at Levi's compliment. "Thanks, but let's wait until after the event to give praise. This might all fall apart."

"Bullshit. This is going to be great," Jade says, and I'm happy she has enough optimism for the two of us.

"I have to make a speech and I'm probably going to faint. It'll be fine," I say sarcastically.

"It will be and if you're so freaked out, I can get you a shot of something upstairs to take the edge off," Jade offers.

"Nah, I'll be okay. Maybe."

That makes Levi chuckle and I'm happy to see a smile

on his face. As we load everything into his SUV, I go over my mental checklist one more time.

Chessboards–check.

Pieces–check.

Prizes–check.

Now I just need to remember to go over the speech I prepared to welcome everyone and kick things off.

Levi opens the doors for both Jade and me. I slip into the passenger's seat while Jade climbs into the back. Once we're all settled, Levi takes off and we're on our way.

As we drive to Oak Terrace, I can't stop fidgeting with my hands. I know I should review my speech, but my nerves are getting the best of me. I take a deep breath and dig into my bag to pull out the notebook I brought, flipping to the page with my speech. I planned to welcome everyone and explain the format of the chess tournament. Although it is simple, I'm still panicking. Not to mention that sometimes when I'm in a car and not driving, I get nauseous.

As I start reading the words, I'm trying to keep my nerves in check and my gag reflex under control. I get through the first couple of lines and my attention is diverted to Levi when he speaks.

"Bump."

"Wait what?"

"There was a bump in the road, and I was warning you about it. Because I know you get nauseous sometimes in the car. Amplify that with everything else going on…"

"I swear on everything if you guys aren't endgame, I'm going to lose my shit because that's the sweetest thing I've ever heard."

"Jade!" I look back at her before I turn to Levi. "She's right though and that is super sweet. Thank you."

Levi shrugs. "I do what I can."

I stare at him for a while longer before I go back to reading over my speech. As I scan over my words, I start to tweak and edit. A phrase here, a sentence there. I want it to sound natural, but also convey my point while appearing to be as excited as I can be. Jade pipes up from the back seat occasionally with suggestions and Levi helps by warning me when we're about to hit a bump in the road.

By the time we pull up at Oak Terrace, I feel much better about my speech and about everything in general. Levi and Jade help carry everything inside while I confirm final details with Mrs. Rafferty. Once that is settled, we head into the main hall and make quick work of setting everything up.

The chessboards are arranged on tables and chairs are set up for the residents and guests; snacks and drinks are ready to go. Several members of the chess club have arrived to help out, and for the most part, I'm happy.

My nerves start to creep back up as I glance at the podium and microphone at the front of the room. Jade gives me an encouraging nod as she finishes placing informational flyers on a table by the door. Levi walks over and gives me a warm hug.

"You're going to be amazing," he says.

I snort. "I'll try. At least if I completely bomb, the chess tournament itself will hopefully make up for my terrible public speaking skills."

Levi laughs. "Hey, don't sell yourself short. You're passionate about this event and about helping the community. That'll come through in your words."

Just then, the double doors open, and the first few residents begin filing into the room. Mrs. Rafferty greets them with a big smile. I take a deep breath and smooth my hands over my dress, preparing to welcome everyone. Levi gives my arm one last reassuring squeeze before going to help Jade direct people to seats.

As more guests arrive, I find my dad near the back of the hall, and I make my way over to him. He's standing with who I assume is Angela, and they're leaning toward one another as they speak quietly.

"Hey, Dad," I say.

He shifts his gaze toward me, his eyes lighting up when he sees me. "Hailey! This is quite the production you've put together."

"Thanks." I glance at Angela. "Hi, Angela. It's lovely to meet you, and I'm glad you could make it."

"Of course, I wouldn't have missed it. Your father tells me you've worked very hard on this event." Her voice is warm and kind.

I nod. "Well, I had a lot of help too." Across the room, I spot Jade ushering an elderly woman to a seat near the front. I know I need to get back so that I can help out.

I give my dad and Angela an apologetic look. "I should get back to helping everyone get to their seats. But I'm really happy you're both here and I'll have to introduce you to Levi, my boyfriend, later."

My dad freezes for a moment before a smile appears on his face. He pulls me in for a quick hug. "I can't wait. We'll be cheering you on. Now go on and show them what you're made of."

I help a few people find their seats before making my way up to the front of the room where Mrs. Rafferty waits by the podium.

She gives me a small smile. "Whenever you're ready, dear."

I take a deep breath and step up to the microphone. The chatter in the room quiets down as all eyes turn to me. I spot my dad and Angela near the back, Jade and Levi over by the snack table.

"Welcome, everyone, to our first community chess event!" I say, pleased that my voice comes out steady. "I want to thank you all for being here today and supporting this idea of mine to bring people together through the game of chess."

I go on to explain the format, recognizing the local chess club members who are helping run the mini tournament, and express my hope that this will become a recurring event. The words flow smoothly, and I find myself relaxing as I speak.

As I wrap up my welcome, applause fills the room. I spot Levi whistling loudly and Jade pumping her fist in the air. Laughing, I step away from the podium and Mrs. Rafferty takes over to direct people toward their first match.

I let out a huge sigh of relief as I walk over to where Jade and Levi are standing.

"See, I told you you'd do well," Jade says, pulling me in for a hug.

"Seriously, Hailey, you nailed it. I got chills listening to you speak so passionately about bringing people together," Levi adds.

I grin at their praise. "Thanks, you guys. I'm just relieved I made it through without messing up too badly."

We make our way over to the snack table as the first round of chess matches begins. I grab a brownie from the snack table and take a bite. It's not as good as the brownies at Brewed Beginnings, but it is still pretty tasty. As I chew, I scan the room and I can't help but smile as I take in the scene I've helped create.

"This was an amazing idea, Hailey," Jade says, looping her arm through mine. "Just look how happy you've made everyone."

I nod, blinking back the sudden tears that are starting to form. I'm going to cry more today than I have in weeks apparently. After over a month of planning and late nights making decorations with Jade, seeing it come to life is incredibly rewarding.

Looking around, I see people from all walks of life drawn together by a shared love of chess. My heart swells with happiness. This event has exceeded my expectations, but let's also be real, my expectations were in the gutter anyway.

I see that Jade has walked away to talk to her grandmother, who I wave to, and I spot my dad and Angela across the room. He has his arm around her waist and whispers something that makes her laugh. Seeing him happy and moving on mostly makes me glad he has found someone who seems to be having a positive impact on his life. When they make their way to the table and appear to be preparing for a match themselves, I feel Levi take a small step closer to me.

I'm pulled from my thoughts all together as he slides his arm around me. "What do you think? Was all your hard work worth it?"

I smile up at him. "It was, absolutely. Seeing everyone so engaged and happy is... It's more than I could have asked for," I reply, my gaze dancing around the room to catch the various groups immersed in their games.

Levi's gaze follows mine. "Since everyone is focused on their games, how about we take a minute for ourselves? There's a little sitting area I saw earlier. It's quiet and pretty secluded. You could use a break, and I... I'd love a few moments alone with you."

The suggestion surprises me, but the idea of stepping away for a minute with Levi is appealing. "Lead the way."

Levi takes my hand and leads me out of the main hall and down a quiet hallway. We walk around a corner and enter a cozy sitting area with plush couches and chairs. A large window looks out over the courtyard where I can see a couple of birds bouncing between the trees that have lost a lot of their leaves.

Levi sits and gently tugs me down next to him. I smooth my dress and wait expectantly.

"I wanted a minute to tell you how amazing you are, Rook," he says, his blue eyes intent on mine. "Seeing you up there, speaking with such passion, you took my breath away. You've worked so hard for this and I'm so proud of you."

"Thank you, Levi. It means a lot."

He brushes a strand of hair from my face, his fingers leaving a tingling trail on my skin. "There's something else I wanted to tell you as well. I know this isn't the optimal time to tell you and it's not exactly the place where I wanted to tell you, but I need to say this before I burst."

My eyes widen. "What's wrong?"

"Absolutely nothing. I wanted to tell you how much I love and adore you."

I'm momentarily stunned into silence as his confession sinks in. He loves me? My heart races and I know without a doubt, I'm going to cry again.

"Levi..." I begin, still trying to find the right words. "I

care about you so much. Over these past few weeks, you've become such an important part of my life. You've seen parts of me no one else has," I continue softly. "You make me feel safe, understood. Like I can just be myself with you."

I reach out and take his hand, interlacing our fingers. "What I'm trying to say is... I love you too." The words come out in a rush, and I let out a small, relieved laugh.

Levi's face lights up as he squeezes my hand gently. "You have no idea how happy it makes me to hear you say that."

He leans in and presses a soft, lingering kiss to my lips. In that moment, everything else fades away. And for the first time in a long time, I feel completely happy and at peace.

38

HAILEY

A few weeks later, Jade and I are standing next to Levi's parents as we're watching the Red Wolves play another match. The game is close and with the time ticking down, we are all hoping that this game goes the way we want it.

I rub my fingers down the number nineteen on my chest, praying that this brings the Red Wolves luck.

"Look at you, you have no issue rocking his jersey now!" Jade elbows me playfully.

"Shut it." I laugh, rolling my eyes, but secretly loving the heavy fabric draped over my shoulders. But it's more than that. I'm loving the fact that his last name and number are on my back.

The crowd erupts into cheers as Levi breaks away with the puck, his powerful strides carrying him down the ice. He maneuvers around defenders and the more he pushes, the more I find myself leaning toward Jade with my hands clasped together.

He shoots and the puck sails past the goalie's outstretched glove into the top corner of the net. The arena explodes with celebration. I'm on my feet, screaming and clapping along with everyone. Beside me, Levi's parents are beaming with pride.

"That's my boy!" his dad shouts over the noise as his mother breaks out into a grin.

Jade playfully shakes my shoulders in excitement. "Looks like your good luck charm is working!"

I grin and smooth my hand over his number again. Win or lose, I know Levi has given his all today and he should be proud of himself, no matter what the score says.

I quickly glance at the bench and notice something I haven't seen before. A young woman is hunched over with a professional looking camera, taking pictures. Who is she?

"Ever seen her before?" I nod toward the photographer, shifting Jade's attention away from the ice.

"Nope," she says and doesn't elaborate.

"Given how close she is to the team, I assume she was hired by them to take photos." The girl is wearing a Red Wolves hoodie and a pair of jeans. A white bow is tying part of her blonde hair back, keeping it out of her face.

"Wait a minute, that must be Coach Johnson's daughter. She transferred here a couple of weeks ago and I guess she got a job with the team."

"His daughter?" My eyebrows shoot up. "I don't know if I'd want to work with my dad."

"Never mind that. Check out Asher."

I follow her gaze and spot Asher stealing glances at the photographer while he's resting on the bench.

"I wonder what that's all about," Jade says before turning her attention back to the game.

"You're guess is as good as mine," I admit.

As the game continues, I find myself being more curious about the dynamics off the ice than on it. Coach Johnson's daughter is focused on doing her job, seemingly oblivious to Asher's attention when he's not on the ice.

The rest of the game is a blur of fast-paced action with the Red Wolves dominating the game. The tension in the arena builds as the clock ticks down, everyone on edge as we wait for the final buzzer.

When it sounds, the arena erupts in a deafening roar. The Red Wolves won the game. I turn to Jade, and we jump up and down, hugging each other in celebration. Looking over at Levi's parents, his dad has a proud smile on his face as he hugs Levi's mom.

Down on the ice, the team crowds around each other, helmets and gloves flying as high fives are exchanged as they congratulate one another. I catch a glimpse of Levi's grinning face before he's dragged into the huddle. When he manages to escape, his eyes find mine in the stands and he gives me a little wink that sets my body ablaze.

Or it could have been because I just saw Levi crush it and now, I wish that he would fuck me silly. Either or.

"Damn," Jade chuckles as we make our way out of our seats to join the crowd filing out of the stadium, "you have it bad for him, don't you?"

"Yep, and it's because I love him."

Jade scoffs as she rolls her eyes. "You two are disgusting. I'm only kidding by the way."

"You act like I care," I tease and bump her hip with mine as we join Levi's parents and make our way to the hallway near the locker rooms.

We wait for what feels like forever before Levi, now showered and changed, emerges with the rest of the team. They are all smiles as they head over to their families and significant others.

I wait patiently as Levi hugs his parents. Levi's relationship with his father has slowly been mending since the day Frank Jamison apologized. Ironically, I learned what his first name was when we were finally introduced to one another while he was still in the hospital. The heart attack was a wakeup call that Frank needed to try to fix things with his son, and based on what Levi tells me, things are going much better.

As I wait for Levi to finish talking with his parents, I spot the team photographer slipping out of an office nearby. She has a camera bag slung over her shoulder and looks eager to leave. Before I can point her out to Jade, Asher emerges from the crowd and touches her arm.

I can't tell what they are saying to each other, but it looks pretty tense. I'm not much for getting into people's drama, or being around people in general when I don't have to be, but I can't help but want to get closer to see if I can hear... something.

I glance at Jade and gesture to the couple that is talking just across the way. Asher leans forward to tell her something and the photographer shakes her head sharply as if the last place she wants to be is there with him.

As I'm plotting how I'm going to get closer to them, Levi appears at my side. He glances at me, and then Jade, and then at the couple we were staring at. "What are you up to?"

"Nothing. Absolutely nothing," I answer quickly.

Before Levi can question me further, Wilder comes over with his parents and swoops in to give Jade a big hug, leaving Levi and me in our own little world.

"Great game tonight," I say, hoping to distract Levi from whatever drama may be unfolding behind him.

Levi grins. "Thanks. Everything really came together in the end. But there's one thing that's missing."

"What's that?"

"My congratulatory kiss."

I'm happy to oblige. "We can't have that now, can we?"

"Nope," he says as he uses his finger to lift my chin. "Or I'll get very cranky."

I stand on my tiptoes and press my lips to his. The buzz that I feel whenever we kiss is stronger than ever as

Levi deepens the kiss by wrapping his arms around my waist. For a blissful moment, it feels like we're the only two people in the crowded hallway.

When we finally break apart, Levi rests his forehead against mine. "That's much better," he murmurs.

Levi takes a step away from me and I look over his shoulder. I notice Asher and the photographer have disappeared. Their interaction lingers in my mind, but I shove it to the side to pay attention to the man in front of me.

"Ready to celebrate?" he asks, taking my hand.

"With you? Always."

As Levi takes my hand and leads me through the hallway. We make our way outside and we walk over to Levi's car. Before he opens the passenger's side door for me, he stops me by holding both of my hands in his.

"I couldn't have asked for a better end to the night," he whispers.

I smile up at him. "Me neither."

"I love you so damn much."

"And I love you."

With that, our lips meet again, and I know that, without a doubt, no matter what troubles we face, we'll make it through.

Together.

EPILOGUE
HAILEY

Five Years Later

The moment Levi parks his SUV in the parking lot, it's like stepping into a time machine. I can't believe we are back on Crestwood's campus where it all began.

"Feels like eons ago, doesn't it?" I say, glancing over at Levi.

His confident stride hasn't changed a bit and I wonder if that came with all of the things he's accomplished over the years. He'd been drafted by the NHL right after graduation, a dream come true for him. His success on the ice has only grown from there and I'm happy to be along for the ride. My job as an environmental consultant allows me the flexibility to travel so I do attend more hockey games than I would have thought possible, especially as someone who disliked sports only a few short years ago.

But all of that fades to the side as I watch Levi take in the fact that we are back on our college campus. It's clear the place still holds a piece of his heart.

"Come on, slowpoke," Levi teases. "Brewed Beginnings is waiting for us."

"Calm down. It's not going to close on us," I say as we walk toward the coffee shop where I used to work and where we first met.

Hand in hand, we make our way into the coffee shop. Though it's been years since I've been here, Brewed Beginnings looks just as I remember. It still has its rustic charm with the exposed wooden beams and the local art is still on the walls.

"Hello and welcome to Brewed Beginnings!" the barista greets us cheerfully. "What can I get started for you?"

Levi orders an Americano while I choose a chai tea latte with almond milk and a brownie. As we wait for our drinks, we find a table by the window, the same table where we used to meet and play chess at.

"Remember how we used to come here when you got me to *teach* you how to play chess?" I ask Levi.

He grins. "Of course. It is the best idea I've ever had."

"Oh come on. You don't have to kiss my ass now. We're already together."

That makes Levi chuckle. "First off, I do like kissing your ass. And it is the best idea I've ever had. You've changed my life for the better, Rook."

His compliment and use of the nickname he gave me warms me from the inside out. Him still being able to do this to me after the years we've been together makes me fall even more in love with him.

Before I can respond, the barista calls Levi's name and he stands up to get the items we ordered. While he's away, I take the time to scan the shop, noting some of the changes that have happened in the years since I've been gone. My observations are interrupted when Levi returns, placing our drinks on the table we decided to occupy.

Levi slides into the chair opposite mine and pushes the steaming chai latte and brownie toward me. "I can't believe it's been five years since graduation. It's still weird to think about."

I wrap my hands around the to-go cup. "It's like no time has passed at all," I reply, taking a sip. When I take a bite of the brownie, I nearly groan. It's still as good as I remember it.

Levi reaches across the table, capturing my free hand. "I think it's about time to add a new memory to this place," he says softly.

"Wait what?" I ask, confused about what he could be talking about.

My heart does a somersault in my chest as he stands up and walks over to me. The chatter around us fades to black as he gets down on one knee right beside our table. When he reaches into his jacket pocket, I swear my world tips upside down and I find myself holding my breath.

"Hailey Reed," Levi starts, his voice steady despite his hand trembling. "From us meeting for the first time here to you teaching me chess—which was just a ploy to spend more time with you—to supporting me through every win and loss, both on and off the ice, you've been my rock, my confidante, my best friend. I couldn't ask for anyone more perfect for me than you." He pulls out a small velvet box and opens it to reveal a simple but stunning princess-cut diamond ring that catches the light in the most beautiful way.

My hands shoot up to my face, covering my mouth which dropped open. I can feel eyes on us now, but I don't care. The only thing that matters is the man in front of me, who has dropped to his knee to ask me one of the most important questions I will ever hear in my life.

"Will you make me the happiest man alive and agree to be my partner for life? Will you marry me?"

My gaze drifts from the ring to the expression on Levi's face. I've known how I would answer this question for a while, but I didn't know he would ask it this weekend.

"Yes," I say as I move my hands to touch one of his. There is no use in trying to hide my tears because they are already flowing down my cheeks. "Yes, I'll marry you."

Cheers erupt from the patrons in Brewed Beginnings as Levi slips the ring onto my finger. Of course, much like everything Levi does, it's a perfect fit.

"I love you," Levi whispers as he stands up to pull me into his arms.

"I love you too," I whisper back, as I stand up before tilting my head up for a kiss that seals the promise we've just made to each other.

As if on cue, the front door of Brewed Beginnings swings open, and I'm shocked to see some familiar faces. Our friends from Crestwood walk in, their arms filled with balloons and wrapped boxes and gift bags. I assume they are for us because I don't know of anyone else's birthday or a big event that is happening right now.

"You did say yes, right? All of this would be for naught if you didn't," calls out Jade.

I roll my eyes at her. "Of course I said yes," I say as I hold up my left hand to show off my latest piece of jewelry.

Jade squeals and runs over to me. We hug, and just as we're breaking apart, someone else walks into Brewed Beginnings, making my mouth drop open.

"Dad!"

"Oh, my sweet girl," he says as he walks into the coffeeshop. He's followed by his wife, Angela, and I stroll over to give them both giant hugs.

I lean back, looking up at the man who's been my

anchor in every fathomless storm life has thrown at me. "Dad, you drove all the way here for this?"

He chuckles and ruffles my hair, just like he used to when I was a kid. "Hailey, did you really think I'd miss this? Seeing my girl get engaged? There was nothing going to stop me from getting here today."

Angela gives me a warm smile that I return tenfold. She's been more than just a stepmother; she's filled spaces in our lives that we didn't realize were empty until she arrived.

I feel Levi's hand on the small of my back. He leans in close and whispers, "I wanted everyone who matters to us to be here. Your dad and Jade helped me plan it."

"Thank you so much to all of you. I couldn't have imagined a better surprise."

"You're very welcome, but something else is missing," Jade says as she appears at my side. She looks at my ring once more before giving me a big grin.

"And what's that?"

"Champagne! We need to celebrate."

We all laugh just before Levi pulls me closer to him. He places a quick kiss on my forehead before putting a longer one on my lips.

Here we are, surrounded by the people we love, getting ready to embrace change once more as we shift from dating to being engaged. I think back to years ago, when I would have been wary of anything like this because I liked being in the little box I created for myself.

But times have changed, and I have grown to trust in myself and in my relationship.

And I wouldn't have it any other way.

IF YOU WOULD LIKE to read a bonus scene featuring Hailey and Levi, you can grab it here.

Asher's story will be the next book in this series.

ACKNOWLEDGMENTS

To say that this entire experience has been a whirlwind is an understatement.

To my family, and especially my Mom, for encouraging me endlessly to pursue this dream. Without you, I wouldn't be here, and this book wouldn't be anything more than a thought in my head.

TK and CB, I'm truly grateful for your friendship. Just thinking about how much you've both helped me with this entire process makes me want to cry (happy tears, I promise).

Andra, you perfectly encapsulated my dream for this cover. I still can't believe this is real.

Ellie, I'm not sure how many ledges you've talked me down from at this point, but thank you. Your hard work with promoting this book is more than I could have ever hoped for. I apologize for all of the rambling voicememos I've sent you, but I promise there are more coming soon ha!

Chrisandra, Athena, Darlene, and Elizabeth, I can't thank you all enough for jumping on this project. Your hard work is immensely appreciated, thank you.

Morgan and Samantha, thank you so much for your thoughtful comments about the very ROUGH draft of this book. Your input helped me check this item off of my bucket list.

And I can't not thank every single reader for picking up this book. You taking time out of your day to read my words means the world.

Thank you.

ABOUT THE AUTHOR

Emery Paige is a dreamer, a word crafter, and a wine lover. She has been a writer and reader for as long as she can remember. Being able to call herself a romance author is a dream come true.

When she's not pouring her soul into her next romance, Emery can be found indulging in her love for music or watching YouTube, where she enjoys everything from travel vlogs to fashion and cooking.

If you would like to keep in contact with her, please visit her website (www.emerypaigebooks.com) or sign up for her newsletter to receive the latest information about her and her books.

She's also on Instagram and TikTok.

Printed in Great Britain
by Amazon

55708958R00238